Miss Morton and the Deadly Inheritance

Books by Catherine Lloyd

Kurland St. Mary Mysteries
DEATH COMES TO THE VILLAGE
DEATH COMES TO LONDON
DEATH COMES TO KURLAND HALL
DEATH COMES TO THE FAIR
DEATH COMES TO THE SCHOOL
DEATH COMES TO BATH
DEATH COMES TO THE NURSERY
DEATH COMES TO THE RECTORY

Miss Morton Mysteries
MISS MORTON AND THE ENGLISH
HOUSE PARTY MURDER
MISS MORTON AND THE SPIRITS OF
THE UNDERWORLD
MISS MORTON AND THE DEADLY INHERITANCE

Published by Kensington Publishing Corp.

Miss Morton
and the Deadly
Inheritance

CATHERINE LLOYD

KENSINGTON
PUBLISHING CORP.

www.kensingtonbooks.com

KENSINGTON BOOKS are published by

Kensington Publishing Corp.
900 Third Avenue
New York, NY 10022

All Kensington titles, imprints, and distributed lines are available at special quantity discounts for bulk purchases for sales promotion, premiums, fund-raising, educational, or institutional use. Special book excerpts or customized printings can also be created to fit specific needs. For details, write or phone the office of the Kensington Special Sales Manager: Attn. Special Sales Department, Kensington Publishing Corp., 900 Third Avenue, New York, NY 10022. Phone: 1-800-221-2647.

Library of Congress Control Number: 2024936506

The K with book logo Reg. US Pat. & TM. Off.

ISBN: 978-1-4967-4064-9

First Kensington Hardcover Edition: September 2024

ISBN: 978-1-4967-4066-3 (ebook)

10 9 8 7 6 5 4 3 2 1

Printed in the United States of America

Thanks to Ruth Long for reading this at the last minute and Edie for the extra comma editing!

Miss Morton
and the Deadly
Inheritance

Chapter 1

London, 1838

Miss Caroline Morton picked up the morning post from the silver tray the butler had placed beside her plate. It was a bright, cheerful morning, and Caroline was alone in the breakfast parlor of the rented house on Half Moon Street. Her employer, Mrs. Frogerton, slept on after a late night at a society ball where Mrs. Frogerton's daughter, Dorothy, had danced the night away.

Caroline had attended the ball, but since she hadn't danced, she'd hardly exerted herself and had risen at her usual time to start the day. The Season was drawing to a close, and Caroline would soon need to decide whether she remained in Mrs. Frogerton's employ or sought another position in London.

Her employer had strongly indicated that even if Dorothy chose to marry at the end of the Season, which seemed more than likely, Caroline would be more than welcome to accompany Mrs. Frogerton back north. Despite her initial trepidation in taking a paid position after being left penniless by her feckless father, Caroline had come to admire Mrs. Frogerton. She treated Caroline like a daughter and had already supported her through several trying events, including a family murder.

Caroline set the stack of invitations to one side and considered the rest of the post. There were two letters for her, including one from her sister, Susan, who was now at school in Kent. Susan still hadn't forgiven Caroline for sending her away to school, and her letters tended to be stilted, short, and remarkably accusatory. According to Susan, every ill in the world, including the weather, the unfairness of her French teacher, and her lack of fashionable new dresses, was somehow Caroline's fault.

Caroline put the letter in her pocket. It was a pleasant day, and she was looking forward to visiting Hyde Park and strolling along the paths with Mrs. Frogerton and her dogs. Reading Susan's new list of grievances would depress her spirits, especially when she didn't have the power or necessary finances to change anything. Mrs. Frogerton had generously paid Susan's fees, and Caroline was very careful not to expose her employer to Susan's complaints.

Her hand stilled over her pocket. She'd asked Susan if she wished to accompany her to their recently deceased aunt's funeral at Greenwood Hall. They were supposed to be leaving in two days. She knew she should open the letter to see whether Susan wanted to come. With a resigned sigh, she took the letter out, unfolded it, and began to read. It did not take long.

> *Dear Caroline,*
> *I do not wish to accompany you anywhere. If you hadn't meddled, I would have stayed with Cousin Mabel and not been forced to attend this terrible school. Please send my condolences to my cousins.*
> *Susan.*

Caroline put the letter back in her pocket. Susan had spent most of her childhood at Greenwood Hall under the care of Aunt Eleanor, and Caroline was disappointed she couldn't bring herself to attend the funeral in person. It was all well and good for Susan to resent Caroline's part in the recent ructions within their family, but to refuse to mourn the dead? Caroline found that hard to accept.

"Whatever is the matter, lass?" Mrs. Frogerton asked as she came into the breakfast room. "You look like someone murdered your favorite pet."

She was already fully dressed in a crimson silk gown with lace trimmings and a matching cap. Her dogs milled around her with great enthusiasm as she settled into the chair opposite Caroline, her lively face aglow with interest.

Caroline fought a sigh. "Susan does not wish to accompany me to Aunt Eleanor's funeral."

"Well, there's no surprise in that, surely? Your sister hasn't forgiven you for taking her away from Greenwood Hall and sending her to school." Mrs. Frogerton paused to allow the butler to set a pot of coffee at her elbow. "For what it's worth, my dear, I still think you did the right thing."

"Hopefully one day Susan will realize that for herself." Caroline rose to her feet. "May I get you a plate of food, ma'am? There are some very nice coddled eggs and mushrooms."

"That sounds delightful." Mrs. Frogerton helped herself to some coffee. "And look on the bright side. If Susan doesn't come with us, we'll have more space in the carriage on the journey into Norfolk."

Caroline set the plate in front of her employer. "I don't expect you to accompany me, ma'am. I have enough money saved for the mail coach."

"As if I'd let you go to that place alone." Mrs. Frogerton frowned at her. "As a previous guest of the house, I do feel some obligation to honor your aunt's passing. I have already ordered the carriage for tomorrow morning at eight. I must warn you that I have no intention of staying at Greenwood Hall. If we are unable to complete the journey back to London after the ceremony, we will stay at one of the local inns and resume our travels the following morning."

"I have no particular desire to linger myself, ma'am." Caroline repressed a shudder. "As my aunt was a practical woman, I suspect her funeral arrangements will be relatively straightforward."

"I agree. And your cousin Nicholas doesn't seem the type to go for an elaborate funeral repast," Mrs. Frogerton said. "He doesn't have a wife to organize such things or the staff to carry it off." She ate some of the egg and beamed at Caroline. "This is very good, indeed! Do I detect a hint of mustard in there?"

"I'll ask Cook. She'll be delighted that you approve." Caroline passed the two piles of correspondence over to Mrs. Frogerton. "Your business and personal correspondence are on the left, and the invitations on the right."

Mrs. Frogerton gave a theatrical groan. "Perhaps you could consult with Dorothy as to the invitations? I must confess that I am eager to return home and never attend another society ball in my life."

"You don't mean that, ma'am. You are a much-liked guest."

"Only for my money. Don't forget that."

"And for yourself. Many people find you . . . refreshing."

"As in, loudmouthed and too honest?"

"An original," Caroline said firmly, and took the pile of invitations back. "I will speak to Dorothy when she comes down. She has developed decided preferences as to which events she wishes to attend, which makes my job much easier."

When Dorothy had first entered society, Caroline had guided her as to which balls would be advantageous to attend in her quest to marry into the peerage. As Dorothy had recently secured the attentions of a viscount, she no longer needed to be seen at all the events and, much to her mother's relief, had scaled down her social activities considerably.

"I'm looking forward to a much quieter month," Mrs. Frogerton said as she sipped her coffee. "Between all Dorothy's goings-on and that business with Madam Lavinia, I am quite done in."

"I agree, ma'am." Caroline turned her attention to the second letter she had received in the post. It was from a very respectable address near Grays Inn. She opened the letter and read the contents.

> *Dear Lady Caroline,*
> *Regarding the will of your late father, the Earl of Morton. Please reply to this missive and let me know when it will be convenient for me to call on you.*
> *Yours sincerely,*
> *Mr. Jeremy Smith*
> *Smith, Smith, Potkins, and Jones, Solicitors.*

Caroline repressed a sigh.

"Don't tell me you have more bad news, lass?" Mrs. Frogerton asked.

"It's not bad news, ma'am, but it is rather tiresome. My father's solicitors wish to speak to me about his will, and I cannot imagine why." She paused. "Unless they have discovered more of his debts and expect me to pay them off."

"I don't think that would be legal," Mrs. Frogerton said. "It is one of the rare instances when being female protects you from a gentleman's mistakes."

"From his gentlemanly debts of 'honor,'" Caroline murmured. "I can't even imagine how much money he let flow through his fingers gambling and speculating."

"Enough to bankrupt his own estate and steal his children's inheritance without shame." Mrs. Frogerton rarely minced words, and her disdain for what Caroline's father had done to his fortune and his family had no bounds. "One might think he would've stopped there, but apparently not."

"The solicitor didn't specify, but it can't be good news."

Caroline ripped the letter in half, took it over to the fireplace, and threw it onto the coals. It burned brightly for a moment before turning to ash. "If it is important, I'm sure he will write to me again."

"That's the spirit, lass," Mrs. Frogerton said. "No need to court trouble." She dropped her toast crusts onto the carpet for her dogs, who gobbled them up in an instant. "If he becomes impertinent, let me know and I'll set my Mr. Lewis on him."

Having witnessed Mr. Lewis deal with the highest echelons of the Metropolitan Police and emerge victorious, Caroline was certain Mrs. Frogerton was correct. It was also comforting to know Mrs. Frogerton would use her wealth and power to support her employee.

"Speaking of the Metropolitan Police, have you heard from Inspector Ross?" Mrs. Frogerton asked.

"Whyever would you think he had time to bother with me, ma'am?" Caroline avoided her employer's bright gaze and busied herself re-sorting the invitations.

"We both know why, miss." Mrs. Frogerton paused. "He is from a very good family."

"Then he certainly wouldn't want to have anything to do with me," Caroline countered. "My father shamed us all."

"Inspector Ross doesn't seem to think so," Mrs. Frogerton said. "And what about Mr. DeBloom? I saw him skulking around at that funeral we attended recently."

Caroline reminded herself that very little escaped her employer's eye.

"I have quite enough to do without concerning myself as to their whereabouts," Caroline said briskly. "If they wish to pay their respects to you or Dorothy, ma'am, I will of course be in attendance."

"I don't think either of those gentlemen wish to speak to me, my dear. Between them and our dear Dr. Harris, you are quite the belle of your own ball."

Caroline met her employer's amused gaze. "I . . . truly do not want any attention. I am quite happy as I am."

"You don't want to be a wife and a mother?"

"I always assumed that would be my destiny, but my circumstances have changed considerably. I try not to think in those terms."

Mrs. Frogerton reached across the table and patted her hand. "You'll come about, lass. I'm sure of it. Some young gentleman will make you forget all about your circumstances, sweep you off your feet, and that will be that."

"I suppose one can always dream, ma'am." Caroline smiled. "But I can assure you that I am fully committed to ensuring that Dorothy marries well and that you are able to return home in triumph."

"Now that is a worthy goal, indeed," Mrs. Frogerton said. "Shall we finish our breakfast and get ready for our walk? I believe it is going to be a very nice day."

Three days later, and in a very different part of the countryside, Caroline held an umbrella over Mrs. Frogerton's head as the Norfolk rain poured down on them. There were very few mourners at her aunt's graveside. It wasn't surprising, as the family had recently been the subject of immense social speculation and gossip. Her cousin Nicholas, who had inherited his father's title, hardly ever came to the estate, preferring to lodge in London and socialize with a group of gentlemen Caroline privately considered wastrels.

He'd been furious when his mother had died from a stroke, leaving him without her guidance and making him completely responsible for his family. Caroline couldn't help but worry about the employees at Greenwood Hall who were now dependent on the whims of a man who had no wish to manage the estate or any intention of living there unless he was forced to.

Caroline could easily see that happening, because she

suspected that unless Nicholas employed a competent agent—and he'd never been a good judge of character—he'd simply bleed the estate to fund his life in London until there was nothing left. Then he'd either have to sell up, which would be difficult with the entail, or live in the countryside until he could regroup and raise funds.

After the short service, Nicholas strode toward Caroline, the rain glinting on his coat and tall black hat. He was alone, as his younger brother George had decided not to attend the service and had stayed at his university.

"Cousin, it was good of you to come."

"Thank you for inviting me," Caroline said.

"Susan didn't accompany you?"

"No, she is rather too far away to make the journey by herself," Caroline said. "She sends her regrets and particularly wished to be remembered to you." She turned to Mrs. Frogerton. "May I introduce you to my cousin, Nicholas, the new Earl of Greenwood, ma'am?"

Mrs. Frogerton looked Nicholas up and down. "My condolences, sir."

Nicholas nodded. "Thank you. I believe you met my family earlier in the year."

"Yes, your mother invited me and my daughter to a house party." Mrs. Frogerton didn't elaborate, which was most unlike her, but Caroline was grateful.

"Would you like to come up to the house for some refreshment before you leave?" Nicholas asked. "There is to be a reading of my aunt's will, and the solicitor suggested you should be present, Caroline."

"Yes, of course. We will follow in Mrs. Frogerton's carriage, Nicholas."

Her cousin turned away and walked by himself to a glossy, closed carriage drawn by two plumed black horses.

"He has no one to support him?" Mrs. Frogerton asked as they made their way back to their own vehicle.

"Not that I am aware of. He chose not to associate himself with his family here and preferred to live his life in London."

"That might have to change," Mrs. Frogerton commented as she got into the coach. "From what I recall, the household needs a strong hand like Lady Eleanor's."

Caroline sat down and let the coachman shut the door before she spoke again. "Between you and me, ma'am, Nick isn't interested in managing the estate. He has always seen it as his source of funds and never questioned how my aunt wrested those sums from such an inhospitable landscape."

Her gaze was drawn to the flatness and grayness of the fens with the deep dykes cutting between them. Half of the land was unusable because of the overflowing marshlands, and the rest was pitted with dry, flint-filled soil on which very little thrived. If Nicholas wanted to continue his current life, he'd need to invest in the land or marry very well indeed.

"I'll wager he won't provide a proper funeral repast," Mrs. Frogerton commented as she looked out of her window.

"I assume the household staff will provide some form of refreshment. Even my cousin needs to eat."

Mrs. Frogerton snorted.

"You didn't take to him, ma'am?" Caroline turned to look at her employer.

"With all due respect, my dear, I find your whole family somewhat of a mystery."

"They have certainly been beset by . . . trouble recently."

"All of their own making," Mrs. Frogerton said. "But to be fair, all families have their crosses to bear."

Caroline was well aware of the somewhat fractious relationship Mrs. Frogerton shared with her only son, who was currently running the family businesses while his mother was busy in London. Many lengthy letters passed between them, and on more than one occasion, Mrs. Frogerton had threatened to pack her bags and return to the north to take back control of her empire.

"Ah, we're here," Mrs. Frogerton commented as the carriage turned left onto the drive up to Greenwood Hall.

Caroline found it difficult to imagine the house without her uncle and aunt inhabiting it and half the staff already gone. There was an unfamiliar housekeeper waiting in the entrance hall to accompany them upstairs to leave their cloaks and tidy up, and no sign of a butler. The house was quieter than she remembered, with no children in the nurseries. Several of the rooms they passed had the shutters closed and the furniture covered in dust cloths, which gave the place an unlived-in feeling.

The housekeeper accompanied them down to the drawing room, where tea was being served. Caroline's cousin Eliza looked up as they entered the room. She wore black and her usual sour expression.

"Caroline. I knew you would come." She paused. "If I were in such reduced circumstances, I suppose I'd be attending every funeral, even if my cause was futile."

"Cousin." Caroline curtsied. "I am sorry for the loss of your mother."

"Despite all your efforts, I was her favorite child." Eliza turned to Mrs. Frogerton. "Good afternoon, ma'am. Would you like some tea?"

"Yes, please." Mrs. Frogerton took a seat opposite Eliza. "Are your family well?"

"Yes indeed. My son is thriving, and my husband's business interests have expanded considerably." She smiled complacently and turned to Caroline. "And you, Caroline? Are you still working for your living?"

"She is, and I am most grateful that she continues to put up with me," Mrs. Frogerton spoke before Caroline could form a reply. "She has worked wonders with my daughter, Dorothy."

"Thank you, ma'am." Caroline smiled at her employer.

Eliza looked up as Nicholas came into the room accompanied by the vicar and another man who looked vaguely familiar.

Nicholas beckoned to Eliza and Caroline. "Come along. This won't take a minute. Mr. Smith needs to return to London as soon as possible."

"Off you go, dear." Mrs. Frogerton smiled at Caroline. "I'll be perfectly fine chatting to the vicar."

Caroline smoothed down the skirts of her black dress and followed her cousins into her uncle's study. Nothing had changed, and she fought a pointless wave of nostalgia for how things had been before his untimely death.

"Please take a seat." Mr. Smith took up a position behind the desk. "Lady Eleanor's will is a lot less complicated than her husband's and deals mainly with monies that came down the maternal side of her family."

Nicholas repressed a sigh and leaned one shoulder against the bookcase. "Please proceed. The sooner we finish, the quicker we can leave this backwater."

Mr. Smith put on his spectacles, unrolled a parchment, and cleared his throat.

"This will is dated the thirteenth of October, 1832."

Eliza sat up straight. "She didn't amend her will before she died?"

"Not to my knowledge." Mr. Smith looked at Eliza. "Are you suggesting you witnessed her doing so?"

"No, I just assumed . . ." Eliza looked around at her brother. "I thought she would have changed certain *aspects* of it to reflect her changed preferences." She returned her gaze to Caroline and positively glared at her.

"Can we just get on with it, Eliza?" Nicholas took out his pocket watch. "If you stop interrupting, we'll find out what Mama decided to do in a trice."

"I'm just saying . . ."

Mr. Smith looked down at the document as if waiting for them to stop bickering. Caroline had to assume that such disagreements were common during the reading of wills.

"Pray continue, Mr. Smith," Nicholas said.

"Thank you, my lord. 'I, Eleanor, Margaret, Mary Greenwood, née Morton, of sound mind and body do hereby decree that on this day . . .'"

"With all due respect, Mr. Smith. Can you get to the important parts about who gets what and spare us the unnecessary legal jargon?" Nicholas was beginning to sound impatient. "I'm fairly certain my esteemed mother has left me nothing, and I'd like to get on."

"As you wish, my lord." Mr. Smith scanned the document and placed his finger on the appropriate section. "There are some small legacies to her dresser, cook, and housekeeper, but the bulk of her money goes to her two daughters and her two nieces."

"That can't be right," Eliza said. "Mama promised everything would come to me!"

"She probably said that to make you stop nagging her, Eliza. She never appreciated being told what to do." Nicholas faced the solicitor. "My sister Mabel is currently abroad, and my cousin Susan is a minor who resides at a boarding school in Kent. Caroline and I can take care of the monies meant for them."

"How much?" Eliza demanded. "How much does she get?"

Mr. Smith looked as if he wanted to leave. "Which lady are you speaking of, ma'am?"

"Her!" Eliza pointed at Caroline. "The person who consistently tried to usurp me in my mother's affections."

"She didn't need to try, Sis." Nicholas laughed. "You did that all by yourself. And if you ask me, it serves you right for being so mean-spirited to our cousins."

"You—" Eliza shot to her feet, her hands clenched into fists.

Mr. Smith looked at her. "If I might answer your question, ma'am?"

"Please. Go ahead."

"Lady Caroline and her sister are to receive a lump sum of five hundred pounds each."

Silence fell, and Eliza's jaw dropped. "*How* much?"

"Five hundred pounds," the solicitor repeated patiently. He looked at Caroline as Eliza started to pace the room and rage, while her brother continued to laugh. "I understand you are currently living in London, my lady. If you prefer, I can call on you there. I already need to speak to you about your father's will, so it won't be any trouble."

It was Caroline's turn to stand. "I think that might be a good idea." She caught Nicholas's eye. "Will you excuse me? I think Mrs. Frogerton wishes to return to London with the greatest of speed."

Nicholas winked at her. "Go ahead, Cousin. I'll deal with Eliza. Thank you for coming all this way in the first place. Perhaps I might call on you in London? I hear Miss Dorothy Frogerton is in possession of a large fortune and is looking to marry into the peerage."

"I fear you are too late, Nick. She has already made her decision." Caroline headed for the door at some speed.

She didn't bother to say goodbye to Eliza, who appeared oblivious to reason and was loudly claiming she and her husband would contest the will. Caroline went into the drawing room, where Mrs. Frogerton was sitting with the vicar. Her employer immediately stopped speaking and set her cup and saucer down on the table beside her.

"A pleasure to see you again, vicar, but I fear we must be off." She rose to her feet and hurried toward Caroline. "I'm glad I told our coachman to wait outside the door. If you can fetch our cloaks and bonnets from upstairs, we can depart this place immediately."

They stopped for the night at an inn on the outskirts of London, and it wasn't until they were settled in their private parlor having dinner that Caroline regained the ability to speak. Since they'd left Greenwood Hall, Mrs. Frogerton had kept up a constant flow of chatter that required no answers, and she hadn't pressed Caroline for any details, which was most unlike her.

"Now, then, lass." Mrs. Frogerton poured them both a glass of wine. "Are you feeling more the thing?"

"Yes, ma'am." Caroline took a steadying breath. "I was just . . . surprised. I assumed my aunt Eleanor required my presence at the reading of the will to berate me for my disobedience and to publicly disinherit me."

"And she didn't do so?"

"No." Caroline took a large sip of wine. "I thought that after her stroke she would amend her will, but it appears she left it as it was."

"I am surprised by that. She didn't strike me as a very forgiving woman," Mrs. Frogerton said. "I thought I heard your cousin Eliza screeching about something and wondered what it was. I suppose she thought she would inherit everything?"

Caroline nodded. "She did, but Aunt Eleanor left her an equal share with Mabel."

"Oh, dear."

"And, even worse in Eliza's view, she left Susan and me some money as well." Caroline met her employer's eyes and spoke in hushed tones. "Ma'am, she left us five hundred pounds each!"

"Well, that must have been a very pleasant surprise, indeed," Mrs. Frogerton said encouragingly. "With a sum as large as that, you could hand in your letter of resignation right now."

"I have no intention of doing any such thing," Caroline said. "Unless you insist."

Mrs. Frogerton smiled. "Good girl. There's no need to rush. Let's get my Dorothy settled first, and then there will be plenty of time to decide what you want to do next."

Chapter 2

"It has been two weeks since our return from Greenwood Hall, Caroline, and you have still not heard from Mr. Smith, your family solicitor."

Caroline looked up from the letter she was writing to Susan. "I'm fairly certain my petty legal concerns aren't a priority and that Mr. Smith has far more important issues to deal with."

Mrs. Frogerton folded her hands in her lap. "One might almost think you were pleased about that."

"I must admit to some reluctance to engage with him," Caroline said. "On our last encounter in London, he and his partners told me I was penniless and then presented me with an enormous bill for their services and the privilege of having delivered the news to me in person."

"You saw Mr. Smith at Greenwood Hall, and he gave you some excellent news," Mrs. Frogerton said. "Have you forgotten that?"

Caroline sighed and set down her pen. "But what if the only reason he wishes to see me is so that he can share the excellent news that my aunt's bequest will go toward paying off my father's creditors?"

"That cannot happen," Mrs. Frogerton said. "And, if there is even a suggestion of such impertinence, I will instruct Mr. Lewis to deal with the matter on your behalf, and we'll soon see who's begging your pardon."

"Thank you, ma'am, but you do not have to exert yourself on my behalf on every occasion. I must attempt to deal with my problems myself."

"Why, when I have the money and the power to do things for you?"

"Because . . ." Caroline paused. "I am merely employed as your companion."

For a second, Mrs. Frogerton looked hurt. "I don't think of you as such, lass."

Caroline rushed over to sit on the sofa beside Mrs. Frogerton. "And I appreciate that beyond measure, ma'am. I am so lucky to be in your employ and to be held in such high regard. I know my fate could've been far worse."

"You're like a daughter to me." Mrs. Frogerton reached out and patted Caroline's hand. "Now don't say anything more, or I'll get cross, and that will never do."

Caroline resisted the impulse to burst into tears and throw herself onto her employer's bosom. Instead, she squeezed her fingers and nodded.

"Thank you, ma'am. I promise I will write to Mr. Smith after I've finished my letter to Susan apprising her of her good fortune."

"Don't give her all the details," Mrs. Frogerton said. "You don't know who's reading her letters, and we don't want anyone getting any ideas, now, do we?"

"That's a very good point, ma'am." Caroline went back to the desk. "I'll simply say that Aunt Eleanor left her something in her will and that I will explain more when I come to visit her after the Season has finished."

"Good, and after you've finished your letter to Susan, we'll have our luncheon and take Dotty to her musical gathering. Her fiancé's mother can chaperone her." Mrs. Frogerton paused. "And while we've got the horses out, we'll just pop by your solicitors' office. It's hardly out of our way, and it will save you from having to write another letter."

Caroline sighed. When her employer got an idea in her head, it was impossible to divert her attention, which meant that fairly shortly she would be speaking to the family solicitor whether she wanted to or not.

"Lady Caroline, Mrs. Frogerton. What a pleasure." Mr. Smith bowed as he ushered them through to his office. "I didn't realize I had the honor of your company today."

"That's because I prevailed upon Caroline to come here," Mrs. Frogerton said as she took a seat. "She was reluctant to return to an establishment where she appears to receive only bad news."

"Hardly that, ma'am." Mr. Smith smiled as he sat down. "In truth, I delivered far happier news to Lady Caroline about an inheritance from her late aunt Lady Eleanor Greenwood only last month."

"Well, one hopes such positivity will continue," Mrs. Frogerton said. "Because for the life of me, I can't imagine how you allowed her father to steal her dowry from right under your noses."

"That was . . . unfortunate, I agree." Mr. Smith polished his spectacles. "Some of our senior partners are a law unto themselves."

"And yet they are rarely held to account," Mrs. Frogerton said. "If it were up to me—"

Caroline cleared her throat. "I understand there was a specific reason why you wished to see me, Mr. Smith?"

"Indeed." The solicitor looked relieved to direct his attention toward Caroline. "As is usual with such complex matters as a peer's will, there were some . . . discrepancies that needed to be tidied up."

"Please don't tell me you found more creditors."

"Oh, no, it was rather more complicated than that." Mr. Smith hesitated. "One of our partners, Mr. Emerson Smith—no relation of mine—recently passed away. His senior clerk has been reviewing his work, archiving his cases, and redistributing anything still outstanding among the other partners of this firm."

"And?" Mrs. Frogerton prompted as Mr. Smith stared down at his desk.

"It appears that among his possessions the clerk found a copy of a new will filed by your father before his death."

"I beg your pardon?" Caroline blinked at him. "It is almost two years since my father's death, and you have only discovered this document *now*?"

"Mr. Emerson Smith was quite unwell for several years, my lady, and I fear his work suffered as a result."

Mrs. Frogerton sniffed loudly. "If I'd employed him, he would've been out on his ear as soon as he proved incapable of doing his job."

"It is rather . . . hard to dislodge the founding member of a firm, ma'am," Mr. Smith said. "Especially when he is reluctant to admit he can no longer cope."

Mrs. Frogerton's opinion of such antics was clear on her face.

Caroline hastened to intervene. "This will that you found. Is it legal?"

"From what we can ascertain, the answer is yes."

Caroline sat back. "I'm not sure what difference it makes to me, Mr. Smith. In truth, if my father made the will closer to his death, his financial affairs were probably in worse shape than ever. I have nothing of value left to offer his creditors except my current salary and the bequest from my aunt."

Mr. Smith looked shocked. "We would never take your personal money, my lady. We do have some standards."

"You let her father squander her dowry, sir. No wonder she is alarmed," Mrs. Frogerton interjected. "I have already suggested she take your firm to court to rectify that!"

"Once again, I must remind you that such decisions were not made by me, ma'am." Mr. Smith swallowed hard.

"I inherited the case after Mr. Emerson Smith became ill and long after most of Lady Caroline's father's assets had been . . . dissolved."

"Do you have a copy of the new will?" Caroline asked. "Mrs. Frogerton has very graciously offered me access to her own solicitor to review the document."

"Because of Mr. Smith's untimely death, I will have to get permission from my partners to release the will to you, my lady." Mr. Smith paused. "From what I have seen, it makes very interesting reading."

"How so?" Caroline asked.

"I cannot disclose that to you." Mr. Smith folded his hands together on the desk. "Without permission."

Mrs. Frogerton rose to her feet. "We are wasting our time, Caroline. I will speak to Mr. Lewis, and he will act for you in this matter." She glared at Mr. Smith. "Please have a copy of the new will delivered to my residence by tomorrow at the latest. If we do not receive it by three o'clock, please expect us back to collect it in person!"

She took Caroline's arm in a firm grip and swept them both out of the office, leaving Mr. Smith red-faced and stuttering.

"What a ridiculous charade," Mrs. Frogerton said as they settled into the carriage. "The *gall* of the man after all the harm he and his measly mouthed colleagues have allowed to befall you simply to appease the whims of a peer of the realm."

"He certainly wasn't helpful."

"You are too kind, lass. He was deliberately obstructive, which makes me wonder why." Mrs. Frogerton pursed her lips. "He must be aware that his firm's reputation could be damaged by such revelations of mismanagement."

"Perhaps he is simply not used to being hurried," Caroline suggested. "The legal profession is not known for its speed. My father's former will hasn't passed probate yet."

"We'll see what Mr. Lewis says about that!" Mrs. Frogerton said. "We'll send a note to him the moment we get back. I'll wager there's money involved somewhere, and that's why they are being so cagey."

Caroline doubted that. Her father had existed in a world where paying his debts of "honor" as a gentleman was a priority, while he kept his staff and tradesmen waiting years to be reimbursed. On occasion, Caroline's mother had used her pin money to pay the servants' wages, while her father had been off on one of his jaunts abroad. Any new money would go to satisfy his creditors.

She looked out the window as the carriage went down the street. Her initial reluctance to meet the solicitor had been confirmed a hundredfold. Nothing good ever came from her father, and she rather wished she could forget the whole affair. She glanced over at Mrs. Frogerton. Not that her employer would let the matter drop now. When she was determined to solve a problem, very little was allowed to stand in her way.

Mrs. Frogerton caught her gaze. "I know this is difficult for you, lass, but I can't sit by and let you suffer when I have the means to make things right."

"I appreciate that, ma'am."

"I must confess that being in London twirling my thumbs while Dotty picks a husband has bored me to tears. I'm not used to being idle." Mrs. Frogerton met Caroline's gaze. "And I acknowledge that I might be interfering too much."

"I don't know what I would do if I didn't have your support." Caroline met her employer's frankness with her own. "Since I lost my status in society, I've come to realize that one has to fight for one's rights with all the resources available."

"That's my girl." Mrs. Frogerton offered her a smile of approval. "I like to see the fight in you." She opened her reticule to find her handkerchief. "And if we don't hear back from Mr. Smith by tomorrow, we will return."

Caroline smiled at her. "I never doubted it for a second."

* * *

To her credit, Mrs. Frogerton did allow Mr. Smith the full twenty-four hours to comply with her request for a copy of the will before she ordered the carriage and sallied forth with Caroline at her side. It was a dreary day, and the streets were awash with rain and accumulated filth that slowed their journey and endangered any pedestrian unwise enough to be out.

When they reached the solicitors' office near Grays Inn, the coachman stopped the carriage as close to the front door as he could manage without the horses mounting the pavement. Mrs. Frogerton paused as she descended.

"Why on earth would they have the front door open in this weather?"

Caroline, who had followed closely with an umbrella, was simply glad they could walk right into the lobby without having to wait for admittance. Inside, there was a veritable hum of voices followed by a high-pitched screech that made Mrs. Frogerton jump.

"Good lord! What was that?"

The answer appeared as a woman ran down the main staircase clutching her bosom. "He's gone! Thieves have taken him!"

Three older gentlemen followed her, two of them puffing quite heavily.

"Mrs. Patterson! Calm yourself!"

Mrs. Frogerton tapped one of the men on the shoulder.

"What is going on?"

Mrs. Patterson spoke before the man could answer. "He's been abducted, I swear it!"

"Who?"

"Our Mr. Smith! We have to send a message to the police!"

While the solicitors conferred, Mrs. Frogerton moved toward the stairs. "Come with me, Caroline."

"Mrs. Frogerton . . ."

Her employer failed to pay heed and was already on her way upstairs.

"Shouldn't we wait for the police?" Caroline asked.

There was no answer, and with a resigned sigh, Caroline trudged after Mrs. Frogerton.

"Goodness gracious!" Mrs. Frogerton stood in the doorway of Mr. Smith's office. "The room has been ransacked!"

Chapter 3

"No wonder Mrs. Patterson was concerned," Caroline said as she stared at the open drawers of the desk, the files scattered all over the floor, and the parchment scrolls that had rolled off into the corners of the room. "I wonder what happened to Mr. Smith?"

"That is a very good question." To her credit, Mrs. Frogerton had ventured no farther than the door, although she was obviously eager to explore further. "One has to wonder whether he fled when an intruder burst in—which might explain why the front door was open—or if he did this himself."

"Why would he destroy his own office, ma'am?" Caroline asked.

"Perhaps he had misplaced something and was searching for it."

"In such a fashion?" Caroline indicated the chaos. "Surely solicitors are trained to treat legal documents with more respect."

"Perhaps someone demanded something from him, and he panicked when he couldn't immediately hand it over." Mrs. Frogerton wasn't done speculating. "Mayhap he and the intruder were working together?"

"None of those suggestions would reflect well on

Mr. Smith, ma'am," Caroline pointed out. "It is far more likely that someone broke in, Mr. Smith discovered them, and the intruder was chased out of the building in a panic."

"But why would Mr. Smith leave the building as well? That woman suggested he'd been kidnapped. Wouldn't he simply run downstairs, alert the staff, lock all the exits, and await the arrival of the Metropolitan Police?" Mrs. Frogerton countered.

Caroline had no answer for that, and Mrs. Frogerton nodded.

"I suggest we adjourn to the lobby and await the arrival of the police."

"Or we could go back to Half Moon Street and allow things to return to normal before we bother them again," Caroline suggested.

Mrs. Frogerton rolled her eyes and set off down the corridor. "Come along, lass. It might be a long wait."

By the time a familiar figure strode into the lobby of the solicitors' office, Caroline was rather hungry and had begun to hope Mrs. Frogerton would show signs of wanting to leave. None of her subtle hints about Dorothy's whereabouts or potential callers at Mrs. Frogerton's house had encouraged her employer to move, but the lack of a cup of tea had begun to wear on her.

"Lady Caroline, Mrs. Frogerton!" Inspector Ross of the Metropolitan Police stopped beside their couch and doffed his hat. He wore a long dark-blue coat over black trousers and serviceable boots and carried a cane. "Whatever brings you here?"

They both stood to curtsy. "We had an appointment with Mr. Smith," Mrs. Frogerton explained, which wasn't exactly true. "We arrived just after he'd gone missing."

"You didn't happen to see him on the streets, did you?" Inspector Ross's gaze stayed on Caroline as he smiled. He was an attractive dark-haired gentleman with a sympathetic way to him that belied his sharp instincts and his surprising choice of career. "That would at least give us some idea about what happened to the poor blighter."

"We saw nothing of particular import, Inspector, except that the front door was wide open when we arrived," Caroline said. "It was raining quite hard."

"Do you think he was attacked in his own office?" Mrs. Frogerton asked.

"I only know the bare minimum of the situation, ma'am. I will have a far better idea after I've spoken to my constable."

"Of course." Mrs. Frogerton sat back down. "We shall await you here."

Inspector Ross's amused glance met Caroline's resigned one.

"Have you given your statements to my constable yet, ladies?"

"Yes, of course." Mrs. Frogerton nodded. "It was the first thing we did when he arrived."

"Then there is really no need for you to inconvenience yourselves further. Might I suggest you return home, and I will come to visit you when I have more to share about the case?"

"If you are quite certain there is nothing more we can do." Mrs. Frogerton sounded quite disappointed. "We are obviously concerned about Mr. Smith."

"I'm sure you are." Inspector Ross turned back toward the front door and opened it. "Shall I call up your carriage? I noticed your coachman is just down the street."

"The poor man must be soaked," Caroline murmured, slightly in awe of the deft way the inspector had handled Mrs. Frogerton's objections. "And the horses have been standing in the rain for almost an hour."

Mrs. Frogerton sighed. "Then we will go." She shook out her skirts. "I am relying on you, Inspector."

He bowed. "I promise I won't let you down, ma'am. By the time I visit, I hope to have a more complete story and a resolution."

"That would be wonderful." Mrs. Frogerton turned to Caroline, who was smiling at Inspector Ross. "Do you still have the umbrella? I think we might need it."

True to his word, Inspector Ross came to the house just before the dinner hour and was welcomed into the drawing room by Mrs. Frogerton. He warmed his hands in front of the fire and then took a seat beside Caroline on the couch. He'd changed out of his work attire into something less formal but far better tailored.

"Would you like some tea, Inspector?" Caroline asked.

"No, thank you." He smiled at her. "It is rather late, and I'm sure you are ready for your dinner."

"You are more than welcome to join us," Mrs. Frogerton offered. "We always enjoy your company, don't we, Caroline?"

Caroline pretended she hadn't heard the question and turned to Inspector Ross. "Have you located Mr. Smith yet, sir?"

"Unfortunately not. He did not go home and has not returned to his office." Inspector Ross frowned. "It is most peculiar."

"Do his colleagues have any idea as to what he was working on when he was attacked?" Mrs. Frogerton asked. "I assume he was the victim and didn't simply ransack his own office and run away."

"One of the clerks was passing through the lobby when he saw an unknown gentleman enter the premises and head up the stairs," Inspector Ross said. "He assumed the man was a client who knew where he was going and thought no more of it until Mrs. Patterson started screaming."

"One has to wonder what Mr. Smith, who, forgive me, seems like a man of little importance, was involved in to attract such violence," Mrs. Frogerton mused. "Do we know what was stolen from his office?"

"His clerk is still searching through the debris trying to

work that out, ma'am." Inspector Ross hesitated. "He did, however, note that some of the documents laid out on Mr. Smith's desk had a familiar name on them."

"Whose was that?" Mrs. Frogerton asked.

"Yours." Inspector Ross looked directly at Caroline. "I understand that the firm has been the family solicitors for the Morton estate for generations."

"Yes, that's why we were visiting them," Caroline admitted somewhat reluctantly. "There has been some recent discussion about my late father's will."

"Was that on the desk?" Mrs. Frogerton intervened. "Because Caroline would dearly love to see it."

"I'm not sure, ma'am," Inspector Ross said. "The junior clerk was still clearing up when I left."

"I doubt my father's will is relevant to what happened to poor Mr. Smith," Caroline said. "If the attacker had wished to avail himself of the document, he would hardly have needed to ransack the office if it was in plain sight on Mr. Smith's desk."

"That is true." Mrs. Frogerton nodded. "But we don't know if the will is still there, do we?"

"Not yet, ma'am, but if it was swept off the desk, then it will surface eventually. I wouldn't concern yourself too much." Inspector Ross rose to his feet. "It is far more likely the rogue was after something far more valuable. I'm sure by tomorrow we'll have a better idea of what that was."

"You don't think Mr. Smith was involved in the incident?" Mrs. Frogerton asked.

Inspector Ross paused. "As in acting as an accomplice to the intruder?"

"We wondered why he ran out of the door rather than raising the alarm with his colleagues to alert the authorities."

"People can act very strangely when they are faced with violence, ma'am. It's quite possible that Mr. Smith panicked and is currently lost somewhere in London."

"If that is the case, then one has to worry for his safety." Mrs. Frogerton frowned.

"We have a constable stationed at his home address and one will remain at the office in case he returns," Inspector Ross said. "I'm hopeful he will turn up."

Mrs. Frogerton looked over at Caroline. "Will you escort Inspector Ross out, my dear, and ask the butler what time dinner will be served?" She smiled at her guest. "Are you quite certain you can't stay?"

"I have to return to the office and write up my report, ma'am." Inspector Ross bowed. "But I would be delighted to join you on a different evening if the invitation still holds?"

Mrs. Frogerton beamed. "We'd like that very much, wouldn't we, Caroline?"

Caroline rose to her feet and walked Inspector Ross down to the hallway below. He retrieved his cloak from the butler and put on his hat.

"Thank you for taking the time to set Mrs. Frogerton's mind at rest," Caroline said.

"It's always a pleasure to be of service to you both." He smiled. "Although one does have to wonder at your employer's propensity to get caught up in criminal enterprises."

"She has a very inquiring mind, sir." Caroline returned his smile. "Although, in this case, her concern was all on my behalf."

"You mentioned your father's will?" She went to speak, and he carried on. "I know it is none of my business, but I am aware of the circumstances surrounding his death. If you require any assistance, I am more than willing to aid you."

"Thank you," Caroline said.

"You already know I believe that you and your sister were very badly served by your family. Despite my somewhat lowly occupation, I do have excellent connections in high places if wrongs need to be righted. I insist that you call on me if you need them."

"That is very kind of you." Caroline stood back as the butler opened the front door and a gust of wind brought in the rain. "Do you have your carriage? It is still rather wet out there."

"I don't mind the rain." He looked down at her. "If it becomes too bad, I can always hail a hackney cab. Take care, Lady Caroline."

She watched him walk down the street, his head lowered to avoid the wind, until he turned the corner and was out of sight. She knew exactly which families he was connected to by birth, and he hadn't overstated their influence in both political and social circles. But she had also learned that every offer of help came with a price . . .

She spoke to the butler and then went back upstairs to the drawing room.

"Well?" Mrs. Frogerton looked at her expectantly. "Did Inspector Ross say anything interesting?"

"Only that he marveled at our ability to turn up in the most awkward of circumstances." Caroline sat down. "The butler says dinner will be served in half an hour. Are we still expecting Viscount Lingard?"

"As far as I am aware, he is coming with his mother," Mrs. Frogerton said. "A great concession on her part to enter the house and sit down to dine with a woman engaged in *trade*."

"The aristocracy has always managed to hold their noses and endure when needs must, ma'am, and even a family such as the Lingards require endless funds." Caroline picked up her embroidery but found it hard to concentrate.

"We shall ask Inspector Ross to join us early next week for dinner."

"If he is able to come. His job is rather demanding."

"Does that put you off?" Mrs. Frogerton inquired.

"Off what?"

"Him."

"I wasn't aware that my feelings as to his availability had any bearing on anything at all, ma'am."

"Come now, lass. You must have noticed how he looks at you."

Caroline shrugged. "I have a pretty face. Men often look at me. It means nothing."

"Who has a pretty face?" Dorothy came in with a rustle of skirts. She wore her favorite yellow, a shade that didn't particularly flatter her but that Caroline had failed to dissuade her from wearing. Her skirt had three large ruffles of lace around the hem, and her neckline was fashionably low. "Don't tell me—you're discussing Caroline again."

"You're very pretty, too, my dear," Mrs. Frogerton said briskly. "And you look very nice in your new ball gown. Are you intending to go out after dinner?"

"No." Dorothy glanced down at herself. "I just thought I'd make an effort because Augustus and his mother are coming to dinner."

It was rather a grand dress for a quiet family dinner, but there was no point in saying anything. Caroline knew Lady Lingard would notice but not comment because she'd reconciled herself to the marriage and wouldn't wish to upset her son, who was besotted with his future bride. Dorothy was obviously happy with the new dress and her decision to accept Viscount Lingard's proposal at the end of the Season.

The butler appeared at the door.

"You have a visitor, ma'am."

"Goodness me, our guests are early for once." Mrs. Frogerton went to stand up.

"No, ma'am. It's Dr. Harris."

Dorothy gave an exaggerated sigh. "What on earth does he want?"

"Please send him up." Mrs. Frogerton glanced over at

Caroline. They were very familiar with Dr. Harris, who often aided and abetted them in their various adventures, and occasionally was the cause of them. "Were you expecting him, my dear?"

"Not at all, ma'am."

"Well, whatever it is, he'd better be quick, because I don't want him here when Augustus and his mother arrive," Dorothy said. "He's far too rude for polite company."

"He certainly speaks his mind," Mrs. Frogerton agreed. "But I like that."

Dr. Harris came in and bowed. "Good evening, ladies. Might I have a word?"

Dorothy glanced pointedly at the clock. She and Dr. Harris were old adversaries. "Only if you are finished and on your way in ten minutes."

"I have to be back at work within half an hour, Miss Frogerton. I won't trouble you for long."

"Don't be rude, Dotty." Mrs. Frogerton advanced toward the doctor, who looked his usual disheveled self. "How can we assist you?"

Dr. Harris directed his attention at Caroline. "I have a patient on my ward who arrived at the hospital three hours ago. He appears to have cracked his skull on the pavement and has yet to regain consciousness."

"And?" Dorothy asked. "Why on earth are you telling us?"

For once, Dr. Harris ignored Dorothy's provocation and continued to address Caroline.

"It appears he was robbed, but whether that happened before or after his injuries, I cannot yet tell. We did discover something on his person. In the inside pocket of his coat there was an empty envelope." He paused. "It was addressed to you, Miss Morton."

Caroline pressed her hand to her throat. "I beg your pardon?"

"The envelope had your name on it. I am hoping you might be willing to visit the ward in the morning to see if you know this gentleman."

"That's ridiculous," Dorothy said. "How do you know it's even her? There must be hundreds of Miss Mortons in London."

"Agreed, but this was addressed to Lady Caroline Morton, of which, to my knowledge, there is only one."

Caroline glanced over at Mrs. Frogerton, who nodded slightly. "I could come with you now, Dr. Harris."

"There is no need. He'll be in far better shape tomorrow. I'd like to keep him quiet overnight."

"You think he'll live?"

"Head injuries are always difficult, but he's well-nourished and doesn't appear to have any other medical issues. I'm hopeful for a complete recovery."

"What time would you like me to attend you?" Caroline asked.

"At nine? That's when I start my shift. I can meet you at the entrance to the hospital and take you to the ward." He reached for her hand, and then stopped himself, and bowed. "Thank you, Miss Morton."

"You are most welcome, Dr. Harris."

He nodded and turned to the door. "If anything changes overnight, one of my colleagues will let me know. I won't trouble you unless it's urgent."

"Good, because she needs her sleep." Mrs. Frogerton's practical tones broke through Caroline's bewilderment. "We will see you in the morning at St. Thomas's, as agreed."

Dr. Harris left, and Caroline looked helplessly at her employer.

"What on earth is going on?"

"I'm not sure, lass, but whatever it is we will deal with it." Mrs. Frogerton came over to squeeze Caroline's hand. "I don't know why Inspector Ross thinks I'm the one who always ends up in trouble when I'm beginning to believe it's you."

"Maybe she's cursed." Dorothy sounded quite cheerful at the prospect. "Like the heroines in those gothic novels you love to read, Mother."

Caroline shuddered.

The butler returned and looked inquiringly at his mistress. "Your guests have arrived, ma'am. Do you wish me to bring them up here, or will you go down and join them?"

"We'll go down," Mrs. Frogerton said. "Thank you."

She looked at Dorothy and then at Caroline. "Now, not a word of this to the Lingards."

"As if I'd mention Dr. Harris in polite company," Dorothy said. "I do hope he left by the back door and didn't bump into Augustus on the way out."

Mrs. Frogerton shook her head. "I would never have believed you'd become so high in the instep, Dotty. You've not married into the peerage yet, my girl."

"But I will be." Dorothy's smile was triumphant. "And then Caroline won't be the only one with a title, and I believe I will outrank her."

She swept out of the room, her head held high, and Mrs. Frogerton followed. Caroline took a moment to compose herself. She was beginning to fear Dorothy was right and that she was something of a curse on any household. Part of her wished she could run upstairs to her bedroom and hide for the rest of the evening. But duty called. Mrs. Frogerton relied on her to make polite conversation with their titled guests, and to steer Dorothy away from saying the wrong thing, and she would do the job she was paid for.

Caroline took a deep breath, went down the stairs, and headed toward the receiving room from where the gentle hum of conversation already emanated. She'd been taught from the cradle how to conceal her emotions, and her training stood her in good stead. No one would know how out of sorts she was, because despite her current circumstances, she was still a lady—and a lady carried on, regardless.

*   *   *

After a sleepless night, Caroline alighted from the carriage outside St. Thomas's and turned to assist her employer, who had insisted on accompanying her.

Dr. Harris awaited them at the main entrance. He was already dressed for work and was consulting his pocket watch as they approached.

"Good, you arrived in a timely manner. Come along."

"Good morning to you, too, Dr. Harris," Mrs. Frogerton called out. "Always a pleasure."

They followed him into the building, which smelled of disinfectant and other unmentionables.

They went up two flights of stairs at some speed, and then he stopped abruptly in front of a door to his right. "Wait here."

Mrs. Frogerton, who was still puffing from the stairs, waved an airy hand at him. "Go ahead."

He returned within a few minutes, his expression concerned. "I had them move the patient into a smaller room where you can speak to him more privately, Miss Morton. He doesn't appear to remember his own name, so if you can identify him, it would be a great help."

"I'll do my best, Doctor Harris."

Caroline followed him through the door, her gaze taking in the long narrow ward with beds on either side filled with patients. There was a deathly stillness along with the stench of poverty that spoke of lack of hope, despite the valiant efforts of the very few staff to keep their charges alive.

"In here, Miss Morton." Dr. Harris opened a door to his left and ushered them inside. "Do you recognize this man?"

"Yes," Caroline said with a sense of resignation. "It's Mr. Smith." She moved toward the bed. "He appears to have lost his spectacles, but I'm quite certain it is him."

"I agree," said Mrs. Frogerton. "That might explain why he had an envelope with your name on it in his pocket, Caroline."

"Mr. Smith?" Caroline spoke softly to the patient, and his eyes fluttered. He had an ugly wound on the right side of his face with extensive bruising and the beginnings of a black eye. "Do you remember me?"

He squinted at her and visibly flinched. "Lady Caroline!" He grabbed hold of her wrist. "I did my best!"

"Of course you did, sir." Caroline attempted to soothe his agitation. "Now that we have established your identity, I'm sure Dr. Harris can alert your family and your employers as to your whereabouts."

He shook his head and groaned. "No, I cannot go back—" His grip tightened, and Caroline glanced over at Dr. Harris, who had come to stand on the other side of the bed. "Be careful!"

His eyes closed and he fell back, releasing her hand.

Dr. Harris took his pulse and gestured for them to leave the room.

After rejoining them in the ward, Dr. Harris said, "I'm glad you recognized him, Miss Morton. Can you give me his full name and address?"

"He is Mr. Jeremy Smith, a partner at Smith, Smith, Potkins, and Jones—my family solicitors near Grays Inn. I don't know his home address." Caroline considered what to say next. "You might also wish to contact Inspector Ross at Great Scotland Yard who is investigating Mr. Smith's disappearance."

"What has he done?" Dr. Harris asked. "Embezzled the firms' funds?"

"He was attacked in his office and ran away."

"That certainly explains his current condition. Although, how did he manage to get himself out of the building and end up in Southwark?"

"I saw no blood in his office, did you, Caroline?" Mrs. Frogerton asked. "One has to suspect that his injuries occurred after he left."

"Any fool running around the streets of London in a blind terror will eventually bump into someone willing to relieve them of their belongings and possibly their life," Dr. Harris said. "We see it every day."

"Then I'm glad Mr. Smith ended up in your care," Mrs. Frogerton said. "And that he will make a full recovery."

"We'll have to see about that, but I'm fairly optimistic he'll come about." Dr. Harris bowed to them both. "I must get back to work. Thank you for your help, Miss Morton. I'll inform his employer and Inspector Ross of Mr. Smith's current whereabouts."

They left the building and went to the carriage. Mrs. Frogerton told the coachman to take them back to Half Moon Street, and the horses moved off.

"One has to wonder what Mr. Smith had in that envelope addressed to you, my dear."

"I suppose he could have decided to hand deliver my father's will to me," Caroline suggested. "He probably wasn't expecting you to be true to your word and return for it so promptly."

"If that is the case, where is it?"

Caroline looked up. "Lost, I assume."

"Or taken, along with his pocketbook and watch. Although, what would a thief do with such a thing?"

"Parchment has value," Caroline said. "It can be reused."

"Then one has to hope Mr. Smith wasn't bringing the original with him."

"To be honest, ma'am, I have no objection to the will disappearing for good."

"You can't mean that!" Mrs. Frogerton looked truly shocked. "Mr. Smith implied that it might change matters for the better."

Caroline looked out the window. "I sincerely doubt anything involving my father could improve my current circumstances."

"I just want you to have what is yours, lass." Mrs. Frogerton folded her hands together on her lap. "You deserve that, at least."

They completed the rest of the journey in silence as rain threatened and the low clouds took on an ugly black hue. When they arrived at the house, the butler hurried out to greet them.

"Mrs. Frogerton, you have guests in the drawing room. Miss Frogerton is entertaining them by herself."

"Oh, good lord, we can't have that." Mrs. Frogerton took off her bonnet and cloak. "Goodness knows what she'll be saying. Why did you let them through the door?"

"Miss Frogerton saw the carriage approach from the upstairs window and came down herself to open the door."

"Then we'll have to make the best of it." Mrs. Frogerton set off up the stairs. "Bring some refreshments. Caroline and I could do with something to warm us up."

"Yes, ma'am." The butler bowed. "I was just on my way to the kitchens when I spied your carriage."

Caroline followed Mrs. Frogerton, who was muttering something about impropriety and her daughter's willfulness. She could only hope her employer and her daughter would refrain from having an argument in front of the guests, whoever they might be.

Caroline almost bumped into Mrs. Frogerton's back when her employer stopped dead in the doorway and screeched.

"Good Lord! Samuel!"

"Mother." An auburn-haired man came toward her, his face wreathed in smiles. "Are you surprised?"

Dorothy clapped her hands and grinned at her mother. "Isn't this wonderful? Samuel has come to London!"

Caroline, who had remained by the door while her employer was surrounded by her children, almost jumped when someone to her right cleared their throat.

"Miss Morton. What a happy reunion to witness."

She turned to see the DeBloom family regarding her with various expressions of delight and disapproval.

"Mrs. DeBloom, Miss DeBloom, Mr. DeBloom." She curtsied.

"Miss Frogerton invited us to call and take tea with her today," Mrs. DeBloom said. "It appears she forgot her brother was to arrive."

"I'm not sure he was expected at all, ma'am," Caroline responded. "Mrs. Frogerton didn't mention it to me."

"Perhaps you are not privy to all the family secrets, Miss Morton," Mrs. DeBloom said sweetly. "You are . . . employed, are you not?"

"Very happily employed, ma'am," Caroline replied with a smile. "I am quite certain Mrs. Frogerton would wish you to stay and share this joyous occasion with her." She stepped forward and caught her employer's eye. "Ma'am?"

Mrs. Frogerton came straight over to shake Mrs. De-Bloom's hand. "I do apologize for my rudeness! I was not expecting my son to take a trip to London."

"I'm sure you'd prefer him to be toiling away on your behalf up north, wouldn't you?" Mrs. DeBloom said. She glanced at her daughter. "Miss Frogerton invited Clarissa for tea. Luckily, my daughter is not the kind of girl to take offense when her plans are overset by others' thoughtlessness."

Caroline noticed Mrs. DeBloom's tongue was far less sweet now that her son had failed to secure the Frogerton heiress as his bride.

"Dorothy?" Mrs. Frogerton held out her hand to her daughter. "Come and apologize to the DeBlooms."

"I certainly didn't mean to offend," Dorothy said. "I was just as surprised as you were to see Samuel coming up the stairs behind you." She smiled beguilingly at Mr. De-Bloom, who had remained remarkably quiet. "Please do join us. I promise I won't neglect any of you again."

Caroline excused herself and went to make sure that the butler had allocated an appropriate room for Mr. Froger-ton's use, and that a maid would be sent up to light the fire and to make sure the bed linen wasn't damp. On her way back up the stairs, she noticed Mr. DeBloom loitering on the landing.

The last time she'd seen him he'd insisted his mother had involved her late father in a nefarious scheme to defraud him of money, and that he intended to set things right. At the time, Caroline had wished he'd remained silent. That feeling had only intensified since the muddle over Mr. Smith and the new will.

Mr. DeBloom grinned at her. "There's no need to look so worried, Miss Morton. I don't intend you any harm."

"In my employer's house?" Caroline asked. "With your entire family around you? One would hope not."

"That's my girl."

Caroline went to move past him, and he took hold of her elbow. "I meant what I said when we last met."

She resisted the urge to pull away from his firm grasp and simply stared past him.

"I intend to recompense you for your father's losses."

"So you keep saying." Caroline set her jaw. "I have yet to see a smidgeon of proof for such a grand claim, and until I do, I would ask you to stop bothering me."

He let go of her arm and looked hurt. "You don't mean that."

"I can assure you I do." She raised her chin. "Your attentions to me are unwelcome, and this pretext of . . . restoring my fortune smacks of deceit, and I am tired of it."

Not waiting to see how he reacted to her sharp words, she went into the drawing room where Mrs. Frogerton's family and guests had grouped themselves around the fireplace.

To her secret dismay, Mrs. Frogerton was regaling her audience with an account of their adventures at the solicitors' office and what had happened to poor Mr. Smith. Not for the first time, Caroline wished her employer's tendency to enjoy the thrill of a drama was less pronounced. She took a seat and found herself being closely observed by Mr. Frogerton, who didn't look particularly happy.

When the butler appeared with two of the parlor maids

and the promised refreshments, she jumped up to help distribute the tea. Mrs. Frogerton poured, and Caroline handed out the cups.

Mr. Frogerton looked up briefly as she set the tea beside him. "Thank you, miss." He paused. "Is it miss or my lady? My mother uses both in her letters."

"I prefer to be known as Miss Morton, sir."

"Why?" He had something of his mother's directness and an even broader accent. "If I had a title, I'd use it on every occasion."

"With all due respect, Mr. Frogerton, if you acquired a title, you will have earned it through your own hard work, whereas I simply inherited mine through my father, who did nothing to deserve his."

He frowned. "One assumes your ancestors did something to merit the title."

"They supported the accession of William of Normandy to the throne of England and fought with him to secure it."

"Then many would say you deserved what you got." He sat back and looked up at her.

"I am certainly proud of my ancestors, sir."

"But not of your father."

She smiled. "May I offer you some cake?"

"I'd rather have a proper meal." He patted his stomach. "It was a long journey."

"I can arrange for a tray to be brought up to your room?" Caroline offered.

"Or I can take myself down to the kitchen and eat there." He drank his tea in one gulp and stood up. "I don't like to make a fuss."

He wasn't particularly tall, which meant Caroline didn't have to constantly look up at him. He had the same bright brown eyes and charming smile as his mother, but there was a hardness in his gaze that spoke of hidden strength. Caroline had a sense she was being judged, but whether he approved of her or not, she couldn't yet tell.

Mr. Frogerton strode over to his mother and bent to whisper something in her ear. She nodded and waved him off. He left the room after a perfunctory bow to the De-Blooms. Caroline resumed her seat, dividing her attention between Clarissa and Dorothy, who were comparing their upcoming social events.

She could only hope Mr. DeBloom would heed her words and leave her alone. Experience told her that he was persistent to the point of obnoxiousness, but there was nothing she could do about that except maintain her distance. She could mention the matter to Mrs. Frogerton, but her employer was a romantic at heart and still considered Mr. DeBloom as a potential husband for Caroline. And, as Caroline had pointed out earlier, it really wasn't fair of her to expect Mrs. Frogerton to solve all of her problems.

She drank her tea and maintained her fake interest in the general conversation until the DeBlooms left and she was able to retire to her own room for a few hours of much-needed contemplation and solitude.

Chapter 4

When Caroline entered the dining room early the next morning after a sleepless night, she was surprised to see Mr. Frogerton was already awake and sitting at the table eating a hearty breakfast. He wiped his mouth with his napkin and stood up as she approached.

"Good morning, Miss Morton."

"Mr. Frogerton." She made her way to the sideboard to select her usual toast and marmalade. "I see you are an early riser."

"I'm used to getting up at the crack of dawn to make sure my workers are where they should be—earning me money."

"It speaks well of you that you still take on that responsibility yourself, sir." Caroline sat down, and the butler brought her a pot of tea and the morning correspondence.

"My mother insists." He made a face. "She says she used to do it after Father died, and there is no reason for me to stop."

"Mrs. Frogerton is an admirable woman," Caroline said.

"She's certainly a forceful one." Mr. Frogerton got up to replenish his plate. "Very few people dare cross her in our part of the world."

Caroline tried not to smile at the image of her employer surrounded by a cowering group of men. "How wonderful."

"I can see why my mother approves of you," Mr. Frogerton murmured.

Caroline drank some tea and turned to her correspondence. She was just about to open a letter from Susan's school when Dr. Harris strode into the room. He was still dressed in his hospital garb and appeared somewhat agitated.

"I'm sorry to disturb you, Miss Morton, but—" He stared at Mr. Frogerton. "Who is this?"

Mr. Frogerton raised his eyebrows. "I was about to ask you the same question. Do you often burst into my mother's house without permission?"

Caroline stood up. "Mr. Frogerton, this is Dr. Harris, a friend of the family."

Dr. Harris bowed. "My apologies, sir." He returned his attention to Caroline. "He's dead."

"Mr. Smith is dead?" Her stomach twisted.

"Yes. I wanted to tell you as soon as I heard. He died last night."

"You did say that head injuries could be unpredictable."

"But I don't think that's what killed him." Dr. Harris looked furious. "I wasn't there when he died. I'm going to have to wait until tonight to speak to the doctor who was on duty. He's sleeping now. I don't know where he lives, or I'd go and wake him up myself."

Caroline took an unsteady breath. "Thank you for letting us know, Dr. Harris. I'll inform Mrs. Frogerton when she wakes up."

"Good." He bowed. "I'd better get back or I'll be missed." He paused. "You look a bit white around the gills. You're not going to faint or anything, are you? Because I don't have time to attend to you."

"I'm fine, thank you." Caroline gripped the back of the chair and slowly lowered herself into the seat. "May I suggest you tell Inspector Ross what has transpired?"

"I'll tell him if no one else has." Dr. Harris nodded at Mr. Frogerton. "Keep an eye on her, sir. She has a tendency to panic in such situations."

He left, and Caroline took another deep breath, aware that Mr. Frogerton was watching her with some concern.

"Despite what Dr. Harris just said, I am not prone to panicking, Mr. Frogerton."

"I hesitate to disagree with a lady, but you do look a bit shaken." Mr. Frogerton frowned at her.

"I'll come about." Caroline drank more tea and slowly buttered her toast. She would not think about the ramifications of Mr. Smith's sudden death. "I've faced far worse than this."

"So I've heard. My mother is an excellent correspondent, and some of her letters from London have been remarkably like the gothic novels she so enjoys."

Caroline couldn't even raise a smile, as his comment was rather too on point.

"One might suggest you've brought a whole new level of excitement into my mother's life."

"I can assure you that none of it has been intentional."

Mr. Frogerton finished his coffee, his gaze never leaving hers. "The aristocracy are known as being a law unto themselves."

"I wouldn't know much about that, sir, as I was cast out for daring to be the daughter of an aristocrat who killed himself rather than face his debtors."

There was a short silence punctuated only by the ticking of the clock on the mantelpiece.

"My mother didn't tell me that." Mr. Frogerton set down his cup with some care. "She speaks of you in the highest terms of praise—especially concerning your good influence on Dorothy."

"That is most kind of her." Caroline was grateful for his change of subject. "Now, if you will excuse me, I'll go up and tell Mrs. Frogerton about Mr. Smith."

"What is he to you?"

"Mr. Smith?" Caroline paused. "He is, or was, my family's solicitor."

"Then what does he have to do with my mother?"

"Nothing, sir. She is simply trying to help me with some legal matters."

"Ah." His faint smile died. "I do hope she hasn't advanced you a loan while you await the arrival of your fortune."

A furious retort trembled on her lips, but she made herself wait to reply until she gained some modicum of calm. "I have taken nothing from Mrs. Frogerton except my salary."

He raised his eyebrows. "I have offended you."

"Not at all. I've become used to having my character and morals dissected by people who have no knowledge of my circumstances."

"Or your pride."

She raised her chin. "My pride is free, sir, and owes nothing to anyone."

She left the room and was almost up the stairs before she took a ragged breath and clutched at the banister. How *dare* he assume she was on the make? Was that why he'd decided to come to London? To make sure his mother wasn't being bamboozled out of her money by a fortune hunter? If he thought she could deceive his mother, he didn't know either of them very well.

She knocked briskly on Mrs. Frogerton's bedroom door and went in to find her employer sitting up in bed chatting to her dresser, who was laying out her morning garments.

"Caroline! Have you been for a walk? Your face is flushed."

"Not yet, ma'am." Caroline forced a smile. "We had an unexpected visitor. Dr. Harris came to tell us that Mr. Smith died last night. He is not convinced it was of natural causes."

"Good Lord!" Mrs. Frogerton shook her head. "The poor man." She threw back her bedclothes. "I must get up."

"There is no great rush, ma'am," Caroline said. "I'm sure you'd rather be spending time with your son than worrying about a matter that really only concerns me."

Mrs. Frogerton cast her a curious look as the maid poured hot water into a bowl for her to wash her face.

"And there is nothing we can do about it anyway. Dr. Harris said he would be speaking to Inspector Ross."

"It still is most peculiar," Mrs. Frogerton said. "I am beginning to wonder whether it has something to do with your father's will, after all."

"Whereas I'm convinced it's the opposite," Caroline said. "If someone did kill Mr. Smith, it must have been for something far more important than an old will."

"But what if the will *is* of vital importance?"

Caroline gathered herself and looked Mrs. Frogerton right in the eye. "I have the bequest from my aunt, ma'am. I am no longer without financial security. I believe we should let the matter drop and allow Dr. Harris and the authorities to deal with the situation from now on."

"Now why on earth would you say that?" Mrs. Frogerton asked.

"Because as I constantly remind you, ma'am, you do not have to . . . involve yourself in all my problems. I am very grateful, but—"

"Caroline."

"Yes, ma'am?"

"I wish to finish dressing. I will see you in the dining room when I'm ready for my breakfast."

Caroline curtsied and left the room, aware that she'd offended her employer, but what else could she do? She couldn't allow Mr. Frogerton to believe she had some sway over his mother when he had obviously come to London prepared to think the worst of her. The affair with Mr. Smith was a Morton family matter, and there was nothing anyone could do now that Mr. Smith was dead.

She went into the dining room and was relieved to see Mr. Frogerton had departed. She sat down in her chair and poured herself some more tea. She tasted it and shuddered, realizing it had gone cold. There was correspondence to sort through, and she focused on that mundane task as she tried to regain her composure.

She'd never been at outs with her employer before. After her first few difficult weeks of employment, she'd willingly accepted Mrs. Frogerton's attempts to make her feel like a valued member of the household. In truth, she'd needed the reassurance and support, but had she overstepped her bounds and allowed herself to consider Mrs. Frogerton as her friend?

It was a pertinent reminder that she was paid a salary and had been engaged as a companion to smooth the Frogerton ladies' passage through the highest levels of society. She looked down at the invitation in her hand and placed it on the pile for Dorothy's perusal. The next letter came from Susan's school but wasn't addressed in her sister's hand.

Caroline opened it and checked the signature at the bottom—it was the headmistress's.

> *My dear Lady Caroline,*
> *I have recently discovered that Susan has been receiving letters from her cousin Mabel concealed within other correspondence from an 'aunt' in Folkestone. I have not alerted her to this discovery because I would appreciate your instruction on how best to proceed. I will hold any further letters from this person and keep them for your inspection on your next visit. I enclose the letter I found tucked into one of Susan's books.*
> *I can only apologize for my lack of vigilance in this*

*matter and assure you that we will be keeping a close
eye on Susan to make sure she is not receiving messages
by other means. I do hope you are able to visit soon so
that we can clear this matter up.*

   Yours sincerely,
   Mrs. Jane Forester, Headmistress

Caroline read through the letter again, a sense of numbness enveloping her. Would her troubles never end? How dare Mabel use Susan—a child who had always worshipped her—to gain information about her estranged family? Caroline was doubly glad she'd been vague about the inheritance Susan had received from their aunt Eleanor.

She opened the enclosed letter and recognized Mabel's handwriting immediately.

   Dearest Susan,
   *I cannot say I'm sorry to hear that Mother is dead.
She wasn't kind to me at the end. I <u>would</u> like to know
what she's done with my share of the family money. Can
you find out? I'm sure if you write to Nick, he'd tell you.
He was always on my side just like you are. I can't bear
to think of spiteful Eliza getting everything, can you?*

   *Hopefully we can talk about these things in person
soon. I can't wait to see you.*

   With love, your cousin, M x

Caroline heard Mrs. Frogerton approaching and quickly refolded both letters and put them in her pocket. She returned to sorting out the correspondence as her employer entered, followed by the butler bringing Mrs. Frogerton fresh coffee.

"Where is Samuel?"

Caroline kept her attention on the mail as she replied. "I believe he breakfasted and then stepped out for a walk, ma'am."

The butler added, "Mr. Frogerton said he would present himself in your study at ten to discuss some business matters, ma'am."

"If you see him return from his walk, tell him I will be available at that time." Mrs. Frogerton glanced over at Caroline. "Would you like a fresh pot of tea, lass?"

"That would be most welcome." Caroline smiled at the butler. "Now, what can I get you to eat, ma'am?"

"A little of everything, please."

Caroline put the plate in front of her employer as the butler poured her coffee.

"Thank you."

Mrs. Frogerton ate steadily, leaving Caroline to finish sorting the correspondence and marshal her arguments. She knew Mrs. Frogerton would come about and attack the issue from a new perspective.

"Did you receive anything from your solicitors?" Mrs. Frogerton asked.

"No, ma'am."

"I can't say I'm surprised." Mrs. Frogerton chewed thoughtfully. "Do you intend to write to them?"

"It seems unnecessary. If they find the will, I'm sure they will contact me."

"Hmm." Mrs. Frogerton's expression wasn't hopeful. "I'll ask Mr. Lewis to write to them."

"There is no need to bother him, ma'am. I'm sure he has far more important things to do than chase a phantom will."

"You don't think it exists?"

"If it was in Mr. Smith's possession when he was attacked and robbed, then I doubt it has survived." Caroline paused. "Perhaps it is for the best."

Mrs. Frogerton set her fork on her plate with a clatter. "What's wrong, lass?"

"Nothing, ma'am. I assure you—"

"Balderdash. Something happened, and I'd like to know what it is."

Caroline sighed. "Perhaps it occurred to me that I was . . . taking liberties and becoming over familiar."

"You're not my scullery maid."

"You treat all your employees well, ma'am."

"Who said you were taking liberties?" Mrs. Frogerton persisted.

"Why would you assume I couldn't work that out for myself?"

"Is it because of your inheritance?"

"What?"

"Is the boot on the other foot and you've suddenly decided you're too grand for me?"

"No, ma'am!" Caroline reached across the table to touch her employer's hand. "That has nothing to do with it at all! How could you ever think such a thing when I owe you such gratitude for your kindness, your consideration, your—"

Mrs. Frogerton patted Caroline's fingers. "Then if it has nothing to do with your inheritance, who intimated you were taking advantage of me?"

Caroline went to speak and then stopped.

Mrs. Frogerton nodded. "Who, lass?"

"No one in particular, ma'am," Caroline said carefully. "As I already mentioned, it recently occurred to me that I was taking advantage of your good nature."

Mrs. Frogerton raised an eyebrow. "And what if you are?"

"Perhaps I feel I should be responsible for solving my own problems," Caroline suggested.

"As if I could stop you worrying yourself half to death about things." Mrs. Frogerton sat back and folded her hands in her lap. "If it pains you, I will not ask Mr. Lewis to intervene on your behalf on this matter."

"Thank you, ma'am," Caroline said. "That is most helpful."

"But if things develop further, I *will* do what is necessary to keep you safe." Her steely tone reminded Caroline of Mr. Frogerton.

"That is very kind of you."

Mrs. Frogerton sighed. "I'm not being kind. I have a bad feeling about this, lass—that you are somehow involved—and I simply wish to keep you safe."

"I can only hope you are wrong, ma'am." Caroline slid the pile of correspondence over to Mrs. Frogerton. "And that you can enjoy your son's visit without worrying about me in the slightest. Now, do you wish to go out and visit the milliner before you see Mr. Frogerton at ten?"

"I doubt the milliner will be open until at least eleven." Mrs. Frogerton finished her coffee. "I'll attend to the post, speak to Samuel, and then we can go out."

After their trip to the milliner, Mrs. Frogerton decided she'd take a nap. Despite her best efforts to avoid going near the study earlier, Caroline couldn't help overhearing the shouting match between mother and son that had gone on for at least half an hour. Mr. Frogerton had stormed out, and his mother had emerged from the study with a face like thunder and, for once, reluctant to speak about what had occurred.

As she had no wish to become involved in the politics of the Frogerton family, Caroline hadn't asked any questions and had instead concentrated on discussing fashionable hats and how many feathers one could add to a brim before it became too much.

She was sitting in the drawing room composing a letter to Mrs. Forester when the butler announced a visitor.

"Mr. DeBloom, Miss Morton."

Caroline turned to tell the butler to deny the gentleman admittance only to find Mr. DeBloom smiling down at her.

"I'm sure you don't want to see me, but it is imperative that I speak with you."

With a mingled sense of resignation and apprehension, Caroline rose from the desk and went to sit beside the fire. Mr. DeBloom took up position on the hearthrug, his hands clasped behind his back.

"You asked for more proof, Miss Morton. I want to explain my suspicions about my mother's machinations and request that you at least give me the courtesy of a hearing."

Caroline gestured to the chair opposite hers, and he sat down.

"Thank you." He cleared his throat. "You must understand that it is quite difficult for me to admit that someone in my family has not been entirely honest."

"I know the feeling, sir."

"Perhaps I should start at the beginning. My family do have genuine mining concerns in South Africa. My father's family are originally Dutch, whereas my mother's came from England. Apparently, my grandfather made his peace with the British and continued to acquire mining contracts for coal and copper, which made him rich, but there is always conflict there, and the family fortunes have fluctuated. One of the reasons for my mother's trip to England is to increase the size of our interests here."

Caroline nodded, as he seemed to require some response.

"At some point, the company began exploring for new mining opportunities, which they mapped out with the proper geological surveys for future use. This information is used to encourage speculative buyers to invest in potential new mines before they break ground. None of this is particularly illegal, by the way, Miss Morton. Opening a new mine is a risky business involving massive costs." He paused. "What *is* illegal is to solicit investors in mines that exist only in the imagination."

He stood and walked over to the window. "When my mother insisted on taking complete control of the company after my father's death, things became difficult. As you might imagine, a lot of businesses did not want to work with a woman, and it became hard for her to secure the necessary funds to continue."

"That is hardly her fault," Caroline said.

"Agreed, but her methods for continuing to raise funds became murkier. She would attend parties and gatherings at the homes of the English elite and charm gentlemen with stories of fabulous wealth just waiting to be dug out of the earth on her land. If they showed interest, she would invite them to visit her at the family mines and show them her speculative maps of where the precious metals and gems would be located. Several gentlemen accepted her invitations and many of them invested money."

Caroline met his gaze. "You're suggesting my father was one of those gentlemen who was duped by your mother."

"Yes."

"Have you contacted any of the other investors?"

He raised his eyebrows. "Why would I do that?"

"To pay back their money, too?"

"With respect, Miss Morton, my mother still runs the company and controls the books. I imagine that many of the gentlemen who did invest in the speculative mines either are content to wait to see if their gamble pays off or have already written off the amount as a loss."

"Which is probably what my father did."

Mr. DeBloom hesitated. "Your father was a slightly different case."

"How so?"

"Allegedly, he and my mother developed a . . . close relationship."

"They were lovers?"

"I cannot say for certain. I would not wish to hurt you by implying I know the exact truth."

"I am no stranger to my father's long list of infidelities, Mr. DeBloom. The jewelry he lavished on other women often came from my mother's family and was supposed to come down to my sister and me."

Mr. DeBloom looked stricken. He slid his hand inside his coat and brought out a letter.

"You asked for proof. This is one of the bank drafts your father gave my mother."

Caroline took the much-folded piece of parchment and opened it. "He paid her *five thousand pounds*. That's a small fortune."

"Yes, and I'm fairly certain that wasn't the only draft from his bank."

Caroline raised her head to look at him. "How did you get this if your mother controls the accounts?"

He shrugged. "I was in her office one day waiting for her to return, and this piece of parchment had fallen to the floor. I picked it up, stuffed it in my pocket, and almost forgot about it until I met you at the Frogertons' and realized who you were."

Caroline almost said, "How convenient," but kept it to herself. She had a sense that Mr. DeBloom wasn't being quite as honest as he purported to be, and that made her doubt his words even with the evidence of her father's profligacy right in front of her.

"Might I keep this, sir?" She indicated the bank draft.

"Unfortunately, I cannot allow that. It is the only piece of evidence I possess as of now."

"Then may I write down the pertinent details?" She was fairly certain she could discover whether the payment had actually gone through from her father's bank records. "My father wasn't known for honoring his debts or his cheques, Mr. DeBloom."

"You're suggesting it might never have been paid by the bank." Mr. DeBloom smiled. "That would serve my mother right, but please, go ahead and check. I will attempt to find more evidence, but it is difficult when either my mother, Mr. Kruger, her business manager, or her secretary are present."

"Mrs. DeBloom has an office in London?"

"Yes—which is convenient for her but makes it more difficult for me to infiltrate, because there is always someone about."

"I thought you ran the company with your mother?"

"I do, but to be honest, Miss Morton, she barely allows me any authority whatsoever."

There was a hint of grievance in Mr. DeBloom's voice that was hard to ignore. It made Caroline wonder how much his resentment affected his opinions of her business dealings.

Caroline copied out the bank details and handed the draft back to Mr. DeBloom, who had reclaimed his seat.

"This is all very interesting, Mr. DeBloom, but with respect, I cannot see how what happened in the past between my father and your mother on a different continent has any impact on the present."

Mr. DeBloom sat forward. "As I said, I intend to repay you."

"My father made many bad business decisions. No one is required to reimburse him for his own foolishness."

"He was duped by my mother," Mr. DeBloom repeated. "She pretended to care for him and stole his money. That is not acceptable. When I gain control of the company, I will right that wrong."

"That is very admirable of you, Mr. DeBloom." Caroline stood up. "Now, if you will excuse me, I need to attend to Mrs. Frogerton."

Mr. DeBloom rose to his feet, too. "You don't believe me."

Caroline walked toward the door and opened it. "I have no opinion on the matter, sir."

"You don't think I'll do it, do you?"

"As I said—"

"I'm willing to expose my own mother as a thief, and you still doubt me." He walked toward her and paused in the doorway.

"Mr. DeBloom . . ."

He grabbed her hand, brought it to his lips, and kissed it. "I'll prove you wrong, and when you beg my pardon, I'll accept your apology on the condition that you take me more seriously in future."

Luckily, before she could form a reply that would not have been complimentary in the slightest, he released her hand, winked, and walked away.

Caroline peered over the banister to make sure he left and then returned to the drawing room, her thoughts in turmoil. Surely Mr. DeBloom must realize that if he ruined his mother, he'd destroy the family business as well. Even with her limited experience, she suspected that any company accused of defrauding investors would not survive long if they were exposed.

And if the company was lost, how would he pay his debts then? Not that she wanted his money. It came with too many obligations attached to it—her gratitude, her acceptance of him as a suitor—things she hadn't asked for.

She was still pondering the matter when Mrs. Frogerton appeared, much refreshed from her nap. They went down to the dining room, where there was no sign of either of her children.

"Dotty is taking Samuel out for a jaunt around London," Mrs. Frogerton explained. "She's going to show him all the sights, and this evening Augustus is coming to dinner to meet him."

"How pleasant for Dorothy to have her brother's companionship," Caroline remarked as she helped herself to the dishes laid out on the sideboard. "I often wished I had an older brother."

"If that was the case, lass, you'd probably not be in the financial straits you're in. Any brother worth his salt would've stopped your father spending his money like water." She paused. "Samuel and I have our differences, but I know he wants the best for our business ventures and for his family."

Caroline recalled the shouting earlier and could only marvel at the way the Frogerton family communicated. But even though they fought, she could tell they loved each other dearly.

"May I ask you something, ma'am?" Caroline took her seat at the table.

"Is it about Inspector Ross?" Mrs. Frogerton looked up. "Did I forget to tell you?"

"I wasn't thinking of him, specifically, but is there something I should know?"

"He's coming to dinner tonight." Mrs. Frogerton smiled at her. "He said he does have some police business to discuss, but that we will be his last call, and after that he is off duty and can dine with us."

"Did you mention it to Cook?" Caroline asked.

"Yes, dear. I just forgot to tell you," Mrs. Frogerton reassured her. "Now, what was it you wished to ask me?"

"It's about a business matter, ma'am." Caroline had thought long and hard about how to phrase her question without being too obvious. "I read something in the paper about a business owner's practices being challenged by his son. I wondered how much power the son would have to make such a challenge. Would it depend on how much of the company he owned himself?"

"What was the dispute about?"

"Money." Caroline hesitated. "The son believes the owner has not been dealing ethically with his customers."

"You mean he's engaged in fraud? Or he's taken out loans on false pretenses or assessment of assets?"

"I'm not quite sure what some of those terms mean, ma'am, but I believe that is something like what might have occurred."

"And does the son think he has evidence of these crimes?"

"What would such evidence look like?" Caroline asked cautiously. "And what if it was from several years ago?"

"He'd need copies of the full accounts, the banking details, and any correspondence relating to such matters," Mrs. Frogerton said briskly. "It's not an impossible task. I've known at least two mill masters who were exposed by their own families."

"And what happened to the businesses if the owner is declared a fraud?"

Mrs. Frogerton looked at her. "Are you concerned about me, lass? Even though Samuel and I disagree on a lot of things, he wouldn't be able to accuse me of stealing a penny, because I run my business honestly."

Caroline put down her fork. "I . . . never meant this to be about you, ma'am. I can only apologize if I gave that impression."

"It's just that it's unlike you to be interested in such commercial matters."

Caroline decided she would have to give Mrs. Frogerton a version of the truth if she wished to get some answers. And if she shared her concerns, it might stop her employer from considering Mr. DeBloom as a potential suitor for her.

"Mr. DeBloom mentioned something about his mother's control of the company, which made me wonder about the matter, ma'am."

Mrs. Frogerton beamed at her. "It is very wise of you to consider his financial circumstances before you commit to anything, lass."

"I have no intention of committing to anything at all. I merely wondered at his sense of grievance against his own mother."

"And you wondered whether Samuel feels the same about me?" Mrs. Frogerton nodded. "It is a valid point. From what I have observed, Mrs. DeBloom doesn't involve her son in her business dealings at all, whereas Samuel already owns thirty percent of our company and will own more as time goes on."

"I have no idea whether Mr. DeBloom owns anything," Caroline said. "He hardly shows any interest in working and spends his days escorting his sister to social events."

"You prefer a man who works for his living like Inspector Ross." Mrs. Frogerton nodded. "Quite right."

"I don't prefer any of them, ma'am, but I have learned to detest idleness and appreciate those who make their own way in the world."

"I can't argue with that."

The butler appeared and offered Mrs. Frogerton a note on a silver salver. "This has just been delivered, ma'am."

"Thank you." Mrs. Frogerton read the note and looked up at Caroline. "It's from Inspector Ross. He says they have a description of the man they believe robbed Mr. Smith in Southwark."

"Have they apprehended him?" Caroline asked.

"No, and the inspector does go on to say that finding a large man with a previously broken nose and a foreign accent in that particular part of London might be difficult."

"Which means nothing will happen."

Mrs. Frogerton refolded the note. "We could go and visit the solicitors' office."

"For what purpose, ma'am?"

"To remind them we are still awaiting a copy of your father's will and maybe to ask whether the intruder was the same man who attacked Mr. Smith in Southwark."

"You think he might have followed him from the solicitors' office?" Caroline frowned. "It seems unlikely."

"It probably is, but as we need to ask about the will anyway, an additional inquiry won't hurt, will it, lass?" Mrs. Frogerton rose to her feet and tossed the note in the fire. "Why don't you order the carriage while I put on my bonnet?"

"We don't have to go anywhere at all, ma'am . . ." Caroline was left talking to herself as Mrs. Frogerton headed for the stairs.

Her efforts to dissuade her employer from involving herself in the matter of the will had so far proved fruitless. Caroline sighed, and as she was not in a position to argue with the person who paid her wages, she supposed she'd just have to go along with it.

Chapter 5

The front door of the solicitors' office was closed this time, and they had to wait for admittance. Mrs. Frogerton asked to see whoever was dealing with Mr. Jeremy Smith's affairs. There was some confusion as to exactly whom that might be, and the head clerk went off to inquire, leaving the ladies in the entrance hall.

Mrs. Frogerton glanced up the stairs. "I wonder if we should avail ourselves of the opportunity to wait in Mr. Smith's office and stop cluttering up the hall. Surely no one can object to that?"

Caroline knew it was pointless to object as her employer set off with some speed up the staircase. The door to Mr. Smith's office was open. A man in his twenties was standing beside the desk and looked up as they came in.

"May I help you, ma'am?"

"I do hope so." Mrs. Frogerton smiled at him. "We have been trying to ascertain who has taken on poor Mr. Smith's work while he is in hospital."

Caroline paused to wonder whether Mrs. Frogerton had decided not to mention that Mr. Smith was dead in case the solicitors hadn't been informed through official channels, or whether she was just being tactful.

"I'm his junior clerk, ma'am. James Thettle. I've been setting his office to rights since the burglary."

"The police believe something important was stolen?" Mrs. Frogerton asked. "How terrible."

"The thief took the clock and candlesticks off the mantelpiece, Mr. Smith's silver ink pot, and his walking stick."

"Quite a haul," Mrs. Frogerton said. "Did he steal any important documents as well?"

"That's difficult to say, ma'am. I'm still trying to sort out what was taken." He gestured at the stack of papers on the desk.

"Did you see the assailant yourself?" Mrs. Frogerton asked.

"I heard the altercation, and I believe I might have seen the man in question on the stairs." Mr. Thettle paused and gave an impressive shudder. "It could've been me he tried to murder."

Luckily for them, it appeared that Mr. Thettle was as big a gossip as Mrs. Frogerton . . .

"Was he a big man?" Mrs. Frogerton asked eagerly. "Did you hear him speak?"

"I didn't notice such details at the time, ma'am, because I thought he was just one of our regular clients." Mr. Thettle sighed.

"We did hear from a very reputable source that the man who attacked Mr. Smith was a foreigner." Mrs. Frogerton paused expectantly and looked at the clerk.

Mr. Thettle pursed his lips. "The only foreigner I've heard shouting at Mr. Smith was in here a while ago."

"I wonder if it was the same man?" Mrs. Frogerton looked at Caroline. "That is probably impossible to prove."

"I would assume so." Caroline hastened to dampen her employer's enthusiasm. "London is a very cosmopolitan city. It would be a remarkable coincidence."

For a moment both Mrs. Frogerton and Mr. Thettle looked discouraged.

Caroline was just about to suggest they return to the hall when Mrs. Frogerton spoke again. "Do you remember what the man you heard arguing looked like? Or do you have his name from Mr. Smith's appointment book?"

"Now that you mention it, I haven't found his appointment book, ma'am." Mr. Thettle looked at the desk. "It might be there somewhere, but I haven't come across it yet."

"How disappointing." Mrs. Frogerton sighed. "Did you see the foreign man who had the argument with Mr. Smith?"

"Only briefly when he emerged from the senior partner's office, and—"

Mrs. Frogerton interrupted him. "Which senior partner was that?"

"Mr. Emerson Smith, ma'am. May he rest in peace. The man I saw was probably in his thirties, had fair hair and blue eyes, and was fashionably dressed."

"Lady Caroline? Mrs. Frogerton?"

Caroline turned to see an older gentleman in the doorway.

"Yes?"

The man bowed. "I understand that you wish to discuss your father's will." He gestured to the door. "I do apologize for the delay. Would you care to come to my office?" His gaze drifted over to the junior clerk. "Thank you, Thettle. You may continue with your work."

"Yes, Mr. Potkins."

Caroline and Mrs. Frogerton followed Mr. Potkins along the landing and into his much larger office that faced out over the park in the square.

"Please sit down." Mr. Potkins retreated behind his desk. "How are you faring, my lady?"

"Apart from being homeless and penniless and having to work for my living, I'm in remarkably good health," Caroline said. "Have you met my employer, Mrs. Frogerton? She has become a staunch defender of my rights."

Mr. Potkins blinked at her. "I see you are as forthright as your father."

"But far more trustworthy." Caroline smiled at him. "Have you discovered the whereabouts of my father's supposed new will?"

"We believe it was in Mr. Smith's possession when he last left the building."

"You mean when he was attacked in his office and ran away," Mrs. Frogerton said. "How convenient for you."

"Yes, that is somewhat unfortunate."

"Unfortunate?" Mrs. Frogerton snorted. "I've dealt with many solicitors and lawyers in my time, Mr. Potkins, and I must say that your firm are the most incompetent bunch I have ever encountered."

"I must heartily disagree with you there, ma'am. This firm was founded by honorable men."

"Who allowed this woman's father to ignore any legalities he chose, steal his daughter's dowries, and plunge his estates into such enormous debt that even he realized he'd never pay it off and so killed himself?"

"We can only advise our clients. We are not responsible for their decisions."

"How very convenient for you." Mrs. Frogerton looked down her nose at the solicitor. "And yet it appears that you can't even keep your hands on a simple will."

"These . . . circumstances are somewhat unusual." Mr. Potkins turned to Caroline as if seeking an ally. "Surely you can see that, my lady? Our firm has been closely associated with your family for generations."

"But I agree with Mrs. Frogerton, sir." Caroline smiled. "In fact, as soon as this matter is solved to my satisfaction, I will be taking my business elsewhere." She stood up. "You no longer have the new will, so nothing has changed. Thank you for your time, and don't you dare send me a bill for this meeting, or I will return it ripped to pieces."

Mrs. Frogerton rose, too. "Well said, my dear. I'm sure Mr. Lewis will handle your affairs far more competently, starting with that inheritance from your aunt." She looked at Caroline. "Make sure they hand the money over as soon as it becomes available. You don't want them losing that as well!"

Mr. Potkins stood up too, his mouth open. They left his office, and on the landing, they bumped into Mr. Thettle, who obviously made a habit of listening at doors.

He grinned at them. "I've never heard Mr. Potkins lost for words before."

"Maybe it will be good for him," Mrs. Frogerton said as she headed for the stairs.

Caroline pressed her gloved fingers to her lips to conceal her smile. Despite everything, her employer's forthright way of dealing with incompetence was very refreshing. She could only hope one day to emulate her.

At dinner that evening, Caroline made no effort to avoid Mr. Frogerton or attempt to engage his attention. She couldn't change his opinion of her, and she wasn't prepared to try. He was also far more interested in meeting his sister's potential husband and interrogating him as to his current financial status, his designs toward Dorothy, and his future plans. To his credit, Viscount Lingard took the grilling rather well, having obviously become accustomed to the Frogerton family's direct way of speaking. Caroline was glad his mother wasn't there to be offended on his behalf.

With Mr. Frogerton focused on the viscount, Caroline and Mrs. Frogerton could enjoy the affable company of Inspector Ross.

"Now, sir, have you made any progress in your investigations?" Mrs. Frogerton asked.

"I've spoken to Dr. Harris and the nurse who was on the ward when Mr. Smith died, and neither of them believe Mr. Smith died of natural causes." Inspector Ross paused. "They both think he was suffocated."

"And nobody noticed?"

"He was in a room by himself right by the door to the ward," Inspector Ross explained. "It would've been easy for someone to slip in there, place a pillow over his face, and hold it down until he breathed no more."

Caroline shivered.

"I'm sorry if this is upsetting to you, my lady." He immediately gentled his tone. "I forget how hardened I have become to such incidences."

"I hardly knew the man," Caroline admitted. "But to be murdered . . . for what?"

"We still aren't sure about that." He frowned. "Although some items were stolen from his office, I have a sense that it is more complex than a simple burglary."

Mrs. Frogerton nodded and pressed her hand to her bosom. "I feel the same, Inspector. Do you think it is connected to the late Earl of Morton's new will?"

Caroline hastened to intervene. "I'm sure Inspector Ross doesn't believe that."

He held her gaze, his expression full of sympathy. "I wish I could agree with you, Lady Caroline, but one has to ask oneself what Mr. Smith was dealing with when he was attacked, and that, unfortunately, was your father's will."

"Which has disappeared."

He acknowledged her comment with a nod of his head. "All investigations have to start somewhere. There is always the chance further evidence will emerge and move the case away from your family and toward others."

"While we were at the solicitors' today, we did inquire as to whether Mr. Smith had met with any large men with foreign accents recently," Mrs. Frogerton said helpfully. "But the clerk could only recall a heated meeting with both Mr. Smiths and some unnamed foreign man who was blond."

"You thought there might have been some previous

contact between Mr. Smith and the man who attacked him on the streets?"

"We thought to ascertain if his assailant was the same man who went to his office," Mrs. Frogerton clarified. "The details of the other meeting were shared with us while we were there."

Inspector Ross said, "One has to wonder whether if, after ransacking the office, he couldn't find what he was looking for and pursued Mr. Smith for more information."

"Or for what he had on his person . . ." Mrs. Frogerton looked meaningfully at Caroline. "It would be helpful if we had Mr. Smith's appointment book, but that appears to have gone missing as well."

"How convenient." Inspector Ross grimaced.

"Perhaps you might check the older Mr. Smith's appointment books?" Mrs. Frogerton suggested.

"For meetings between both Mr. Smiths and a foreigner." Inspector Ross nodded. "That might certainly help."

Caroline stood up abruptly. "Excuse me. I need to check what time dinner will be served."

She left the room and continued walking in such a haphazard fashion that she found herself facing the linen cupboard at the end of a long corridor that went nowhere. She took a few deep breaths. It was all very well for Mrs. Frogerton and Inspector Ross to speculate over her father's missing will, but she hated having to be party to it. Her father had caused enough harm in his life without reaching out from beyond the grave to cause more. Her fingers curled into fists. She hated him so much . . .

"Lady Caroline."

She turned to see Inspector Ross standing a respectable distance behind her.

"Yes, Inspector?"

"I fear I have caused you some distress."

She shrugged. "Not at all, sir."

"My work can sometimes lead me into difficult avenues." He hesitated. "I do try to be aware that there are consequences to every decision I make and that I am dealing with the lives of real people and not just theories."

"Which is why you're very good at your job." She mustered a smile. "I already have reason to be thankful for your diligence with regard to Dr. Harris. I'm sure you'll manage this matter with your usual competence and diplomacy."

"I'll certainly do my best." He stepped back as she came toward him. "Would you prefer it if someone else kept you informed about the case?"

She stopped opposite him. "In truth, I'd rather it was you. I appreciate your professionalism."

His smile was rueful. "Whereas, I am beginning to wish you saw the man rather than the job."

"I suspect they are interchangeable, sir, seeing as you chose this occupation when I'm fairly certain your family did not approve."

"They did not," he agreed. "Something else we have in common, Lady Caroline."

"I chose my occupation through necessity."

"Forgive me, but *I'm* fairly certain someone in your large and well-connected family would've offered you and your sister a home."

"At a price."

He nodded. "My family wanted me to become . . . my brother's keeper. I refused. If he wishes to drink and gamble himself to death, I'm not willing to restrain him or be held accountable for his failings."

"I quite understand."

"Thank you. If you prefer, I could communicate directly with Mrs. Frogerton."

"I'd much rather you spoke to me." Caroline paused.

"Mrs. Frogerton means well, but this is a Morton family matter."

"Understood. She does have a decided ability to place herself in the middle of things."

"Because she wishes to help me," Caroline said. "And while I appreciate that—"

"You do not wish to burden her with your personal business." He nodded. "I quite understand. I fear it will be impossible not to involve her because of her genuine concern for you, but I will do my best."

"Thank you."

He offered her his arm. "Now, will you accompany me back to the drawing room? Mrs. Frogerton will be wondering what has happened to us."

She set her hand on his sleeve. He spoke of trivial things that soothed her until they arrived at the dining room, where the other members of the party were already sitting down. Mrs. Frogerton glanced over as they came in but didn't say anything, her attention on Dorothy, who was complaining that the drooping lace on her sleeves might inhibit her eating.

Inspector Ross pulled out Caroline's chair and bowed. "Lady Caroline."

"Thank you."

For the first time that evening she offered him a genuine smile. Unlike Mr. DeBloom, he never tried to take advantage of her precarious social status and always treated her with respect. It was refreshing and a balm to her troubled mind.

"*Lady* Caroline?" Mr. Frogerton spoke from the other side of the table. "I thought you preferred Miss Morton."

Inspector Ross sat down beside Caroline and smiled at Mr. Frogerton. "She does prefer it, sir, but I grew up considering her a titled lady, and I find it difficult to address her as anything else."

Mr. Frogerton's sharp gaze ran over Inspector Ross. "You're a bit of a mystery man, Inspector. You sound like a toff, you have an occupation, but everything you wear is handmade from the most expensive cloth."

"My son runs the textile side of my business, Inspector," Mrs. Frogerton interjected. "He knows cloth."

"My family are titled, sir." Inspector Ross didn't seem bothered by Mr. Frogerton's rather familiar remarks. "And, as I'm sure you'll appreciate, good cloth is made to last."

"That's the truth." Mr. Frogerton raised his glass to the inspector. "It'll last you a lifetime."

Inspector Ross glanced down at his waistcoat. "I hope you're correct, because on a policeman's salary, I can't afford evening coats like this."

"You truly work for your living?"

"I am employed by the Metropolitan Police force."

"Good man." Mr. Frogerton glanced at his mother. "I'll wager my mother has some stories as to how she became acquainted with you."

"I believe I tried to arrest one of her acquaintances." Inspector Ross smiled. "She didn't take it well."

"She wouldn't." Mr. Frogerton signaled to the footman to refill his glass and settled down to enjoy his soup, leaving Caroline and Inspector Ross to eat their own dinner.

Toward the end of the meal, just before Mrs. Frogerton withdrew with the ladies, Inspector Ross touched Caroline's arm and spoke quietly. "I intend to return to the solicitors' office tomorrow if I have time. Do you have the name of the clerk you spoke to? He might be able to help with our investigation."

"Mr. James Thettle," Caroline said. "He was Mr. Smith's junior clerk."

"Thank you." He paused. "I hesitate to tell you what to do, but on the basis of what we *do* know about Mr. Smith's assault and death, might I ask you to take care, especially when you are out and about?"

"Do you think I am in danger?" Caroline asked bluntly. "That seems absurd."

"If the matter is connected to your late father's will, then, yes, I do believe you should be careful. Your name was on that envelope found in Mr. Smith's possession."

"If Mr. Smith did have the will, it was taken, so why would his attacker want me?"

"I suppose it might hinge on what the will said, Lady Caroline." Inspector Ross met her gaze. "And whether you might be a beneficiary."

Mrs. Frogerton stood up and placed her napkin on the table. She was wearing her rubies, and the pins in her hair caught the gaslight and twinkled like drops of blood.

"Come along, ladies. Let's leave the gentlemen to their port."

Caroline rose to her feet, her moment of quiet comfort now disturbed by the very man who had made her feel safer.

Inspector Ross stood too and gazed down at her, his expression serious. "Be careful, Lady Caroline."

She nodded and moved swiftly out of the room. When she reached Mrs. Frogerton's side, she cleared her throat.

"Would you mind if I went straight to my room, ma'am? I have a terrible headache."

"Of course not, lass. I can pour my own cup of tea." Mrs. Frogerton patted Caroline's hand. "Off you go. I'll make your apologies for you."

"Thank you."

Caroline rushed up the stairs and into her room as if Mr. Smith's assailant was behind her, locked her bedroom door, and sat on the side of her bed, her calm destroyed and her breathing uneven. She had five hundred pounds to her name, and nothing could stop her leaving except her own sense of obligation.

But that was enough.

Biting her lip, she started to undress. The headache

she'd alluded to was becoming a reality, and taking refuge in her bed was appealing. There was one perfectly legitimate avenue of escape available to her. All she had to do was ask Mrs. Frogerton's permission and she could be away from London within a day. The thought steadied her, and she was finally able to close her eyes and attempt to sleep.

Chapter 6

Dr. Harris set his cup down on his saucer with a clatter that made Caroline wince.

"I must confess that I am tired of constantly being hauled before the Metropolitan Police and being forced to account for my perfectly legitimate activities!"

"They only asked you for a statement, Dr. Harris," Mrs. Frogerton said peaceably. "They can hardly think you the murderer when you were fast asleep in your bed."

"We both know that isn't the case, ma'am." Dr. Harris was in an argumentative mood. He'd turned up at the house at calling time and outstayed all the other callers by glaring at them until they left. "They are like dogs with a bone. Once they sink their teeth into something, they refuse to let go."

His gaze alighted on the butler, who stood hovering by the door. "Is there any chance of a decent cup of tea? This fancy stuff tastes like something unmentionable in present company."

The butler turned to Mrs. Frogerton. "Mr. DeBloom and his sister are in the hall, ma'am. I informed them that Miss Frogerton was not at home, but they asked if you might receive them instead."

"Of course!" Mrs. Frogerton brightened at the notion of more company. "Send them up and bring some more tea."

Dr. Harris frowned. "Why is that fellow constantly in your house, when Miss Frogerton has obviously chosen another suitor?"

"One might ask you the same question, Dr. Harris." Mrs. Frogerton winked at him.

"I've never considered courting your daughter, ma'am." Dr. Harris looked seriously revolted by the idea. "I only find myself here so often because I am constantly being involved in your antics."

Caroline raised her eyebrows. "You are under no obligation to visit at all, Dr. Harris, especially when you are being rude to your hostess, who has shown you nothing but kindness."

Dr. Harris grimaced. "You're right." He turned to Mrs. Frogerton. "That was unjust of me, ma'am. Sometimes I forget myself in polite company."

The DeBlooms arrived, and Caroline hastily excused herself to speak to the butler. She had no desire to talk to Mr. DeBloom, and with Dr. Harris displaying his usual lack of tact, her headache from the previous evening was fast returning. She lingered for as long as she could in the kitchen but eventually had to return to the drawing room before Mrs. Frogerton began to worry.

Miss DeBloom smiled as she came in. "Dr. Harris was telling us about his recent patient."

Caroline shot Dr. Harris a severe look. "I do hope he didn't go into too much medical detail."

"On the contrary," Dr. Harris said. "I was explaining that it is harder to suffocate someone than you might think. But if your victim is drugged or somehow incapacitated, it becomes easier."

"Hardly drawing room conversation, Doctor."

"It is relevant to Mr. Smith's murder, Miss Morton. I would've thought you'd be interested in that. Inspector Ross came by the hospital to tell me that, on the night in question, one of the patients in the main ward remembers seeing a man enter the ward, check the whereabouts of the night nurse, and then return to Mr. Smith's room, where he remained for several minutes before leaving again. I was merely suggesting that he would've had ample time to suffocate my patient."

Caroline turned to the DeBlooms. "May I offer you some more tea?"

"No, thank you," Mr. DeBloom answered her. "We have an appointment at my mother's office to go over our monthly accounts and receive our allowance." He made a face. "It is never very pleasant, but Clarissa and I endeavor to support each other."

"Your mother has an office in London?" Mrs. Frogerton asked as she accepted more tea from Caroline. "I forget that she is a businesswoman like me."

"She prefers not to mention it in polite company," Mr. DeBloom said.

Dr. Harris snorted.

Mr. DeBloom looked coldly at the doctor. "We are very proud of her."

"As she evidently pays your bills, so you should be."

"I work for her, Dr. Harris." There was a note of annoyance in Mr. DeBloom's voice. "She pays me for my labor. Do you have an issue with that?"

"Not at all. I wish I had the same arrangement with my employer." He paused, and Caroline tensed. "One meeting a month to discuss my monthly accounts and nothing to do in the interim sounds wonderful."

"I'm sure Mr. DeBloom is far more involved in the company than that, Dr. Harris," Mrs. Frogerton said. "As usual, you are jumping to conclusions without having all the evidence."

"Something I wouldn't want in any physician of mine," Mr. DeBloom murmured, and looked at his sister. "We should be going."

"Yes, of course. Mother doesn't like us to be late." Miss

DeBloom jumped to her feet, her nervous gaze moving between her brother and Dr. Harris. "Thank you for the tea, Mrs. Frogerton, and please give my regards to Dorothy when she returns."

They left, and Mrs. Frogerton looked at Dr. Harris. "You were remarkably rude to Mr. DeBloom."

Dr. Harris shrugged. "He lives off his mother and pretends to work. Perhaps it was time someone pointed that out to him."

"This was hardly the place to do so."

"The question you should be asking yourself, ma'am, is why he keeps coming here." He glanced over at Caroline who had resumed her seat.

"To escort his sister, who is a friend of Miss Frogerton's." Caroline met his gaze.

"With all due respect, that is balderdash. Miss DeBloom barely has a word to say to anyone. She comes because her brother wants her to, and I think we all know why."

"Because Mr. DeBloom is also a friend of Miss Frogerton," Caroline replied steadily. "Just because she is practically engaged to another man doesn't mean she can't associate with her friends."

"Mr. DeBloom comes to see you, Miss Morton," Dr. Harris said. "It's patently obvious."

"And what's wrong with that if he does?" Mrs. Frogerton asked.

"You seriously think a man like Mr. DeBloom has honorable intentions toward her?" Dr. Harris pointed his finger in Caroline's direction.

"Why would he not?" Mrs. Frogerton raised her eyebrows. "She would make any man an excellent wife, and if Mr. DeBloom is in love with her—"

"Please." Caroline shot to her feet. "Will you both stop discussing me as if I'm not here."

"He's not in love with her—he's simply fallen for a beautiful face."

Caroline sat down again and pressed two fingers to her aching brow.

"She is far more than a pretty face," Mrs. Frogerton declared.

"Well, *I* know that, but does Mr. DeBloom?" Dr. Harris shook his head. "My advice to you both is to watch him carefully. I don't trust the man." He took out his pocket watch and consulted it. "I must be going. I have to be on the ward in an hour."

He set down his cup, bowed, and left with two small cakes wrapped in his handkerchief.

After a long pause, Mrs. Frogerton looked over at Caroline. "Are you all right, lass?"

"I feel like a discarded bone being picked over by a pack of wolves."

"That is remarkably dramatic for you," Mrs. Frogerton said. "I always found it quite exciting when my suitors fought over me."

"My suitors?"

"Come now, Caroline, you must realize that Dr. Harris dislikes Mr. DeBloom because he wants you for himself."

"I am aware of no such thing, ma'am."

"They are both quite ridiculous, preening and pecking at each other in front of you." Mrs. Frogerton chuckled and shook her head.

"I can only repeat that I desire nothing from either of them."

"Yes, you have a decided preference for Inspector Ross, which makes sense, seeing as he comes from the same social circle."

"I . . ." Caroline looked helplessly at her employer. "Don't want any of them."

Mrs. Frogerton smiled. "I'm sure you're right, lass. Now, can you go and speak to Cook and tell her that it will just be us for dinner? Dorothy and Samuel are going to the theater tonight with the DeBlooms."

* * *

Between Inspector Ross's warnings and Mrs. Frogerton's insinuations as to her potential husband, Caroline wasn't looking forward to another sleepless night, and happily volunteered to stay up to ensure that Dorothy and Mr. Frogerton returned safely from their night out at the theater. The mantel clock was chiming one when she heard someone at the front door.

Recognizing Dorothy's voice, Caroline unlocked the door and held it open for the Frogertons and the DeBlooms to come through.

"You shouldn't be answering the door at this hour," Mr. Frogerton said as he took off his hat. "Where's the butler?"

"I told him to go to bed, sir. There was no point in both of us being up at this hour."

"In truth, there's no reason for anyone to be up. We're not children."

"Mrs. Frogerton worries about her daughter." Caroline offered to take his cloak, but he held on to it.

"I don't expect you to look after my needs, Miss Morton." He headed toward the stairs. "Good night, all."

Caroline turned away and fixed her attention on Miss DeBloom, who had said her goodbyes to Dorothy and was already leaving. Mr. DeBloom strolled toward Caroline.

"You can't avoid talking to me forever, Miss Morton." Mr. DeBloom smiled down at her.

"I have no intention on avoiding you at all, sir. You are always welcome in my employer's house." She walked toward the door. "Is Mrs. DeBloom awaiting you in the carriage?"

"Yes, she has Kruger to guard her, so don't worry about her safety." He remained in the doorway looking down at her. "You know I'd do anything for you, Miss Morton."

"Then perhaps you might move off the threshold so that I can close the door and stop the heat escaping."

He grinned and dropped a kiss on the top of her head. "Always so proper."

Caroline abruptly stepped back and was considering closing the door whether he was clear of it or not when Mrs. DeBloom got out of the carriage and came toward them, the swish of her silk skirts mirroring her irritation.

"For goodness' sake, will you stop attempting to ingratiate yourself with Mrs. Frogerton's companion. I'm sure she has work to do."

The look Mrs. DeBloom shot Caroline was decidedly unfriendly.

"I'm coming, Mother." Mr. DeBloom turned back to Caroline and lowered his voice. "Mrs. Frogerton told us about your father's missing will. If you do recover it, it might be helpful evidence against my mother."

"Will you please leave?" Caroline looked up at him.

"If you wish, but I am always at your service should you need me. Good night, my lady." He bowed low and walked to the carriage, where his mother stood waiting.

Caroline was just about to close the front door when a man crossed the road behind the departing carriage and waved frantically at her.

"Lady Caroline!"

She squinted into the darkness, her breathing ragged. The man stopped in front of the streetlight and pointed at his chest.

"No need to start screeching, my lady. I'm James Thettle from the solicitors' office."

Caroline pressed her hand to her chest and took a moment to regain her composure. Inspector Ross had told her not to be foolish, and she'd already forgotten his advice.

"Mr. Thettle."

He came up to the door, his cheeks pink from exertion.

"I'm sorry to arrive at such a late hour, but I saw the carriage, and I thought I'd take a chance that someone was up."

"This house is surely not on your way home," Caroline said, suddenly aware that Mr. Thettle had been present when Mr. Smith's office had been ransacked and that he'd known his employer was in hospital.

"No, my lady." He delved into his coat pocket, and Caroline tensed. "I wrote you a note. I deemed it safer to bring it to you directly. I was going to leave it at the kitchen door, but when I saw you standing there, I thought I'd deliver it personally." He brought out a sheet of folded paper sealed with wax. "I didn't want it going out with the usual post and having questions asked about what I was up to."

She gingerly took the note he offered her. "Thank you."

"I might as well tell you what it says, seeing as I'm here." He grinned at her.

"Please go ahead."

"I've been working long hours tidying up both Mr. Smiths' affairs, and I found something." He paused expectantly.

Caroline remembered he shared a taste for the dramatic with Mrs. Frogerton and dutifully replied. "What did you find, Mr. Thettle?"

"A few weeks ago, I was asked to write a fair copy of some of the sections of your father's new will. From what I recall, Mr. Emerson Smith wanted to compare the old version with the new and wished to make notes as he did so—hence the need for a copy."

"I see."

"I found some of my notes when I was clearing up. I didn't realize he'd kept them." He gestured at the envelope. "That's what I wanted to tell you."

"Are they in here?"

"I only had time to recopy a couple of them before I had to leave. I'll finish the rest over the weekend."

"Or you could simply give me the originals?" Caroline suggested.

"Oh, I couldn't do that, my lady. That's the property of our office you're talking about."

"One might assume that my father's will would be *my* property."

"Yes, but these are copies made by an employee, which is quite different, my lady."

Caroline was too tired to argue over an issue she wished had never arisen in the first place. "Thank you."

Mr. Thettle bowed. "You're welcome. If you come into the office to see Mr. Potkins, don't tell him what I did."

"How else am I to explain how the information came to me?" Caroline asked.

"I'm sure Mrs. Frogerton will think of some excuse." He touched the brim of his hat. "Pleasure to see you again, Lady Caroline. I'll wish you a good night."

"Thank you."

She was just about to shut the door when he turned back to her. "That carriage that was in front of your house when I arrived. Are you acquainted with the occupants?"

"Yes, why?"

"Because that bloke looked just like the foreigner I told you about who came out of Mr. Smith's office after a right old barney." He pursed his lips. "Some Dutch name—like DeBeers or something. What a coincidence, eh?"

He nodded and went on his way, leaving Caroline to shut the door and make sure that everything in the house was secure. It wasn't until she'd made her way up to her bedchamber that she allowed herself to consider all the ramifications of Mr. Thettle's conversation.

She set the envelope on her desk and decided to delay opening it until the morning. She was too busy wrestling with the notion that Mr. DeBloom had been to her family's solicitors. What on earth had he been doing there? Had he already known about the new will? If he had, it made his current behavior toward her difficult to interpret. He claimed to care about her, but what if his concern was, and always had been, for the contents of her father's new will and the damage it might do to his family business?

There were too many things to think about, and Caroline's mind was awhirl. Knowing she wouldn't be able to sleep, she picked up a book from her bedside table and settled in her chair. If she had to be up, reading one of Mrs. Frogerton's favorite gothic novels would ensure that she not only stayed awake but remained thoroughly alert.

Chapter 7

"Mrs. Frogerton?"

"Yes, my dear?"

Her employer looked up from her knitting. She had no patience for embroidery and preferred to produce something warm and useful. By Caroline's reckoning, she had knitted enough scarves, hats, gloves, and shawls to clothe the entire household five times over.

"May I speak to you about something?"

"Of course. Sit yourself down." Mrs. Frogerton patted the seat beside her. "Samuel and Dotty are still sleeping, I've finished my business accounts, and we've nothing planned until luncheon." She peered closely at Caroline. "You look worn to the bone, lass."

"I didn't sleep very well last night, ma'am," Caroline said. "Which is why I wanted to seek your advice."

"Are you still upset about Dr. Harris and Mr. DeBloom fighting over you?"

"Not exactly." Caroline hesitated. "I am more inclined to wonder if Dr. Harris had a point about why the De-Blooms are visiting so frequently."

Mrs. Frogerton set her knitting to one side. "Because Mr. DeBloom is besotted with you, and his sister looks up to Dotty and lets her chatter away without interrupting, which, as we both know, suits Dotty very well."

"It might not be quite that straightforward." Caroline took a deep breath. "Mr. DeBloom suggested his mother persuaded my father to invest heavily in South African mines that didn't exist."

Mrs. Frogerton's eyes widened. "Oh my."

"He showed me a bank draft supposedly from my father for five thousand pounds. To be fair, my father often promised sums of money he couldn't pay, but Mr. De-Bloom believes the cheque was honored by the bank."

"You could probably confirm that with a visit to the bank," Mrs. Frogerton suggested. "They should still have a record of your father's account."

"I intend to do that, ma'am." Caroline paused. "Mr. DeBloom said it wasn't the only cheque my father wrote to his mother's company."

"May I ask what Mr. DeBloom's purpose was in sharing this information with you? Was he angry? Was he asking for repayment?"

"On the contrary, he was offering to repay *me* because of his mother's duplicity."

"And just how does he think he'll do that? Out of his allowance?" Mrs. Frogerton snorted. "From what I understand, he owns no part of his mother's business, and I'm fairly certain he is not at liberty to disperse her funds."

"He suggested he was willing to destroy the company to expose his mother's lies."

Mrs. Frogerton looked at her for a long moment. "To be honest, lass, that sounds most unlikely. Why would he destroy his own income?"

"That's a very good point, ma'am."

"And what exactly is he suggesting his mother is doing? From what I know of that particular business, investment in speculative mines is not uncommon."

"Mr. DeBloom did mention that, but he implied his

mother had gone beyond seeking investors for legitimate mines and was selling dreams of mines that had no basis in reality." Caroline sighed. "The thing is—it is just the sort of foolish thing my father would be attracted to. And according to Mr. DeBloom, my father was also attracted to his mother."

"Good Lord." Mrs. Frogerton's face was a picture of mingled delight and horror. "Were they *lovers*?"

"Apparently."

"I don't know how you've managed to keep all this to yourself, Caroline. No wonder you've been looking so peaky lately! Dr. Harris was right. One does have to question why Mr. DeBloom keeps turning up here." She leaned forward to pat Caroline's hand. "Now, what can I do to help? Shall I order the butler to deny the DeBlooms entrance to this house?"

"I suspect it's too late for that."

"And it might be better to continue to let them in so we can observe them more closely." Mrs. Frogerton nodded. "Well, I am very disappointed in Mr. DeBloom."

"His attitude toward his mother and his family business does invite some scrutiny," Caroline agreed. "And that isn't all, ma'am."

"What now?" Mrs. Frogerton demanded. "Don't tell me that he is already married and has made an improper proposal toward you?"

"I almost wish it was that simple, but I suspect it is far worse. Do you remember Mr. Thettle telling us about a foreigner he saw at the solicitors' office?"

"Yes indeed."

"Last night, when I was saying farewell to the DeBlooms, Mr. Thettle turned up."

"At this house?" Mrs. Frogerton frowned. "How very peculiar."

"I must admit he gave me a terrible fright when he popped up behind the departing carriage. He said he had written me a note and had come to drop it off personally, because he didn't want his employers to know what he was up to."

"None of that is reassuring, Caroline." Mrs. Frogerton frowned. "You should have shut the door in his face and told him to return at a more proper hour."

"You are right, ma'am, but I was so confounded by his presence that I accepted both his explanation and the note he offered me."

"And what exactly does this have to do with our discussion about Mr. DeBloom?"

"As he was leaving, Mr. Thettle asked me if I knew the occupants of the carriage, because he'd recognized Mr. DeBloom as the foreigner who'd called on the solicitors' office and had a terrible argument with both Mr. Smiths."

Mrs. Frogerton gasped. "Good heavens!"

"To say I was shocked would be an understatement, ma'am. Coupled with what Mr. Thettle told me about my father's will, my suspicions about Mr. DeBloom and his plans only intensified."

"Wait—Mr. Thettle had the will with him?"

"Apparently, he'd been asked to copy out parts for Mr. Emerson Smith to compare more easily with the original. He found those notes when he was tidying up and brought them to me."

Mrs. Frogerton looked thoughtful. "If I am understanding you correctly, lass, you're thinking Mr. DeBloom is somehow mixed up with the matter of your father's will."

"Yes, ma'am. What if he already knew of its existence and has been trying to stop me seeing it?"

"That is quite a leap, Caroline," Mrs. Frogerton said. "How would Mr. DeBloom have known about the new will in the first place?"

"Perhaps his mother told him about it. She and my father were apparently very close."

"But why would Mr. DeBloom care what was in such a document, anyway?"

"Perhaps my father left all his money to Mrs. DeBloom?" Caroline suggested. "Or the will mentions bequeathing the fake shares in the mine to his heirs, and Mr. DeBloom didn't want anyone from the solicitors' office inquiring about the matter and exposing the deception?"

Mrs. Frogerton gazed at Caroline. "I am beginning to suspect you are reading too many of my gothic novels, lass. Your suspicions are almost as far-fetched as mine usually are."

"I cannot think of any other reason why Mr. DeBloom, of all people, would be seen at my family solicitors."

"There might be a perfectly legitimate explanation. Maybe the DeBloom family also have a relationship with one of the solicitors in the office."

"That seems unlikely, as they reside in South Africa. And, even if Mr. DeBloom does have a perfect right to be there, may I remind you that both of the gentlemen he spoke to are now dead?"

"Only one of them died in mysterious circumstances."

"Can we even be sure of that?" Caroline shot to her feet and began to pace the room. "How much of a coincidence is it that Mr. DeBloom argued with two men and shortly afterward they both die unexpectedly?"

Mrs. Frogerton patted the seat beside her. "Is it possible you have been thinking on this matter for too long and are perhaps . . . reading more into it than is warranted?"

Caroline looked at her employer. "I never exaggerate, ma'am."

"Then come and sit down and let us see if we can puzzle this out together," Mrs. Frogerton suggested. "As you are always telling me, there has to be a logical explanation somewhere."

Caroline reached into her pocket and took out the letter Mr. Thettle had given her. "Perhaps we should find out what Mr. Smith's clerk has to say in his note. That might help our investigations."

Mrs. Frogerton uttered a small shriek. "Goodness! I'd forgotten all about that."

"I haven't, ma'am." Caroline resumed her seat. "In truth, I've been almost afraid to open it." They both looked at the folded letter, and Caroline sighed. "I suppose I'd better find out what it says."

She broke the seal, spread out the single sheet, and began to read. "The first part of the letter merely confirms what Mr. Thettle told me in person last night—that this is a copy of some of the notes he made from my late father's will."

"Some of the notes?" Mrs. Frogerton searched for her reading glasses under her discarded knitting.

"Mr. Thettle said he didn't have time to write more, and that if I wished to see everything, I'd have to take the matter up with his employers without mentioning what he'd done."

"Hmm." Mrs. Frogerton frowned. "Mr. Thettle's behavior is extremely odd. One has to wonder whether he is more involved in the matter than we previously thought."

"His reasons for passing by our house at one in the morning were distinctly unconvincing," Caroline said. "And not only is he employed at the solicitors' office, but he has access to both Mr. Smiths' records. If anyone knows what is going on with my father's will, it is probably him."

"I wonder if he's considering blackmail?" Mrs. Frogerton asked.

"Blackmailing whom, ma'am?"

"Mr. Potkins, the DeBlooms, you. It could be any number of people, if he believes the contents of the will are worth paying for."

Caroline continued reading and then looked up.

"What is it, lass?"

"If my father did write this, he was either drunk or ill."

"That is hardly encouraging, but if Mr. Thettle is intent on blackmail, he probably wouldn't give you the more interesting parts to start with."

"So far, he's given me nothing that makes me believe this document was written by someone who was in sound mind, as I believe is required for a will to be valid." Caroline started to read aloud. " 'I have wronged those to whom I owe my fidelity and trust. I have squandered my inheritance and yet I still beg for forgiveness.' "

Mrs. Frogerton raised her eyebrows. "It sounds more like a confession than a will."

Caroline nodded and read on. " 'In an attempt to revive my fortunes, I have been deceived by an immoral woman who has stolen my last penny—my last gamble to restore my children's inheritance.' "

"Now, that last bit does sound like your father, lass," Mrs. Frogerton commented. "A man who's happy to blame everyone but himself for his considerable failings."

"It does seem to suggest he committed money that he didn't have to Mrs. DeBloom's mines and possibly that he has become aware that he has been cheated."

"Money that rightfully belonged to you and your sister and that your fool of a solicitor let him take." Mrs. Frogerton paused. "That does make me wonder whether the loss of this will is also convenient for your solicitors, as they might be shown in a very poor light."

"They have been reluctant to show me the will, ma'am," Caroline agreed. "And Mr. Thettle implied that even giving me a copy of his notes would get him into trouble."

Mrs. Frogerton gestured at her to continue reading. "What else does your father have to say for himself?"

" 'Despite the duplicity of the DB Company, I bequeath my shares to my daughters in the hope that the company will honor them. There is also property in South Africa that I was wrongfully advised had to be held in another's name due to the laws of said country, which should be claimed. Addresses to be added.'" Caroline looked up. "That's all there is."

"It's enough to make me believe your father was attempting to right some wrongs, but how much credence can we give to what he said? He hardly sounds sensible." Mrs. Frogerton frowned. "I suspect even a dead man can be sued if he has defamed someone, and the DeBloom mining company will not like this at all."

"Which is probably another reason why my solicitors were so reluctant to show me the will in the first place," Caroline said.

"They certainly could be in jeopardy," Mrs. Frogerton said. "A solicitor's good reputation is essential to conduct their client's confidential business."

"Then perhaps they will be glad that both of the men who were involved in the matter are now dead."

"Whilst your solicitors have behaved in a most unethical manner, I doubt they had the ability to murder *themselves*, dear, which does lead me to wonder about Mr. Thettle's part in all this." She paused. "I must ask Inspector Ross what Mr. Emerson Smith died of. His death seems more and more convenient."

"What do you think I should do, ma'am?" Caroline asked. "My instinct tells me to visit the solicitors and demand to see all Mr. Thettle's notes and anything else they have about this matter. My father must have corresponded with them about the changes he wished to make to his will. *Someone* must have advised him."

"Normally, I would be the first to agree that we should storm the solicitors' office at once, but I think we should wait for a while."

"Why, ma'am?"

"Because of Mr. Thettle."

"You mean to see if he intends to ask for money before I can see the rest of his notes?" Caroline paused. "I'd almost forgotten. He said he copied these notes from the will—that might not be true."

"That's another reason for caution," Mrs. Frogerton agreed. "And one has to wonder whether he also intends to blackmail his own employer. It might be worth waiting to hear what Inspector Ross thinks of all this, lass."

Caroline considered that. "Yes, I'll write him a note."

"A note? From everything we've discussed so far it will be a fifty-page novel." Mrs. Frogerton shook her head. "What a muddle."

"And we mustn't forget that poor Mr. Smith was murdered," Caroline said. "I was reluctant to admit that his death was connected to my father's will, but I am beginning to wonder if I was wrong."

"Someone wanted Mr. Smith dead, and the last thing he was working on was your father's will," Mrs. Frogerton agreed. "But it is still hard to believe anyone would kill him simply because of some fraudulent mining shares."

"There must be more to it," Caroline stated. "If the will truly is gone, the only way to find out more is to gain access to those missing notes Mr. Thettle made."

"We must endeavor to keep this matter between ourselves, Caroline," Mrs. Frogerton said. "I'd never forgive myself if you suffered harm whilst in my employ."

"In truth, ma'am, there is no need for you to be involved at all. Once I tell Inspector Ross what is going on, I'm certain he'll tell us both to stand down and allow him to do his job."

"When has that ever stopped us?" Mrs. Frogerton asked. "We shall continue to investigate in our own way with as much caution as necessary. I will not say a word to Dotty and Samuel."

"That is probably for the best," Caroline said to her employer. "Thank you for your counsel, ma'am. I was reluctant to burden you with my fears, but you have helped me order my thoughts into a less troubled state."

"That makes a change. It's usually the other way around." Mrs. Frogerton winked at Caroline. "Now, why don't you write your letter to Inspector Ross, and I'll order us some tea."

An hour before they were due to dine, Mrs. Frogerton's butler entered the drawing room where Caroline, her employer, and Mr. Frogerton were sitting.

"Ma'am." He offered her two notes on a silver salver.

"Thank you." Mrs. Frogerton took the letters and opened them. "Excellent news," she said after reading them. "Both Inspector Ross and the DeBlooms can come to dinner tonight."

Caroline looked at her employer, who raised her eyebrows.

"Yes, I know it was rather short notice, and that is not how it is done in society, Caroline, but I thought it worth taking a chance."

"You don't need to subscribe to London society's notions of what is acceptable, Mother. If you want guests at your own dinner table, then ask them." Mr. Frogerton looked at Caroline. "I'm sure Miss Morton would agree."

"Absolutely, sir." Caroline met his gaze calmly. "Mrs. Frogerton is an excellent host, and invitations to her dinner parties are highly coveted."

Shortly afterward, she followed Mrs. Frogerton up the stairs to get changed for dinner.

Her employer paused on the first landing. "I know it's a risk inviting them all here, but I'd like to see their faces."

"I wouldn't recommend bringing up the matter of my father and his will, ma'am," Caroline cautioned, knowing Mrs. Frogerton's tendency toward dramatics.

"I have no intention of doing so. Sometimes it is simply best to sit back and let people talk. You can learn a lot by being silent, Caroline."

"Yes, ma'am."

Mrs. Frogerton continued down the corridor, and Caroline went up the second flight of stairs to her bedchamber. As she had never heard her employer exercise restraint in company, Caroline was far more nervous about the dinner than she wanted to be. She was also aware that Mr. Frogerton would not appreciate any attempts she made to steer his mother's conversation into appropriate avenues. He'd already indicated that he thought she had too much control of Mrs. Frogerton's behavior.

She went into her bedroom and opened the cupboard where her two evening dresses hung side by side. She chose the newest one made of heavy dark-blue silk, which had been a gift from her employer. Even though she had the services of a maid available to her, Caroline tended to care for herself. She no longer needed someone to curl and arrange her hair or care for her jewelry and fine linen.

She sat at her dressing table and considered what to do with her hair. As it was a dinner party, she could relax her severe style a little by braiding her hair into a coronet on top of her head and allowing the front to curl more naturally around her face. She still had her mother's pearl necklace that she'd hidden from the debt collectors who had come to take possession of her family home. She supposed she should be grateful they hadn't searched her or thrown her and Susan out on the street. By all accounts, their courtesy to the daughters of an earl was probably an aberration as to how they usually worked.

Caroline could still remember watching the contents of her home being stripped out—her sister's dolls, her mother's jewelry—almost everything had gone to pay off her father's enormous debts. She'd sat on the steps at the front of the imposing townhouse comforting Susan and waiting for Aunt Eleanor, her father's sister, to arrive and take them to Greenwood Hall.

And now, Eleanor was dead, Susan disliked her intensely, and somehow her father was still putting her life in danger even from beyond the grave . . .

Caroline pushed aside such melancholy thoughts and

got ready. If Inspector Ross was attending the dinner, Caroline needed to speak to him before he encountered the DeBlooms, because unlike Mrs. Frogerton, the inspector did have the authority to ask any questions he liked.

In truth, it was no hardship speaking to Inspector Ross. He was always respectful and reliable—qualities Caroline had come to appreciate in a gentleman. Even if he had to follow orders, he was always willing to listen and never made her feel anything less than a lady.

The nature of his occupation meant he could sometimes be delayed for more pressing events. Caroline hoped this would not be the case on this particular evening. After washing in the warm water the maid had provided, Caroline put on her dress, quickly braided her hair, pinned it up, and found her shawl.

When she came down the stairs, there was a gentleman in the entrance hall. He looked up at her. "Miss Morton."

"Good evening, Mr. Frogerton."

He continued to stare at her. "How extraordinary. Your eyes match the silk of your gown."

Caroline paused at the bottom of the staircase. "Will you excuse me, sir? I need to speak to the butler."

"I apologize." He stepped out of her way. "You're a beautiful woman, Miss Morton."

He sounded almost pained by the admission, which didn't surprise Caroline in the least, as he wasn't one of her admirers.

"Thank you." Caroline barely gave him a glance before noticing the butler advancing toward the front door. "I believe Mrs. Frogerton is shortly expected in the drawing room if you wish to go upstairs and join her?"

To her relief, it was Inspector Ross at the front door. She caught his eye as he came in and gave his hat and cloak to the butler.

He bowed. "Lady Caroline! What a pleasure."

She went over to him, aware that Mr. Frogerton hadn't moved from his position at the bottom of the stairs.

"Good evening, Inspector Ross. You are the first to arrive."

"That makes a change." He smiled broadly at her. "I was contemplating a very dull evening at my club before I return to work at midnight, so Mrs. Frogerton's invitation was most welcome."

"She always appreciates your company, sir." Caroline gestured toward the stairs. "Mrs. Frogerton is awaiting her guests in the drawing room."

Having no desire to be at the front door when the De-Blooms arrived, Caroline accompanied Inspector Ross up the stairs. There was no sign of Mrs. Frogerton in the drawing room, although Dorothy was there. She was talking to her brother, who had come up the stairs ahead of Caroline and the inspector.

Inspector Ross lowered his voice. "I received your letter, my lady. It was most informative."

"I thought you should know all the facts, sir."

"It is certainly helpful, although much of what you surmise remains to be proved."

"I am aware of that. It just felt like there were too many coincidences to be ignored." She looked up at him. "At least you haven't suggested I should be thrown into Bedlam for concocting a jumble of lies."

"One thing I do know about you, Lady Caroline, is that you possess a calm and rational mind, and jumping to fantastical conclusions is not your style at all." He met her gaze, his hazel eyes full of concern. "I will do my best to investigate each and every claim you made. I will reiterate that you must be very careful."

She nodded. "I will do my best. You are not intending to arrest anyone over dinner, are you?"

"Not unless someone has a fit of conscience and confesses their crimes right in front of me. I fear then I'd be obliged to act." He smiled at her. "I will keep my counsel, my lady."

"Thank you."

He nodded and turned toward the door, where Mrs. Frogerton was just coming in with the DeBloom family.

He walked over to greet his hostess. "Good evening, ma'am. Thank you for inviting me for dinner."

Caroline stayed where he'd left her, and Mr. Frogerton came to stand next to her. "He likes you."

"Perhaps he simply has excellent manners and makes an effort to be polite to everyone he meets."

"Unlike me, you mean."

"It was merely an observation of the inspector's character, Mr. Frogerton, and not intended as a reflection on anyone else."

"He's very good with my mother," Mr. Frogerton said.

"As I said, he's charming to everyone." She smiled at him. "Have you met Mrs. DeBloom? She is a business owner like Mrs. Frogerton."

"I met her briefly at the theater. I had no idea that she ran her own business. What does she do?"

"She owns a mining company in South Africa."

"Indeed." Mr. Frogerton's sharp gaze moved to Mrs. DeBloom, who was now speaking to Inspector Ross and pushing her shy daughter to do the same. "One would never guess."

"I believe she has a manager and her son to aid her in her business ventures."

Mr. Frogerton snorted, sounding remarkably like his mother. "I don't think Mr. DeBloom has done much mining, Miss Morton. Have you seen his hands? I doubt he'd know which end of a pickaxe to hold, let alone use."

"Whereas, you would."

"Yes, I've done my time at all the jobs in our businesses. My mother insisted. If you know how a job should be done, you can tell when someone isn't doing it right or how they could do better."

"That's admirable, Mr. Frogerton." Caroline noticed Mr. DeBloom was moving her way. "Will you excuse me?

I need to speak to Mrs. Frogerton about the timing for dinner."

Mr. Frogerton offered her a brusque nod. "I must say, Miss Morton, that you take your responsibilities seriously."

"I'm paid to offer the highest level of service, sir, and I always try to provide it."

"So I've noticed." He cleared his throat. "I said some harsh things to you when we first met. I'd like you to know I've revised my opinion of you somewhat."

"I'm delighted you no longer think I'm out to fleece your mother, sir." Caroline curtsied. "Now, I must get on."

He nodded, and she walked away from him and from the approaching Mr. DeBloom. Mrs. Frogerton was conversing with Mrs. DeBloom and her daughter. It was the first time Caroline had seen Mrs. DeBloom since she'd discovered her father had been involved with her on his visits to Africa. She had no particularly strong feelings about her father's infidelity. It was simply a part of his weak and untrustworthy nature. Mrs. DeBloom was certainly not the first woman he'd bedded.

She was an attractive woman with her fair hair, blue eyes, and rounded figure. She also had the strength of character her father had lacked and was always drawn to in others. It was unsettling to realize that Mrs. DeBloom had known exactly who Caroline was from their first meeting and had made no effort to be pleasant despite the relationship she'd enjoyed with her father.

In truth, she'd gone out of her way to be unkind, constantly reminding Caroline of her lowly status and her paid position. Knowing how easily her father discarded people he no longer found useful or interesting, Caroline wished she could ask Mrs. DeBloom how the relationship had ended. The woman's unflinching hostility indicated that things had gone badly. Perhaps Mrs. DeBloom was glad she'd deceived her lover, taken his money, and given him nothing in return. It might have felt like a fitting revenge. If she hadn't been so intimately involved in the matter, Caroline might even have approved of Mrs. DeBloom's actions.

"Miss Morton?" To her surprise, Mrs. DeBloom was addressing her directly. "Do you have a moment?"

"Yes, of course, ma'am." Caroline followed Mrs. De-Bloom to the far corner of the drawing room, where they had a modicum of privacy.

"I want you to stop encouraging my son to visit you," Mrs. DeBloom said abruptly.

"I have never encouraged him, ma'am."

"Come now, Miss Morton, we are both women of the world. You are in financial straits, and capturing the attention of a gentleman such as my son would restore you to your former position in life."

"Women are often forced to marry, Mrs. DeBloom, but I am not one of them," Caroline said. "I have secure employment with Mrs. Frogerton, and I can assure you that I have no designs on your son."

"I find that hard to believe." Mrs. DeBloom looked down her nose at Caroline.

"In truth, I have been wondering whether to ask for your help in dissuading him from bothering me," Caroline continued. "Mr. DeBloom refuses to listen, and I am reluctant to involve Mrs. Frogerton, who can be very protective of me."

"You're suggesting my son is at fault?"

"Yes, ma'am."

Mrs. DeBloom raised her chin. "I see you still value yourself far too highly, dear. I expect you thought he'd make you an offer of marriage, when all he wants is a mistress."

"I do value myself highly, ma'am." Caroline smiled. "And I would never become any man's mistress."

"You are impertinent." Mrs. DeBloom glared at her. "But perhaps I should have expected that from a member of the Morton family." She thrust her finger at Caroline's face. "Keep away from my son!"

"With pleasure, ma'am." Caroline curtsied. "Please excuse me."

After Mrs. DeBloom stormed off, Inspector Ross came over to Caroline and gently caught her elbow. "Is everything all right, my lady?"

"Yes, of course, Inspector."

"Forgive me for doubting you, but it looked very much as if Mrs. DeBloom was telling you off. Is she concerned that her son appears to be besotted with you?"

Caroline looked up at him and he smiled.

"I am a police officer, Lady Caroline. I am trained to be observant."

"So I see."

"Or was the matter being discussed more serious than that?" Inspector Ross wasn't finished. "Did she mention anything about your father's will?"

"She ordered me to keep away from her son," Caroline said. "I asked for her assistance in doing so, because he is remarkably persistent, and she didn't take it well."

Inspector Ross frowned and looked over to where Mr. DeBloom was chatting to Dorothy.

"Do you want me to have a word with him?"

"And warn him off?" Caroline sighed. "I am not a bone, Inspector. I dislike being fought over."

"I must confess that I have never thought of you in quite that way, Lady Caroline, but I will hold my fire. With the recent revelations about the DeBloom connection to your solicitors, I don't want to muddy the waters."

"Have you spoken to Mr. Thettle?"

"I haven't had the opportunity."

"I think he might have a lot more knowledge of the situation than I first thought," Caroline said. "Not only did he work for both Mr. Smiths, but he was also the witness who saw both Mr. DeBloom and the foreign-looking gentleman on the premises."

"I shall endeavor to speak to him as soon as I can."

"Thank you." Caroline paused. "There is one more thing. Do you happen to know what Mr. Emerson Smith died of?"

Inspector Ross's eyebrows went up. "Are you suggesting his death wasn't natural?"

"I'm hoping very much that it was, but it is strange that both of the men who dealt with my father's new will died shortly after rediscovering it."

"Ah, I see what you mean." He nodded. "I will inquire."

The butler appeared at the door to announce that dinner was served. Inspector Ross bowed and offered Caroline his arm.

"Will you do me the honor of accompanying me to dinner, Lady Caroline?"

"I'd be delighted."

She placed her gloved hand on his sleeve, ignoring both Mr. DeBloom, who was pouting, and Mr. Frogerton, who seemed to find the whole situation highly amusing, and went into the dining room.

She was relieved when, during dinner, Inspector Ross made no efforts to interrogate the DeBlooms. Mrs. Frogerton did start a conversation with Mrs. DeBloom about the obstacles for women who ran businesses, but Mrs. DeBloom seemed disinclined to engage, her attention divided between constantly interrupting her daughter and preventing her son from conversing with Caroline.

As Caroline had no wish to speak to any of the DeBlooms, she focused her efforts on Inspector Ross and Mr. Frogerton, who seemed to get along remarkably well. They had a shared interest in horse racing and shooting game, which kept the conversation moving nicely.

When the ladies withdrew, leaving the men to their port, Caroline was fairly confident there would be no awkward conversations or dramatic confessions between the gentlemen in the dining room. She was less certain how Mrs. DeBloom would behave toward her in the drawing room. When she entered the room, there was no sign of Mrs. De-Bloom, but her daughter was there.

Clarissa rushed over to Caroline. She was a quiet, fair-haired girl who seemed perpetually afraid of her mother. "I know it is none of my business, but was my mother being rude to you?"

"She certainly expressed her opinion, Miss DeBloom, but that is her right."

"I told Philip he was drawing Mother's attention to you." She sighed. "I'll try to warn him that she is annoyed, but I don't know if he'll care. He *insists* that we keep calling on you, and I don't know how to stop him."

"I suspect Mr. DeBloom is hard to dissuade from anything he sets his mind to."

"That is very true," Miss DeBloom agreed. "I'm certain that if he could just try to be more conciliatory toward Mother, she'd let him control more of the business. She and Mr. Kruger work very hard as it is, and I'm sure she'd welcome his assistance."

Mrs. DeBloom entered the room, and her daughter moved quickly away from Caroline. The butler brought in a tray with tea and the small cakes Mrs. Frogerton loved and set it on the table in front of his employer. Even as Caroline distributed the tea, she was thinking about the DeBloom family. How much of Mr. DeBloom's apparent devotion was because he genuinely cared for her, as opposed to his desire to destroy his family business? Did he want to gain her confidence to uncover more evidence to use against his mother, or did he truly wish to restore her fortune to right a wrong?

Her instincts led her to believe the worst of him. Any man who refused to listen when a woman asked him not to pursue her wasn't a true gentleman. When that woman was in an inferior position—where her reputation was already suspect and such a public pursuit could damage her livelihood—it was far worse. If Mrs. Frogerton hadn't been Caroline's staunch defender, she might have found herself without a job or a reference, totally at the mercy of Mr. DeBloom, who would no doubt be delighted to pay for her "companionship."

It would not do. Caroline resolved to be vigilant. She could only hope Inspector Ross and his constables would find evidence to locate Mr. Smith's killer and solve the case without involving the DeBlooms or her father any further.

Chapter 8

With some trepidation, Caroline opened the letter from Susan's headmistress that had arrived in the afternoon post.

> *Dear Lady Caroline,*
> *This morning a letter arrived addressed to Susan from a solicitor in London. As per our previous correspondence, I read the letter on your behalf. It said that Susan had received a five-hundred-pound bequest from a Lady Eleanor Greenwood. The letter was signed by a Mr. Jeremy Smith and had taken over a week to get here from London.*
> *Unfortunately, one of my junior teachers saw the note on my desk and decided to inform Susan of her good fortune. That person has been severely reprimanded. Susan is demanding to see the letter in full, and I wish to seek your advice on this matter.*
> *Yours sincerely,*
> *Mrs. Jane Forester, Headmistress*

Caroline sighed so loudly that Mrs. Frogerton looked up from her reading.

"Not more bad news?"

"I thought I instructed the solicitor not to share the news of Susan's legacy directly with her, but it appears he disregarded my wishes. Through a series of unfortunate events, Susan is now in possession of that information."

"She doesn't have the money yet, lass."

"But I can see her writing to the solicitor and demanding it be sent directly to her."

"She's still a child. Any money owed to her will be sent to you."

"And I intend to use it to pay you back for funding her education and pay for the rest of her school fees," Caroline said. "You have been incredibly generous."

"Oh, don't waste your capital on that," Mrs. Frogerton said. "Speak to Samuel and invest in the funds he suggests."

"I cannot expect you to fund my sister's education forever, ma'am," Caroline said.

"Why not?"

"Because with my aunt's bequest she can now afford to do it herself," Caroline said.

"And I would prefer it if you invested the capital for the next two years while she finishes school and pay me back when you've made a profit," Mrs. Frogerton said firmly. "It's just good business sense."

"Are you sure, ma'am?"

"Yes." Mrs. Frogerton gave a decisive nod. "I am never wrong about how to manage money."

"I must confess I am more concerned that Susan will find a way to share this information with Mabel than what she might do with the money."

"I suspect Mabel would probably relish the opportunity to help herself to the funds." Mrs. Frogerton frowned. "I thought you'd put a stop to their correspondence?"

"I've done my best, but as I am not there, I cannot say whether I've been successful or not. There was that ominous note in Mabel's last letter that she would be in England very soon. You can guarantee that she will seek out Susan in person."

"I don't doubt it for a moment, lass."

Caroline folded up the letter. "All I can do is ask Mrs. Forester to be as vigilant as possible. But if Susan is determined to meet Mabel, it might prove difficult to stop her."

"Perhaps we should pay another visit to your solicitors to make certain they know not to release the funds to anyone but you," Mrs. Frogerton suggested.

"I think I'd prefer to write," Caroline said. "I have no desire to visit Mr. Potkins again."

"He probably wouldn't see you if I was there." Mrs. Frogerton chuckled. "I don't think he'd ever been so insulted in his life."

"Who have you been insulting now, Mother?" Mr. Frogerton came into the drawing room and went to kiss his mother's cheek. "Nobody of importance, I hope."

"Just Caroline's family solicitors. A more incompetent bunch I have yet to meet!"

Mr. Frogerton sat down opposite Caroline. "With all due respect, Mother, perhaps you should leave the matter for Miss Morton to deal with herself."

"I am dealing with it, sir." Caroline smiled at him. "I was just about to write to them with new instructions."

"Make sure you tell them you want all the money by the end of the month," Mrs. Frogerton said. "There is no reason why it should take any longer now that your aunt's estate has been settled."

"They owe you money, Miss Morton?" Mr. Frogerton looked intrigued. "That is highly irregular."

"Caroline and her sister have a bequest from her recently deceased aunt. I was just telling her to ask your advice about the best place to invest it." Mrs. Frogerton looked expectantly at her son.

"Congratulations." Mr. Frogerton turned to Caroline. "Will you be leaving my mother's employ?"

"I hope not," Mrs. Frogerton said. "Although, with five

hundred pounds for each of them invested in the funds with your guidance, Samuel, I'm fairly certain they would have enough to live comfortably off the interest."

"That's a substantial bequest," Mr. Frogerton said. "If I were in your position, Miss Morton, I suspect I would have handed in my notice the moment I heard the good news."

Caroline held his skeptical gaze. "I signed an employment contract with Mrs. Frogerton until the end of the social season, sir. I prefer to honor my commitments."

"And after that?"

"I haven't yet decided."

"And I don't want her to leave." Mrs. Frogerton smiled at Caroline. "If I can get Dotty settled with her viscount, I'll need companionship even more."

"One might imagine Miss Morton has other options to consider, Mother," Mr. Frogerton said. "I noticed Mrs. De-Bloom was most anxious to stop her son from even speaking to Miss Morton last night."

"Mr. DeBloom is a grown man." Mrs. Frogerton flicked her fingers dismissively. "I doubt he cares what his mother thinks."

"As his income depends on her good will, I beg to differ," Mr. Frogerton said. "If she threatens to cut off his allowance, I'll wager he'll come to heel."

"Caroline isn't interested in Mr. DeBloom, Samuel."

"I noticed that, too." Mr. Frogerton gave Caroline an amused glance. "Inspector Ross is a very pleasant gentleman, is he not, Miss Morton?"

Caroline rose to her feet and went over to the writing desk by the window. "I need to write to Mrs. Forester."

"And your solicitors," Mrs. Frogerton reminded her.

Caroline opened the lid of the desk with something of a bang and sat down. The Frogertons' ability to involve themselves in her personal business and discuss her as if she wasn't there was somewhat disconcerting. She opened the drawer, took out a new piece of freshly cut paper, and readied her quill and ink.

Mr. Frogerton strolled over to look out of the window.

"Do you fancy a drive through the park, Mother? We can leave Miss Morton in peace to write her letters."

"That's an excellent idea. I'll just put on my bonnet."

Mrs. Frogerton left the room, and Caroline pretended to ignore Mr. Frogerton who lingered beside her.

"I'm more than happy to help with your investments, Miss Morton. If I do say so myself, I have a good eye for it."

Caroline set down her pen and looked up at him. There was no point in allowing her pride to affect her financial future. "I would appreciate your advice on this matter, sir."

"Good. I'm assuming you'd want an annual income sufficient to support you and your sister?"

"Yes."

"And somewhere to live." He paused. "I'd suggest waiting on buying a property until you are quite certain as to where you wish to be located. It would take a large chunk out of your capital. The later you dig into that, the better."

"My sister is at school for at least one more year. I won't need to look for a permanent home until she has completed her schooling."

Mr. Frogerton nodded. "I'll do some thinking on this matter and come back with my conclusions before I leave London."

"Do you not intend to stay for the rest of the Season?" Caroline asked.

"I need to get back." He paused. "Everything here seems satisfactory, and I have no cause to worry."

Caroline looked at him. "I suppose I should be relieved I have passed muster, Mr. Frogerton."

He smiled. "I must confess that your thousand-pound bequest has reassured me as to your upstanding character immensely, Miss Morton."

Mrs. Frogerton came back into the room, her bonnet in

her hand. "Come along, Samuel. We can discuss the best places to put Caroline's money on the way."

"Of course we can." Mr. Frogerton inclined his head to Caroline and went to join his mother. "I'm coming right now."

When she'd finished writing her letters, Caroline went to find the butler to ensure their quick dispatch. She discovered him in the kitchen with a note in his hands.

"Lady Caroline. I was just about to bring this up to you."

"Thank you."

She took the note, which was written in an unfamiliar hand; gave him the letters with instructions as to their delivery; and went back upstairs. Mrs. Frogerton and her son hadn't yet returned from their carriage ride, and Dorothy was still sleeping. As the note was addressed to her, she opened it immediately.

> *If you want more from your father's will, you'll need to pay for the privilege. Correspondence on this matter can be left at the Boars Head on the corner of Fleet Street. JT.*

Caroline couldn't quite believe James Thettle had signed his name to his blackmail attempt, but she wasn't surprised he'd made the effort. Junior clerks were not well paid, and, as Mrs. Frogerton had predicted, he'd seen an opportunity to make money and taken it. But was Caroline his only contact, or had he decided to include others he thought might be interested in the matter? If he'd found Mr. Smith's appointment diary, he might have access to the addresses of all his clients.

It was not something to be taken lightly, and for once, Caroline was glad Mrs. Frogerton hadn't been with her when she'd read the note. Knowing her employer, she'd be calling the carriage and insisting they head straight for the Boars Head on Fleet Street to confront Mr. Thettle, possibly with a pistol in each hand.

After glancing outside at the weather, Caroline left a note for Mrs. Frogerton and went down to the hall. She found the butler and asked him to hail her a hackney cab. Five minutes later, she was on her way to Great Scotland Yard, where she hoped Inspector Ross would be available to address her concerns.

Her luck was in, and he came down to the crowded visitors entrance to escort her to a more private room where they wouldn't have to shout at each other to be heard over the never-ending racket. He looked his usual calm self, but there was a tiredness around his eyes that spoke of lack of sleep. Caroline felt a stab of guilt for bothering him about something so trivial.

"I do apologize for disturbing you, Inspector. I should have simply written you a note, but I thought you should see this."

"You never disturb me, Lady Caroline," Inspector Ross said. "In fact, you are the brightest thing I've seen all day. I've been dealing with a gruesome double murder that has kept me up for the last two nights."

She handed him the note, and after he read it, he frowned. "I see Mr. Thettle is making threats. I wonder if his employers know about this."

"One would assume that even they wouldn't condone blackmail, Inspector."

"Agreed. May I keep this?"

Caroline nodded. "I was hoping you could advise me how to proceed with this matter."

"Don't contact him unless I say so, and don't give him money."

"I don't have any money, sir."

"Why would he think you did?" Inspector Ross mused. "Or perhaps he hoped Mrs. Frogerton would see this note and offer to pay on your behalf."

"It's probably the latter, which is why I haven't shown my employer the note yet. But as Mr. Thettle is privy to all my financial affairs, he might be aware that I recently received a bequest from my deceased aunt."

"Lady Eleanor Greenwood?"

Caroline nodded.

"I read her obituary in the paper." Inspector Ross made a face. "I'm sorry for your loss."

"Thank you. She left Susan and me enough money to make us financially independent in a modest way."

"You must be relieved." He looked down at the note. "Do you intend to leave London and set up home near your sister's school?"

"Not yet, sir. I have my contract with Mrs. Frogerton to honor."

"Of course." He smiled. "I'd expect nothing less from you."

"Mr. Frogerton will be investing the money on my behalf until Susan finishes school and we can decide where we want to live." She hesitated. "I was considering staying in Mrs. Frogerton's employ until then. Would that be considered odd?"

"You seem to get along remarkably well together, so why not? At least you'd be in a place of safety. Although, with Mrs. Frogerton you never know . . ." Inspector Ross folded the note in half. "I assume she'd be willing to keep you."

"She has suggested as much," Caroline said.

"Then it seems like an ideal plan to me."

"It's not as if my newfound wealth is enough to reopen the doors of society. My reputation will never fully be restored after taking employment for a *wage*. And to be honest, I no longer wish to be part of a world that turned its back on me."

"I have similar feelings, Lady Caroline," Inspector Ross said. "I must confess I quite enjoy earning a wage and not being ordered around by my family."

They smiled at each other, and Inspector Ross cleared

his throat. "Do you ever attend the theater, Lady Caroline?"

"Yes, Mrs. Frogerton enjoys it immensely."

"Would you consider attending such an event with me?"

"I'm certain Mrs. Frogerton would be delighted to invite you to join us, sir."

"Ah, I meant would you be willing to accompany me—with suitable chaperonage of course."

"I think I would like that very much," Caroline said, aware that she might be blushing. "As long as Mrs. Frogerton has no objections, obviously."

He nodded. "I'll speak to her." He put the note in his pocket. "I'll pay a visit to your solicitors today and speak to Mr. Thettle. I doubt he'll admit he's a blackmailer, but I'll make sure he knows I'm watching him. I'll warn him of the consequences if he attempts to extort any money from you."

"Thank you, Inspector."

"And while I'm there, I'll see if I can discover how Mr. Emerson Smith died." Inspector Ross was already moving to open the door for her. "I'll keep you informed of any progress, Lady Caroline."

She was quietly amused by his ability to switch into his more professional manner so quickly.

"Thank you for seeing me." They exited the room together.

"It was my pleasure. I do hope you have a maid with you, Lady Caroline? This isn't the safest part of London."

"I am quite capable of finding my way around, Inspector."

"I'm well aware of your many capabilities, my lady, but Mr. Smith was murdered on the streets after dealing with your father's will, which means you might be at risk." Now he was frowning at her. "Constable Jones?" He raised his voice.

"Yes, sir?"

"Will you find Lady Caroline a hackney cab and make sure she is sent safely on her way?"

"Of course, sir." An elderly constable in the dark blue coat and uniform of the Metropolitan Police came to stand beside her. "Come with me, my lady. I'll get you safely away from here."

Caroline allowed the constable to take her out of a side door that led onto a quieter street, where he instantly found her a hackney cab.

"Where to, miss?" the cab driver called down to her.

"Coutts Bank on The Strand, please." Caroline thanked the constable and got into the cab.

If she was out flouting the rules of polite behavior, she might as well continue to destroy her nonexistent reputation by turning up at a financial institution run by men. She wanted to know more about her father's dealings with the DeBlooms, and who better to tell her than her father's banker?

She alighted from the cab on the busy street and stared up at the imposing double-fronted building of Coutts Bank, which had been established in the seventeenth century. A doorman guarding the front entrance looked down his nose at her as she approached.

"Move along, miss. There's nothing for the likes of you in here."

"On the contrary." Caroline raised her chin and held his gaze. "My family have banked here since before you were born. Please move aside."

He took a small step back as he heard her voice, which still held all the authority of her class.

"I don't know about that, miss . . ."

She smiled and eased past him, fairly certain he wouldn't want an undignified brawl with a lady on the front step of such a venerable institution. She entered a large, echoing hall guarded by a gentleman sitting behind a large mahogany desk that dominated the space. He stood with some reluctance as she approached him.

"Good morning, sir." Caroline decided to take the initiative. "I am Lady Caroline Morton, daughter of the late Earl of Morton. I wish to speak to someone about my father's account."

"Do you have an appointment?"

"No, but I won't take up much of your banker's time. I merely need to see some old records."

"I'm not sure . . ."

Caroline smiled as sweetly as she could and might have fluttered her eyelashes. "I have no living male relatives to send in my stead, sir, or else I wouldn't be here. Please have the decency to at least inquire whether anyone can help me. My family have banked with you for generations."

"The Earl of Morton, you said."

"Yes, my late father." Caroline nodded encouragingly.

The man sighed. "I will inquire." He pointed at a door to his right. "Perhaps you might be more comfortable in our visitors' morning room, Lady Caroline."

"That would be most welcome. You have been most helpful, sir." Caroline went through into the sunny room that faced the street.

She was made to wait for some considerable time. She didn't mind, because it gave her the opportunity to refine what she wished to discuss and how much information to reveal.

Eventually, the door opened to reveal a vaguely familiar face.

"Lady Caroline, what a pleasure to see you again."

She curtsied. "I feel I should know your name, sir, but—"

"You were quite a little girl the last time I saw you." The man chuckled. "You burst into your father's study complaining about something your little sister had done, hotly pursued by said sister and your nurse."

"I can only apologize for my appalling manners, sir," Caroline said. "And here I am bursting in again without an appointment."

He gestured at the chairs beside the fireplace. "Would you care to sit down? My name is Mr. Andrew Castle. I have been with the bank for the last thirty-five years and knew your father very well." He paused. "I was sad to hear of his passing. He was a fine gentleman."

"He left my sister and me penniless and homeless, sir." Caroline sat down.

"Yes, your father's debts were considerable when he died. There was very little capital left to salvage." He paused. "Obviously all the entailed estate goes into trust until the new heir to the earldom can be confirmed."

Mr. Castle's measured tone held very little sympathy, but Caroline wasn't offended. She was fairly certain Coutts had lost money on her father as well.

"If you have come seeking financial recompense, Lady Caroline—"

She held up her gloved hand. "I have no expectations of such a thing, sir. I merely wish to see my father's banking records. Is that possible?"

"Might I ask what you are trying to discover?" Mr. Castle's obvious relief at her not throwing herself at his feet and begging for money showed on his face. "We do hold all the records on his various accounts."

"My father invested a considerable amount of money in mining ventures in South Africa. I am trying to ascertain how much he spent on shares which proved to be for mines that never existed."

"Is there a suggestion that he was deliberately defrauded or did he, like a lot of people, simply make some bad investments?" Mr. Castle coughed gently. "The late earl could be somewhat impulsive in his financial dealings, my lady."

"I am well aware of that," Caroline said. "But in this case, it is possible that he was lied to. I have seen evidence of at least one cheque that was written out of his account at Coutts. I am curious to see whether it was honored, and whether he wrote any more to the same company."

Mr. Castle considered her. "If you can assure me that this bank will not be liable for any costs or legal actions in this matter, I will ask my clerk to find your father's accounts and bring them here for you to peruse."

"I have no intention of involving this bank in any case, sir, but if my father *was* defrauded, I cannot answer as to what a court might choose to ask, and to whom." Caroline held his gaze. "I am more than willing to sign my name to that statement if you wish."

He nodded. "I can accept that." He rose to his feet. "If you will excuse me for a moment, my lady, I'll go and find my clerk."

"Thank you." Caroline smiled at him.

"Would you care for some refreshment, Lady Caroline?"

"That would be most welcome."

He nodded and left the room, leaving Caroline feeling rather proud of herself. She knew Mrs. Frogerton wouldn't approve of her actions—mainly because she hadn't been involved—but this truly was Morton family business, and Caroline preferred to keep it that way. Her family's very public downfall had already provided enough fodder for society gossips. If she could resolve this matter in private, she would be very relieved indeed.

Mr. Castle returned within a half hour. Caroline was served with tea and cakes by a very efficient butler who still managed to convey, without saying a single inappropriate word, that he didn't approve of ladies, titled or otherwise, popping around to the bank.

"Ah, I see you have had your tea."

"Thank you. It was very pleasant indeed."

Caroline set down the cup, her gaze fixed on the enormous leatherbound book Mr. Castle's clerk held in his arms. He set it down on the desk beside the window and withdrew from the room.

Mr. Castle opened the book. "The Morton account goes

back to the 1650s. I assume the information you require is of a much more recent date."

"Yes." Caroline joined him at the table. "The cheque was dated five years before he died. I have the details here."

Mr. Castle took her note and began to turn the pages.

"Is this all for my family?" Caroline asked.

"Indeed. And it will continue on when the new Earl of Morton is discovered and takes his seat in the House of Lords." He paused. "Although there is very little money left, there is still revenue from property, trade, and shares trickling in. If it takes a long time to find the earl, the account might even show a profit."

"I hope for his sake that it does," Caroline said.

"Have you any notion as to whereabouts on the family tree the new heir might reside?" Mr. Castle asked.

"My father didn't maintain close links with his family. We barely met anyone."

Mr. Castle turned the page and ran his finger down the closely written columns, which contained detailed notes as to each transaction as it occurred.

"DeBloom. Here it is." He pointed at a line. "This cheque was honored by the bank at the time it was presented." He read on. "Apparently, it was for shares in a new mine."

"That's what I was told," Caroline said. "Does it give a name for the specific mine?"

Mr. Castle peered closer. "I think that says, *Wonderwerk Myne*. That doesn't sound very English, does it?"

"As the mine was supposed to be located in South Africa, perhaps they are using the local language," Caroline suggested. "May I write these details down?"

"You may, but as I mentioned earlier, they do not constitute any evidence you can use in a public trial."

"I understand."

Mr. Castle furnished Caroline with a pen and ink, and while she copied out the notes, he continued his inspection of the bank account.

"There are two further payments to the DeBloom account." Mr. Castle looked up.

"Two? Totaling how much?" Caroline asked.

"Slightly lesser sums this time. The first is for two thousand pounds, the second for a thousand. One of them has a note that a property was purchased on the earl's behalf." Mr. Castle frowned. "But, if I might say, considering the state of the earl's finances at that point, I would not have advised him to proceed with either transaction."

He read the paragraph beneath the second sum. "Ha! In fact, I did warn him, and there is a note to prove it."

"It was good of you to try," Caroline said. "I doubt he would listen."

"He was not the easiest of clients to persuade to change his mind, my lady. He was always very certain of his intentions."

Caroline bit back what she wanted to say. "May I take a copy of these additional entries, sir?"

"Yes, of course, Lady Caroline." Mr. Castle stood aside to give Caroline better access to the book. "Are you and Lady Susan, well?"

"As well as the recently dispossessed can be, sir. I have a position as a companion, and my sister is completing her education at school."

"Good Lord." Mr. Castle stared at her aghast. "You've been forced to seek *paid employment*?"

"Yes, that's what happens when one of your clients spends all his money and then delves into his capital and his daughters' doweries."

"I . . . am sorry to hear that, my lady." He paused. "Was there no one in the family who could offer you a home?"

"My aunt, Lady Eleanor Greenwood, did just that." Caroline smiled. "She recently passed away, leaving my cousin, who has a similar appreciation for money as my father, in charge of the estate. I did not have confidence in his ability to keep offering us a home and preferred to earn my own living."

"I . . ." Mr. Castle appeared to be at a loss of words.

Caroline took pity on him. She finished writing and sanded off the ink. "As I said, sir, my sister and I are very well and adapting to our new circumstances. There is nothing for you to worry about."

"We tried to restrict your father's spending toward the end of his life. He seemed to accept that. I cannot believe he continued to use . . . other means to extract money from his estate." Mr. Castle frowned. "I'm surprised his solicitors allowed him to tamper with legal trusts."

"I had the same conversation with them, sir. In my opinion they were negligent." Caroline folded the note, placed it in her reticule, and stood up.

"Ah, so that is the point of this investigation." He nodded. "It is very brave of you to attempt such a thing, Lady Caroline, but I must warn you that I fear you won't succeed."

"Why is that, sir?" Caroline put on her gloves.

"With all due respect, my dear, you are a lady. The courts don't tend to listen to—"

"Women like me," Caroline spoke over him.

"Ladies without a husband or a powerful family behind them," Mr. Castle continued smoothly.

"Then perhaps it is time they did." Caroline smiled at him. "Thank you, Mr. Castle. You have been most helpful."

Mr. Castle rang the bell, and his clerk appeared.

"Before you go, my lady, will you run your eye over this letter my clerk has composed as to your understanding of the bank's lack of liability in this matter?"

"Yes, of course." Caroline read the letter. "It all seems perfectly satisfactory."

He offered her a pen, and she signed with a flourish.

"Thank you, Lady Caroline." Mr. Castle beamed at her. "Now, if you will allow my clerk to escort you to your carriage?"

She curtsied, and let the young man walk her out of the building, past the doorman, and onto The Strand.

"I don't have a carriage, but if you could hail me a hackney cab, I'd be most grateful."

He grinned at her. "You're a funny one. Got Mr. Castle all in a tizz this morning."

"Good." Caroline smiled back at him.

"If we walk down to the corner, it will be easier to find a cab." He glanced back at the doorman, who was listening intently.

"If being away from the office will cause you problems, I can attend to the matter myself," Caroline suggested.

"Nah, Mr. Castle would kill me if any harm came to an earl's daughter." He gestured for her to follow him. "Now, come along, and we'll get you on your way home in a jiffy."

Ten minutes later, Caroline was on her way back to Half Moon Street filled with a sense of satisfaction about completing her business. She was far more assured than the scared little mouse when her father died and her world crumbled around her. Mrs. Frogerton had taught her a lot about how to stand up for herself, and she'd always be grateful for it.

Just before they reached the turn into her street, the cab driver shouted down to her. "Traffic's all snarled up ahead. Can I drop you here, luv? It'll save me having to turn around in that mess."

"Yes, of course," Caroline called back.

She alighted from the cab and paid the driver, who tipped his hat, smartly turned his horse around, and was gone before she'd even reached the corner of her street. From what she could see, a brewery cart had broken down and several of the barrels had fallen off the back, blocking the road. The driver of the cart was trying to stop a group of lads from stealing the ale, and a fight was imminent. As she glanced over to see if the police had arrived to offer their assistance, someone bumped into her. She momentarily lost her footing, and an instant later she was slammed against a wall with a man's forearm across her throat.

It was hard to see her assailant's face under the shadow of his tall hat. She tried to draw in a breath, but he increased the pressure.

"Keep your mouth shut."

She stopped struggling and concentrated on drawing in air through her constricted throat. His voice was slightly muffled, as if he'd covered most of his face with his kerchief.

"Stay away from the DeBlooms. Nod your head if you heard me."

She did her best even as black dots swirled in front of her eyes.

"Next time I'll kill you."

He stepped away and pushed her so violently that the back of her head cracked against the wall. She sucked in great gasps of air as unconsciousness beckoned but refused to give in to it. If she collapsed on the street, anything could happen to her. She had to get home. She drew herself upright and staggered forward, almost falling as she rounded the corner, her gaze fixed on the yellow door of the Frogertons' rented house.

She'd barely managed a few steps when someone grabbed hold of her arm. She screeched and swung at them with her reticule and was rewarded with a stream of northern cursing.

"Lay off, Miss Morton. I'm trying to help you."

She recognized Mr. Frogerton's brusque voice and tried to focus on him before collapsing on his chest in a dead faint.

Chapter 9

As Caroline came to her senses, she found herself lying on her bed with her boots still on. Mrs. Frogerton was by her side, while Mr. Frogerton hovered at the doorway looking remarkably concerned.

"Don't just stand there, Samuel," Mrs. Frogerton snapped. "Fetch her maid and the doctor!"

"I would if I knew who they were," Mr. Frogerton said.

"Ask the butler!" She shooed him away and turned her attention to Caroline. "There, there, dear. Don't fret."

"I'm fine." Caroline tried to reassure her employer.

"You are not fine. You collapsed in Samuel's arms. Now let's get you out of your clothes and into bed."

Caroline's maid, Letty, came in, and they both started to undress Caroline.

She winced when Mrs. Frogerton tried to remove her bonnet. "I think I hit my head."

"You fell down?" Mrs. Frogerton sounded rather loud. "Did you trip over something?"

"No, the man pushed me against the wall," Caroline whispered.

"There was a man?" Mrs. Frogerton's voice rose another octave.

Caroline tried to turn her head away. The maid gently settled her back against the pillows.

"I suspect Miss Morton has a headache, ma'am," Letty said. "She seems sensitive to loud noises."

"Oh." For a moment Mrs. Frogerton looked blank. "Am I being too strident?"

Caroline closed her eyes as her boots and stockings were removed.

"Should we let her sleep before the doctor gets here?" Mrs. Frogerton whispered loud enough to wake the dead. "If she has sustained a head injury, we need her to be conscious."

There was a knock on the door and Letty went to answer it. She returned within seconds. "Mr. Frogerton said he's sent for the doctor and told him it's urgent."

"Good." Mrs. Frogerton removed Caroline's cloak and gasped, completely forgetting to be quiet. "What happened to your throat? It looks like someone tried to strangle you!"

"I suspect that was his intention," Caroline croaked. "Luckily, we were in too public a place."

Mrs. Frogerton sat back. "And this is why I tell you not to go out alone, young lady! A woman of your class and beauty should never be unaccompanied in the dangerous streets of London, and now look what's happened to you. Did he steal your reticule or attempt to ravish you?"

"Ma'am," Letty spoke softly. "Perhaps you might wait for the doctor downstairs while I finish helping Miss Morton into bed. You can tell him what has occurred." She paused. "You wouldn't want Mr. Frogerton trying to explain what happened, now, would you?"

"No, he'd get it completely muddled." Mrs. Frogerton let go of Caroline's hand. "I'll watch for the carriage and intercept dear Dr. Finnegan in the entrance hall before Samuel can say a word."

She exited the room, leaving a blissful calm behind her.

"Thank you, Letty."

"You're welcome, miss. I know Mrs. Frogerton means well, but sometimes she becomes a little overexcited. If you can manage to sit forward, I can help remove your dress and stays without you having to stand."

"I don't think I could stand," Caroline confessed. "My legs wouldn't hold me."

"That's probably the shock, miss." Letty tutted. "Mr. Frogerton said he found you practically on the doorstep! It's scandalous how these thieves are behaving these days. Me dad says it's not safe anywhere anymore, and he should know."

"I'm not sure he was a thief. He certainly didn't steal anything apart from my peace of mind." Caroline shivered as she remembered the violence in the man's menacing tone.

"Now lie back down and I'll do the bottom half." Letty could be quite bossy. "I have your nightdress warming by the fire. We'll have you all decent before the doctor arrives."

All Caroline wanted was to be left alone like the small, scared animal she was, but she knew that wasn't possible. The doctor would need to examine her, and then she'd have to face the quite justifiable wrath of Mrs. Frogerton, who didn't employ her to go wandering over London without a care in the world.

She might have proved she was an independent woman capable of managing her own business, but she'd also been reminded of the cost of such freedom. Her assailant had certainly made her feel vulnerable, and she hated it.

Letty stayed beside her until the doctor arrived and then took up a position at the end of the bed to allow Mrs. Frogerton room to speak to Caroline.

"Now, tell Dr. Finnegan what happened, lass."

"I was just about to turn into Half Moon Street when a man grabbed me and pushed me up against a wall." Caroline tried to swallow, but it was difficult.

"Drink some water, lass." Mrs. Frogerton handed her a glass. "And take your time."

"He braced his forearm over my throat and . . . threatened me."

"About what?"

Caroline met Mrs. Frogerton's inquiring gaze. "About a matter we are involved in, ma'am."

"So, it wasn't just bad luck," Mrs. Frogerton said. "Whoever it was deliberately came after you. Did you recognize him?"

"No, ma'am."

Dr. Finnegan gently cleared his throat. "Perhaps it would be best if I examined my patient before we get into the salient details of the whys, and instead concentrate on ascertaining the extent of Miss Morton's injuries."

"Oh!" Mrs. Frogerton sat back. "Please, go ahead."

Dr. Finnegan's fingers were very gentle as he probed Caroline's head and then her throat. Eventually, he sat back and regarded her.

"There isn't any blood at the back of your head; your bonnet took a lot of the impact. And, apart from a few abrasions on your throat, I don't think you'll have much more than bruising to deal with. Despite the soreness across your chest, from what I can see, your assailant didn't break any bones."

"Thank goodness," Mrs. Frogerton muttered. "Or I'd be out in the streets searching for him myself."

Dr. Finnegan patted Caroline's hand. "I'd recommend a couple of days in bed with a liquid diet to help with your swollen throat. You'll probably have a headache for a while, and I'll prescribe something for that. You might feel nauseated when you attempt to stand, so please don't force yourself to resume your duties too quickly." He glanced over at Mrs. Frogerton. "I'm fairly certain your employer will be tolerant of your weakness."

"As far as I'm concerned, she can stay in bed for as long

as she likes, Dr. Finnegan," Mrs. Frogerton said. "I just want her to be well again."

"You are a very kind and generous employer, ma'am." Dr. Finnegan stood and began to repack his bag. "I wish all my clients were so forbearing with their staff."

"I consider Caroline part of the family, Doctor." Mrs. Frogerton smiled at him. "Now, may I escort you downstairs? My son Samuel will see you out."

Letty held up the bottle Dr. Finnegan had given her. "Shall I give Miss Morton a dose of this now, Doctor? She has a horrible headache."

"Yes, of course." Dr. Finnegan looked at Caroline. "It might make you drowsy, but that's not a bad thing after the events of this terrible day. You probably need your sleep."

"Thank you, sir."

Caroline took the medicine, which tasted faintly of mint and poppy seeds, and lay back on the pillows. The medicine had a bitter aftertaste, but Caroline didn't care.

Letty closed the curtains and came back to gaze at Caroline. "If it's all right with you, miss, I'll tell Mrs. Frogerton you're asleep and not to disturb you for an hour or two."

"I would appreciate that. Thank you."

Letty nodded as she gathered up the supplies the doctor had used, along with the bowl of water. "She means well."

"She does."

Letty headed for the door. "I'll be back in a minute to sit with you."

Caroline hadn't eaten since breakfast and could already feel the effects of the potion creeping through her body. The gradual lessening of the pain in her head and throat only made her more conscious of just how agonizing they had been. Would her assailant have killed her if they hadn't been on such a busy street? Because of the melee in the blocked road, an unusually large number of people had been loitering on the pavements, making his task harder.

Even though she hadn't been able to see his face properly, she instinctively knew he was a man who liked inflicting pain on others. An almost anticipatory note had been in his voice when he'd threatened her life, as though he couldn't wait to carry out his promises.

The fact that he'd accosted her practically on her doorstep was worrying. Had he followed her around all morning, or simply lain in wait near Half Moon Street, knowing she'd have to return at some point and that she'd foolishly gone out alone? Neither scenario made her feel particularly safe.

A wave of sleep overwhelmed her and, for once in her life, she willingly embraced it and let herself be carried over into darkness.

The next morning brought a procession of visitors. Letty arrived first to see to her basic needs and to ask her what she wanted for breakfast. Caroline couldn't imagine eating her usual toast and marmalade—every swallow would be agony. Even though she wasn't particularly hungry, she asked for coddled eggs and tea.

While she was eating her breakfast, Mrs. Frogerton arrived and asked whether she would allow Samuel to inquire as to her health while she was still in bed. Caroline acquiesced, and Mr. Frogerton came in looking remarkably uncomfortable.

"Miss Morton." He inclined his head. "How are you this morning?"

"Better than I was yesterday, sir." Her voice was still raspy. "I must thank you for your prompt action on my behalf."

"I hardly had any choice in the matter, Miss Morton. I spotted you reeling around like a drunkard and tried to take your arm, and you attacked me with your reticule."

"I must have assumed my assailant had returned, sir. I can only apologize."

"It's quite all right. You didn't have the strength to do any damage." He frowned at her. "Your throat is bruised."

Caroline's fingers brushed the lace at her neck. "Yes."

"And your voice sounds strained. Did the bastard lay hands on you?"

Mrs. Frogerton, who had remained in the room as a chaperone, spoke up. "He *threatened* her, Samuel."

"But he didn't steal anything." Samuel's shrewd gaze met Caroline's. "How odd."

"Perhaps he was insane," Mrs. Frogerton said.

"Did you think that's the case, Miss Morton, or did his threats make sense to you?" Mr. Frogerton asked.

Caroline looked helplessly at Mrs. Frogerton, who came to stand by the side of the bed. "I think that's enough, Samuel. Poor Caroline is very tired."

For once Mr. Frogerton didn't argue with his mother. He bowed. "I am glad I was there to be of assistance, Miss Morton, and I wish you a speedy recovery."

He had barely departed before Dorothy appeared, still in her nightgown with her hair braided down her back.

"Whatever have you been up to Caroline? My maid said you were attacked on our street in broad daylight!"

"I—"

Dorothy leaned closer and gasped. "Your throat!" She spun around to look at her mother. "That could've been *me*! We should leave this place immediately. I'm sure Augustus and his family would invite us to his townhouse on Grosvenor Square." She paused. "But maybe not Caroline—she should stay here in case she is attacked again."

"Dorothy . . ."

Miss Frogerton was already on the move. "I won't mention it to Augustus, because I don't want him to think that I live on the kind of street where such a terrible thing could happen. And I don't want you to say anything either, Mother. You know how you do run on. Let's keep this between us. Caroline had best stay in bed until her bruises fade and then no one will be any the wiser."

She blew Caroline a kiss and left the room, leaving Mrs. Frogerton, for once, speechless.

"Well," she finally said. "As if I would mention your personal business to Augustus, Caroline. What does she think of me?"

Caroline was glad Letty had brought in her breakfast tray. She was able to drink some tea and attempt to eat her eggs while Mrs. Frogerton went downstairs to have her own breakfast. It was nice to be quiet after all the visitors, but Caroline knew Mrs. Frogerton, at least, would be back. She'd want to know exactly what had happened, and Caroline would be obliged to tell her.

She set aside the tray and kept the tea while Letty measured out a slightly smaller dose of medicine to deaden her ever-present headache. She must have dozed for a while, because when she woke up, the tray had gone and Dr. Finnegan sat by her bed holding her wrist.

"You look much better today, Miss Morton. Are you still in pain?"

"I still have a headache and my throat is sore," Caroline admitted. "But I think I'm improving."

"You've coughed up no blood?"

"None, Doctor."

"That's good." He touched her shoulder. "Any new pain in your ribs?"

"No."

"Excellent." He smiled at her. "We'll have you up and about in no time." He glanced over his shoulder at Letty. "Do you still have the medicine I prescribed?"

"Yes, sir. There's plenty left."

He patted Caroline's hand and rose to his feet. "I'll come back tomorrow. But if anything changes, please ask Mrs. Frogerton to contact me immediately."

"Thank you, Dr. Finnegan."

He bowed and left. Caroline asked Letty for more tea, which led to a discussion about the benefits of honey for a sore throat and how Letty would give the cook her own special recipe. Mrs. Frogerton arrived while Letty was enumerating the benefits of her concoction, and she sent Letty off to the kitchen.

Caroline braced herself as her employer firmly closed the door and came to sit beside the bed. Mrs. Frogerton wore an elegant chestnut-brown morning gown that suited her to perfection and had added earrings made of amber that caught the light.

"Is that a new dress, ma'am?" Caroline asked. "It is very becoming."

"It is new, but let's not waste what voice you have complimenting me." Mrs. Frogerton looked at Caroline, her expression grave. "I think you owe me an explanation, lass."

There was an uncompromising note in her employer's voice that Caroline hadn't heard directed at her before.

"What would you like to know, ma'am?"

"All of it, lass." Mrs. Frogerton paused. "You are in my employ. I have a care for your welfare, and I would feel responsible if anything happened to you."

Caroline took a fortifying sip of tea and prepared to recount her actions on the previous day.

"While you were out with Mr. Frogerton, I received a note from Mr. Thettle. He said that if I wished to see more excerpts from my father's will, I would have to pay for the privilege."

Mrs. Frogerton tutted. "I thought he might try something like that. He seemed the type."

"I decided the best thing to do would be to take the note to Inspector Ross and ask for his advice about how to proceed."

"I don't doubt your decision, lass, but you could've waited until I returned."

"I . . . thought I could manage the matter without bothering you, ma'am," Caroline explained.

"I see. And what did Inspector Ross have to say for himself?"

"He took the note and said he would visit Mr. Thettle and warn him off."

Mrs. Frogerton nodded but didn't comment, which was surprisingly disconcerting.

Caroline licked her lips and continued. "I decided that while I was in the city, I would visit Coutts."

"To find out whether the cheque Mr. DeBloom showed you had been presented at the bank," Mrs. Frogerton said. "And what did they say?"

"The cheque was honored, as were two others to the DeBloom company. One was for the property," Caroline explained. "I have the details written down. The banker said they had tried to warn my father about his excessive spending and that they believed he'd brought it under control."

"How convenient for them."

"I believe they were worried I'd come to beg for money from the estate. They took great pains to remind me that everything remains in trust for the next Earl of Morton."

"Have they not found him yet?" For the first time Mrs. Frogerton sounded like her old self. "You'd think he would've shown himself by now."

"Apparently not."

"Maybe claiming a bankrupt earldom with a tragic past doesn't appeal," Mrs. Frogerton said. "I'm not sure I'd want to take on that debt just for a title."

Caroline drank more tea and forced herself to continue. "The hackney cab I took from Coutts dropped me off just before the corner of Half Moon Street because the road ahead was blocked by a brewery cart." Caroline tried to steady her breathing. "I was looking at the turmoil on the street when someone bumped into me. Before I could apologize, he pushed me against the wall and pressed his arm to my throat."

"Could you see his face, lass?"

"Not really. His hat brim shaded his eyes, and he'd

pulled a muffler or kerchief over the bottom half of his face." Caroline shuddered as she recalled the sense of helplessness that had held her paralyzed like a pinned butterfly against the wall. "I only know he was tall, dark-haired, and wished me harm."

"What did he say to you?"

"To leave the DeBlooms alone," Caroline said bleakly. "Or next time he'd kill me."

Mrs. Frogerton reached for her hand. "Oh, my dear, how horrible."

"It was terrifying, ma'am."

"Are you quite sure it wasn't Mr. DeBloom?"

"Absolutely certain, ma'am, although this man did have a South African accent."

Mrs. Frogerton sat back, her expression concerned. "One has to wonder if this is the same man who was seen at the solicitors' office confronting Mr. Smith."

"I had the same thought," Caroline admitted.

"Did he have a broken nose?"

"I couldn't see anything but his eyes, ma'am." It was something she hoped never to have to see again. "He meant what he said."

"That he would kill you if you didn't leave the De-Blooms alone," Mrs. Frogerton said slowly. "Which makes me wonder whether your father's belief that he was defrauded might be true after all."

There was a knock on the door, and then Letty came in. "There's an Inspector Ross in the hall, ma'am, asking to come up and see Miss Caroline."

Mrs. Frogerton looked at Caroline. "Are you well enough to receive him, lass?"

"Did you tell him what happened to me?"

"I might have done." Mrs. Frogerton shrugged unconvincingly. "I'm fairly certain he would've found out anyway—as he is a police officer. I merely made it easy for him."

"I'll see him." Caroline rearranged her pillows behind

her aching head, and Mrs. Frogerton wrapped her best paisley shawl around her shoulders. "I intend to tell him everything I've told you."

"I wouldn't expect anything less, my dear." For the first time since the attack, Mrs. Frogerton smiled at Caroline. "And if anyone can help us sort out this mess, it'll be Inspector Ross."

She turned to Letty. "Send him up, please and make a fresh pot of tea for Miss Caroline."

"Mrs. Frogerton." Caroline waited until Letty had departed to speak. "I am truly sorry for worrying you. I was merely attempting to deal with my own family issues without bothering you, and now I've just made everything worse."

"I can't deny that I wish you'd told me what you were about, lass, but I understand better than most people about pride and the need to handle your own affairs." Mrs. Frogerton paused. "All I'll ask is that you tell me your plans before you head out next time. Then at least I'll know what you're doing and where to start looking if you don't come back."

Chapter 10

"Lady Caroline."

Inspector Ross came into her bedroom accompanied by Letty, Mr. Frogerton, and Mrs. Frogerton, which made it rather crowded. He looked tired, tight-lipped, and disinclined to smile.

"Inspector Ross. There was no need for you to come, sir. I am hardly a priority." Caroline was already exhausted and was finding it difficult to be polite.

"As Mrs. Frogerton contacted me in some distress, I felt it was necessary to come as soon as possible." He glanced over his shoulder. "I would appreciate a moment to speak to Lady Caroline alone."

"Not in her bedchamber, Inspector," Mrs. Frogerton said crisply. "I will remain. The rest of you can leave."

"As you wish, ma'am." Inspector Ross sat beside the bed and produced a notebook and pen, his formality very different to his usual relaxed manner. "I assume you are well enough to give me your statement, my lady?"

"I wouldn't have granted you access if I wasn't, Inspector."

"Then please tell me what happened after you left Scotland Yard. Constable Jones assures me that he put you in a hackney cab and sent you on your way home."

"He is correct, but I had one more stop to make."

He paused his writing but didn't say anything, so she continued. "I went to Coutts Bank on The Strand."

There was quite a long silence before he looked up at her. "One might have thought that Coutts would send a representative to your home."

"I no longer have a home. It was repossessed by Coutts to pay my father's debts." Caroline met his gaze head-on. "I had to find a way to speak to my father's banker, and being direct seemed the best option."

"And you were assaulted there."

"No, I was attacked on the corner of Half Moon Street on my return journey home."

His brow creased. "Did you walk back from The Strand by yourself?"

"I took a hackney cab. The road was congested due to an accident, and the turn was blocked. The cab driver couldn't get in front of the house without considerable maneuvering and asked if he could let me down just before the corner."

Inspector Ross wrote busily in his notebook before continuing his questions. "Did your assailant steal your possessions?" His gaze moved to her throat. "Or did he take something you were wearing from around your neck?"

"He stole nothing, Inspector."

"I don't understand." He looked over at Mrs. Frogerton. "I thought Lady Caroline had been robbed, ma'am."

"That's what I assumed when she first came in, Inspector, because I have repeatedly warned her not to go out without an escort."

Inspector Ross turned to Caroline, his expression unreadable. "It seems we are in agreement about that, at least, Mrs. Frogerton."

Caroline was perilously close to bursting into tears, and that would never do. "Would you see the inspector out, ma'am? I am remarkably tired, and I see no point in continuing this conversation."

"Caroline . . ." Mrs. Frogerton came forward. "Perhaps you should finish explaining what happened. You did say you wished the inspector to know everything."

"That would be helpful," Inspector Ross said. "Because at the moment I feel somewhat confused."

Caroline looked down at her tightly interlaced fingers. It was most unpleasant to have the two people who generally offered her the most support united in their disapproval of her actions. The fact that she deserved their condemnation for ignoring their well-intentioned advice made things worse. She suddenly found herself unable to speak.

After a moment, Mrs. Frogerton gave an exasperated sigh. "Caroline was attacked by a large man with a South African accent who threatened to kill her if she didn't leave the DeBloom family alone."

"Good Lord," Inspector Ross said. "That does put things in a different light."

Mrs. Frogerton stood up. "If you will excuse me for a moment, Inspector, I'll make sure my son Samuel doesn't leave the house in case you need to talk to him. He was the one who helped Caroline after she was attacked."

She left the door open and was already shouting orders at her staff before she reached the top of the stairs.

Inspector Ross cleared his throat. "Lady Caroline . . ."

Caroline continued to stare at her joined hands until he laid one of his hands over hers.

"I want to apologize. When I saw the damage inflicted upon you . . ." He swallowed hard. "I struggled to separate my intense concern for your well-being from my professional need to ask intrusive questions. I might have been too hard on you."

"It's quite all right, Inspector. I understand that you have a job to do. I can only apologize that Mrs. Frogerton contacted you personally."

"I'm glad she did." He paused. "It certainly confirms my suspicion that whatever was in your late father's will is connected to what happened to Mr. Jeremy Smith."

Caroline nodded, her attention on the gentle motion of his thumb on her fingers. It was curiously soothing.

"I know I do not have the right to tell you what to do, my lady, but in my professional capacity, I am asking you not to go out alone until this case is solved."

"I am more than willing to do as you ask," Caroline said.

"Thank you." He brought her hand to his lips, kissed it, and sat back. "Now, do you remember anything about this man who assaulted you?"

"It all happened very suddenly, Inspector." Caroline heard the returning Mrs. Frogerton on the stairs. "His face was half covered by his kerchief, and he wore his hat low over his forehead."

"What about the rest of him? Did he smell of strong spirits? Was his clothing that of a beggar, a working man, or someone else?"

Caroline was thinking about the questions when Mrs. Frogerton came in and sat down.

"He smelled of tobacco," Caroline said slowly. "I think he was wearing a sturdy wool coat, because the fabric was coarse against my throat."

"Not a beggar or a drunk, then." Inspector Ross wrote something in his notebook. "If I were to take a wild guess, it sounds like the same man who terrified Mr. Smith."

Caroline shivered.

"We had the same thought, sir," Mrs. Frogerton said.

Inspector Ross's sigh was almost inaudible as he scribbled more notes. "We will speak to the households near where the assault took place in case anyone saw this man, but it might be difficult to find him."

Mrs. Frogerton snorted. "I know where I'd start looking for him, Inspector—at the DeBlooms'."

"This might surprise you, ma'am, but even the police have to have a justifiable reason to go into anyone's business premises."

"Then find one," Mrs. Frogerton said. "Because I'll wager that man works for the DeBlooms. That woman probably keeps him on the books simply to threaten her competitors."

"I'll see what I can do, ma'am." Inspector Ross glanced at his watch and stood up. "I have to be back at work in half an hour. I'll return after my shift—if that is acceptable?" He looked from Mrs. Frogerton to Caroline.

"If you have something new to tell us, you'll be most welcome," Mrs. Frogerton said. "I have suspended all my social activities until Caroline is well enough to come downstairs, so you are welcome to join my family for dinner."

Inspector Ross bowed. "That is very kind of you." He paused as he went to put his notebook away. "I almost forgot. I visited your solicitors, Lady Caroline. Mr. Thettle was away visiting his mother in Hackney. I will return when he comes back to work."

"Thank you, Inspector," Caroline said. It was far more pleasant to talk about someone other than herself. "And the matter of Mr. Emerson Smith's death?"

"Ah, that's an interesting one." He flipped a few pages and consulted his notes. "He fell down the stairs while working late one evening at the office and broke his neck."

"I'm almost reluctant to inquire what he was working on at the time," Mrs. Frogerton murmured.

"Only Mr. Thettle can answer that question," Inspector Ross said. "I'll be sure to ask him when I see him."

Mrs. Frogerton escorted the inspector out and returned to sit beside Caroline's bed, her face creased with worry. "I don't like the sound of that at all, do you, lass?"

"No, ma'am," Caroline said, and pressed her fingers to her temple. "I wonder if I might trouble you to call Letty? I think I need another dose of Dr. Finnegan's medicine."

Caroline woke up with a start to find a familiar face scowling down at her.

"There's no need to flap, Letty. I'm a doctor. It's perfectly acceptable for me to be in Miss Morton's bedchamber."

"Not without me chaperoning her," Letty said firmly. "Now, look what you've done—you've woken the poor love up! I'm going to find Mrs. Frogerton."

Letty, seemingly forgetting her chaperoning duties, rushed off, leaving Caroline staring up at Dr. Harris, who was now holding her wrist and consulting his pocket watch.

"I bumped into Dr. Finnegan at the hospital. He told me what had happened to you." He kept his attention on his watch. "You could've asked me to come and attend to you."

"I was in no state to ask for anything," Caroline said. "Mrs. Frogerton chose to call her personal physician."

Dr. Harris relinquished her wrist. "Your heart and lungs seem fine." He looked at her chest. "Mostly superficial bruising. How are your ribs?"

"Not broken according to Dr. Finnegan."

"Good. Now what have you been up to?"

Caroline sat up against her pillows, and Dr. Harris retreated to the chair beside the bed.

"I'm not sure what you mean."

He raised an eyebrow. "You have a remarkable ability to get into trouble, Miss Morton."

"I did nothing wrong, if that's what you're implying."

"I'm sure you didn't, but you and your employer can be remarkably annoying when you get an idea into your heads."

"Such as saving your life?" Caroline asked.

"I didn't say your investigations were unsuccessful," Dr. Harris countered. "You have an uncanny ability to put the fox amongst the pigeons, and in this case that obviously led to your current state."

As this was undoubtably true, and far too accurate a reading of the situation, Caroline chose not to reply.

Dr. Harris nodded. "I thought so. Does it have something to do with your father's will?"

"Who told you about that?"

"Mrs. Frogerton, of course." He looked at her expectantly. "Well?"

"It might be connected in some small way," Caroline said reluctantly. "But I cannot be sure."

Mrs. Frogerton came in with Letty behind her. "Dr. Harris, you could've had the courtesy to come into the drawing room and announce your presence before you sauntered into Caroline's bedchamber."

"I did," Dr. Harris protested. "You were asleep."

"I was not—" Mrs. Frogerton's color rose. "I was merely resting my eyes for a moment."

"I called your name at least three times, ma'am," Dr. Harris continued. "If it hadn't been for the fact that you were snoring quite loudly, I would have worried about your health."

Letty concealed a snort and hastily departed when Mrs. Frogerton turned to glare at her.

"Have you told Dr. Harris about the DeBloom threat to your life?" Mrs. Frogerton adroitly changed the subject.

"Mr. DeBloom was the one who attacked you? Good lord." Dr. Harris stared at Caroline. "Have you told Inspector Ross?"

"It was not Mr. DeBloom himself," Mrs. Frogerton continued. "But I'm convinced it was someone in his employ. I told Inspector Ross to start his investigations there!"

"Wait a moment." Dr. Harris frowned. "You're suggesting Mr. DeBloom ordered someone to tell Miss Morton to stop bothering him when the only person doing any bothering is Mr. DeBloom himself?"

"Not Mr. DeBloom—his mother!" Mrs. Frogerton said.

"Now, that makes more sense." Dr. Harris nodded. "She probably doesn't like her little boy chasing after the daughter of a disgraced earl with no fortune." He looked at Caroline. "To be honest, I would've thought Mrs. De-Bloom would do her own dirty work and warn Miss Morton off personally. To send someone to physically intimidate her seems a little heavy-handed."

"Maybe the hired help decided to take things further than Mrs. DeBloom wanted." Mrs. Frogerton shuddered. "I am simply glad Caroline escaped with her life."

"She's hardly injured, ma'am. If she worked in one of your mills, she would've been back to work the same day," Dr. Harris said.

Luckily for Dr. Harris, Mrs. Frogerton chose not to take offense at his comment, as all her attention was on Caroline.

"Now what am I supposed to do if the DeBlooms come calling?" Mrs. Frogerton exclaimed. "If I allow them in, am I putting Caroline in danger? And what on earth do I say if they ask after her?"

"You do not need to be specific about what happened to me, ma'am." Caroline finally managed to insert herself in the conversation going on over her head. "You can just say I am indisposed. As long as you meet the DeBlooms without me, I'm sure you'll be fine."

"Perhaps it would be good to tell them what happened to Miss Morton," Dr. Harris said slowly. "Then it would be blatantly obvious who knew about it and who didn't."

"I can't risk it," Mrs. Frogerton said. "And we can't avoid the DeBlooms for the rest of the Season. That would require an explanation."

"You could continue the acquaintance at other venues, ma'am, and simply not include them in your dinner parties or admit them on morning visits," Caroline suggested.

"I'd have to say something eventually, lass. You know me. I like to be straight with everyone."

Dr. Harris's gaze met Caroline's, and he nodded. "With all due respect, Mrs. Frogerton, you are known for your honesty and, as you are rightfully indignant about Miss

Morton, I'm fairly sure you'd make your displeasure known."

"I fear you are right. Now what are we going to do?" Mrs. Frogerton considered Caroline. "I wonder if I should arrange for you to convalesce somewhere?"

"I am perfectly fine, ma'am. I intend to get up tomorrow and resume my duties," Caroline said.

"And hide every time the DeBlooms turn up?" Mrs. Frogerton asked. "Because we both know Mr. DeBloom, in particular, is very hard to put off."

Dr. Harris cleared his throat. "I have been thinking of visiting my sister."

Mrs. Frogerton raised her eyebrows. "That is all very well, Dr. Harris, but hardly helpful."

"Dr. Harris's sister, Rose, is a teacher at Susan's school in Kent, ma'am," Caroline explained.

Dr. Harris nodded. "Miss Morton could accompany me."

Mrs. Frogerton went still. "And see her sister. A perfectly reasonable thing to do."

"I have been wanting to visit Susan," Caroline said slowly. "There have been some . . . issues with her correspondence."

"Would that be Mabel stirring the pot?" Dr. Harris made a face. "I thought she'd left the country."

Caroline sometimes forgot Dr. Harris knew her family very well. He'd been present during the house party at Greenwood Hall when two of her aunt's guests had ended up dead.

"Mabel has written to Susan."

"Your sister did seem very fond of her cousin," Dr. Harris continued. "It wouldn't surprise me if Mabel continued to try to influence her."

Mrs. Frogerton sat up straight. "I'll send you and Dr. Harris off to Kent in my carriage. You can stay for a few days, sort out matters with Susan, and regain your health by walking by the sea."

"I think we'd be better going on the mail coach, ma'am," Caroline said. "We don't want anyone thinking you are involved in this matter."

"And while you are gone, I will work out how to disengage myself from the DeBlooms without causing offense." Mrs. Frogerton brightened. "Perhaps I'll ask Dotty to have a falling out with Miss DeBloom. That should stop them both from having a reason to call on us."

"That's not a bad idea, ma'am," Dr. Harris agreed. "Miss Frogerton is very good at being disagreeable."

Mrs. Frogerton stood up. "Come with me, Dr. Harris. We'll make the arrangements for your travel. When can you leave?"

Dr. Harris looked back at Caroline and rose to his feet. "I'd suggest the day after tomorrow when Miss Morton is fully recovered. I'll need to write to my sister to warn her of my arrival and make sure I have cover in place at the hospital. Although, as I haven't taken a day off in months, it's the least someone could do for me."

"Excellent." Mrs. Frogerton continued talking as she and Dr. Harris left the room. "I'll provide you with sufficient funds for a respectable inn. I'm not having Caroline staying anywhere that isn't decent."

Caroline sank back on her pillows. For the first time in days, she felt relief wash over her. She didn't consider herself a coward, but the thought of inadvertently meeting the DeBlooms and triggering her assailant's wrath was frightening. Seeing Susan in person might help to diffuse the misunderstandings that corresponding by post sometimes magnified.

Letty came in with a pot of tea. "You look a bit better, Miss Morton. How's your loaf?"

"My loaf?"

"Loaf of bread head." Letty grinned at her. "Your headache."

Caroline cautiously turned her head back and forth. "It's almost gone."

"That's good, because I hear you're traveling into Kent in two days." Letty poured Caroline a cup of tea. "Now which of your dresses do you want me to pack?"

It wasn't until later when Letty had gone that Caroline considered what Mrs. Frogerton might get up to while she was away. Her employer had a tendency toward the dramatic, and without Caroline to dampen her enthusiasm, she might get herself into trouble.

Caroline got out of bed and walked slowly over to her writing desk. Miss Frogerton wouldn't take kindly to be asked to watch out for her mother, and Mr. Frogerton was as blunt as his parent, which left Inspector Ross as the only possibility. She wrote him a short note and left it on the desk for Letty to take down to the butler to post.

She wrote his name and direction on the front of the letter and sealed it. It was also an opportunity to tell him she would be absent for a few days so that he wouldn't worry. Not that Inspector Ross had much time to concern himself with her whereabouts, but he might be relieved to know she wasn't out causing mischief. Now, all he had to be concerned about, at Caroline's request, was Mrs. Frogerton . . .

After sitting up in her chair to have her dinner, Caroline admitted she was still rather tired and was looking forward to returning to bed. Just as she was finishing her meal, Mrs. Frogerton came in with a note in her hand.

"A message for you, lass. I didn't recognize the hand, so I'd thought I'd bring it up myself so we can open it together."

"I wonder if it's Mr. Thettle again?" Caroline took the note. "He's probably annoyed that I haven't replied to his blackmail letter yet."

She opened it and read the contents before looking up at Mrs. Frogerton. "It's from Inspector Ross. I thought it advisable to inform him of my impending absence."

"I'm sure you did, dear." Mrs. Frogerton winked at her. "What does he have to say for himself?"

There were certain elements of the note that Caroline didn't wish to share with her employer, but others needed to be addressed. "He says Mr. Thettle hasn't returned to work."

"Oh, dear." Mrs. Frogerton frowned. "One has to wonder why."

"Either someone agreed to pay him to receive my father's last will and he's run off with the money, or someone decided to take it for themselves anyway."

"I don't like either of those notions, Caroline. Perhaps there is a logical explanation. His mother might be ill, and he's had to stay by her side."

"One would think he would've informed his employers if that was the case. Unfortunately, it appears we have another reason to be wary." Caroline sat forward. "Are you quite certain that you wish me to leave?"

"Yes, lass. You have to go," Mrs. Frogerton said firmly.

"I suppose that if someone has got the last known copies of my father's will, that might be the end of it." Caroline sighed. "If they are destroyed, there is no more evidence to secure a conviction for anything."

"I suppose that's true." Mrs. Frogerton looked doubtful. "But I still have a sense we're in dangerous territory, and I don't like it at all."

"Which is why when I'm away, you must take Mr. Frogerton with you wherever you go," Caroline said. "He won't allow anyone to bother you."

"That's the truth." Mrs. Frogerton nodded. "I did speak to Dotty, and she was more than happy to stage an argument with Miss DeBloom next time they meet."

"That's very good of her."

"She has become quite fond of you and considers you part of our family."

"That is very gratifying to hear."

Mrs. Frogerton reached over to pat Caroline's knee. "You've been a great asset, lass."

"Despite dragging you into all kinds of trouble," Caroline said.

"Oh, that's half the fun of it. I never know what you'll drag me into next!" Mrs. Frogerton rose to her feet. "I have a few arrangements to complete before I can hand over your travel plans, but I should have all the confirmations by tomorrow. Do you wish to write to the school to tell them you are coming?"

"I've already done so, ma'am. Letty took the letter down earlier this afternoon."

"Good girl." Mrs. Frogerton looked at Caroline. "You're as pale as soured milk, lass. You should go to bed."

"I was just contemplating doing that, ma'am."

Caroline got into bed, and Mrs. Frogerton went toward the door.

"I'll wish you a good night, then."

"Good night, ma'am." Caroline hesitated. "And you will take care when I am gone, won't you?"

"I'm a tough old bird. I think I can manage it." Mrs. Frogerton winked. "Now get some sleep, and I'll see you in the morning."

Chapter 11

As Dr. Harris had refused to give up the seat by the window, Caroline spent the first part of her journey squashed between him and a large farmer returning from his first trip to London. The farmer was anxious to share his every impression with his fellow occupants of the coach and, as Dr. Harris closed his eyes and pretended to be asleep, it fell to Caroline and the other passengers to listen to the farmer's account and offer appropriate comments when required.

Not for the first time, Caroline regretted her inability to be rude, as one by one the other passengers lost interest, and she still felt obliged to respond. Her gratitude when he left the coach at Dartford was profound. When no one else got on to occupy the seat, she was even more relieved. As she rearranged her skirts, she "accidentally" kicked Dr. Harris's ankle, making him turn and frown at her.

"What was that for?"

"Your incivility."

He raised an eyebrow. "I had no interest in what the man was saying. Why would I pretend otherwise?"

"One might have thought you would've had an interest in protecting me from overexerting myself."

"You're perfectly capable of ignoring him."

"I am not. I wasn't brought up to be rude."

"Oh yes, of course, the aristocracy and their endless politeness." Dr. Harris yawned. "Which doesn't actually extend to doing anything useful, like paying fair wages, or—"

"Hear! Hear!" the young man sitting opposite them said. "Down with the aristocracy!"

Caroline pressed her lips together and looked pointedly at Dr. Harris, who had the grace to look embarrassed.

"Present company excepted, of course," he murmured. "By the way, we'll stop for the night in Maidstone. I told Mrs. Frogerton we could probably make the trip in one day, as it's only eighty miles or so, but she was concerned for your comfort."

"For which I am truly grateful," Caroline said.

They'd set off from the Blossoms Inn in Cheapside early that morning in driving rain that hadn't lessened as they'd reached the outskirts of London and embarked across more open spaces. Caroline's headache had returned, and for a moment she wished she'd accepted Mrs. Frogerton's offer of her carriage. She could've slept at will and not had to put up with the conversation of anyone except Dr. Harris.

Dr. Harris nudged her side. "As we have hours of traveling ahead of us, perhaps you'd care to explain why Mr. DeBloom wants to kill you."

"It's a very long story."

"As I said, we have plenty of time." He paused. "You might as well tell me what's happened. Otherwise I'll be asking you questions for the rest of our journey."

"Very well." Caroline sighed. "But you can't interrupt me all the time."

He frowned. "That might prove difficult. You do have a terrible tendency to overcomplicate things."

"And you must promise not to tell anyone what I tell you."

"Who would I tell? The next corpse I lay out?"

Caroline turned to face him and lowered her voice. "It all started when I received a letter from my family solicitor suggesting that my father had made a new will."

"What on earth does that have to do with Mr. De-Bloom?" Dr. Harris demanded.

Caroline gave him a look.

"Please go on," he said, giving her a placating gesture.

"You met my solicitor in the hospital when I had to identify him."

"Mr. Smith." Dr. Harris nodded. "He was suffocated on my ward."

"After supposedly trying to deliver a copy of the new will to me," Caroline said. "But as you know, he never reached me . . ."

It was dark by the time she finished her tale. They'd stopped for a late dinner at Maidstone in a very pleasant establishment Mrs. Frogerton had found for them to stay in overnight.

"It doesn't make any sense." Dr. Harris took an apple from the cheeseboard, brought out his own knife, and began to peel the skin. "If the will is now gone, why are the DeBlooms still so eager to pursue you?"

"I don't know." Caroline accepted the slice of apple he handed her.

"Perhaps they aren't aware of Mr. Thettle's part in all this."

"Mr. Thettle is missing."

"You think the DeBlooms got to him as well?" He paused to eat his apple slice. "I suppose it's possible he was trying to blackmail him."

"Mr. Thettle recognized Mr. DeBloom that night in his carriage," Caroline reminded him. "And he had information on all the clients at work."

Dr. Harris frowned. "I'll return to my earlier point. If the mine never existed, and your father's will mentioning the shares is now gone, why are the DeBlooms still after you?"

"I have no idea," Caroline said.

"Perhaps you need to speak directly to Mrs. DeBloom and assure her that you mean her no harm."

"I'm not the one making threats," Caroline pointed out.

"Then talk to Mr. DeBloom."

Caroline raised her eyebrows, and he shrugged.

"I don't like the man, but I don't think he's likely to threaten you. He's totally besotted."

"It might all be an act," Caroline reminded him. "He might be working with his mother."

"If you tell him what happened, and he does nothing, you'll know he's involved."

"And he'll send his henchman around to kill me for interfering in his affairs again," Caroline said. "Or he'll kill me himself."

Dr. Harris finished his apple. "You are very negative about all this, Miss Morton."

"Perhaps that is because it is my life and death we are discussing?" Caroline countered. "I have no desire to sacrifice myself just to prove a point."

"Write to him, then. While you're here."

Caroline considered that. "I have the necessary funds to send a letter back to London."

"And, as we'll be gone in the morning, he won't be able to find you if he does want to murder you," Dr. Harris said helpfully.

"How reassuring," Caroline murmured.

Dr. Harris stood up. "Shall I go and ask the innkeeper for some writing implements?" He glanced down at the dinner table. "And some more of that excellent cheese."

They arrived in Folkestone the next day and were soon comfortably situated in adjoining rooms in the Rose & Crown, the best hostelry the town had to offer. Caroline had a view of the recently completed fortifications of the western pier and the northeast pier, which offered the town some protection from the ravages of the sea. There were rumors that the railway would be coming and that the port would soon rival Dover.

After a hearty lunch, Caroline and Dr. Harris hired a chaise to take them to the Forester school, where Rose Harris worked as a teacher and Susan was a pupil. It was situated in a small hamlet two miles away from the coast in open countryside.

The school sat in the center of a gated parkland with a wide gravel drive leading up to the porticoed front door. Her previous arrival had occurred at night after a long drive from Norfolk. Caroline hadn't had time to notice much about the surroundings when she'd brought a complaining Susan down to Kent and was pleasantly surprised by the school's situation.

The front door opened as the carriage pulled up, and a woman Caroline recognized as Mrs. Jane Forester, the headmistress, came out. She wore a plain blue dress with a white collar, and her spectacles were perched on top of her head. Dr. Harris snorted as he opened the door to help Caroline alight.

"This is a nice surprise. I'm not usually worthy of Mrs. Forester's attention," Dr. Harris muttered as he held out his hand to help Caroline descend. "I usually have to go around the back with the servants."

Caroline ignored him and concentrated on the headmistress, who looked somewhat agitated.

"Good afternoon, Mrs. Forester."

"Lady Caroline!" The headmistress rushed forward. "How did you get here so promptly? I only sent the note this morning—"

"Is there something the matter?" Caroline asked.

Mrs. Forester took a deep breath and spoke almost to herself. "Of course, you couldn't have received my note, you've obviously just arrived in Folkestone, and I foolishly sent it to London." She visibly gathered herself and turned to Caroline. "With hindsight, perhaps I should not have told Susan you were coming today."

"What do you mean?" Caroline feared she already knew the answer.

"Susan has disappeared."

Dr. Harris put his hand on Caroline's shoulder. "She probably bolted when she heard you were in the vicinity." He looked at Mrs. Forester. "Might we go inside? It's beginning to rain."

Caroline followed the headmistress and Dr. Harris into the entrance hall, which was tiled in white and black and had an impressive chandelier hanging from the dome. The school had obviously started life as a private house. To distract herself, Caroline wondered how it had come into Mrs. Forester's hands and how she'd financed such a venture.

They were ushered into a pleasant morning room while Mrs. Forester ordered tea and asked the maid to fetch someone. Caroline sank down into one of the chairs, her heart thumping so loudly she wondered why no one had commented on it. How could she possibly function when her little sister was so unwilling to see her that she'd run away?

"Chin up, Miss Morton." Dr. Harris looked down at her. "She's probably hiding in the woods hoping you'll give up and leave so she can come out before it gets dark." He turned to Mrs. Forester, who had joined them. "Isn't that so, ma'am?"

"I've already had a team out searching the grounds, Dr. Harris, but with no success." Mrs. Forester took the seat opposite Caroline. Despite her earlier distress she now appeared rigidly in control of herself. "Susan did not come down for breakfast. I sent her form teacher to find her. She reported that Susan's bed was empty and that there was no sign of her."

"At what time was this?" Caroline asked. She was amazed she sounded so calm. But perhaps she wasn't the only person present who was good at masking her emotions.

"Eight o'clock," Mrs. Forester said. "We have been searching for her ever since."

The clock on the mantelpiece obligingly gave three dainty chimes to remind them of the passing of time.

"Then she's been missing for more than seven hours," Caroline said. "Did she leave on her own?"

"Everyone else is accounted for, Lady Caroline."

"Then she must have had help," Dr. Harris said. "Someone must have been waiting for her outside the grounds." His gaze met Caroline's. "Is Mrs. Forester aware of the issue of Mabel?"

"Yes, of course." Mrs. Forester looked at Dr. Harris. "With all due respect, why are you still here, sir? I presume you came to visit your sister in my employ. Surely this matter is between Lady Caroline and me?"

Caroline held up her hand. "Dr. Harris is assisting me. I prefer it if he stays."

There was a knock on the door, and a maid came in with the tea things, followed by a familiar figure. Dr. Harris walked over and embraced his sister. She had similar dark coloring to her brother but not his height or intimidating manner.

"Rose, it's a pleasure to see you."

"Likewise, Oliver." Rose smiled shyly up at her brother and then turned to Caroline. "Lady Caroline. I am so sorry about your sister. We have been racking our brains trying to work out where she has gone."

"Miss Harris is Susan's form teacher," Mrs. Forester said. "She is responsible for her daily well-being."

"But she is not responsible for Susan going missing under *your* care, Headmistress," Dr. Harris cut in, his expression fierce.

"I don't think Mrs. Forester is suggesting that is the case, Dr. Harris," Caroline said. "I'm sure she is well aware of where such responsibilities lie."

Caroline turned to Rose Harris. "Would it be possible to see where Susan sleeps and where she keeps her possessions? She might have secreted further letters from her cousin, which might help us understand where she has gone."

Rose looked at Mrs. Forester. "Would you like me to take Lady Caroline upstairs, ma'am, or do you wish to accompany her yourself?"

"You may take her," Mrs. Forester said. "Dr. Harris must remain down here while I speak to the search party."

"That's perfectly acceptable," Dr. Harris said. "I'll have a cup of tea while I wait."

Caroline followed Rose up the stairs, occasionally catching glimpses of pupils about their business. She heard singing, a piano, and a class reciting French verbs in unison. As a child, Caroline had a governess until her father could no longer afford one. After her mother's death, she'd been bundled off to be brought up in Aunt Eleanor's nursery, where she'd been taught alongside her cousins and the charity children her aunt collected like trophies.

It was there that Susan and her cousin Mabel had grown close—a bond that had only strengthened over the years when Caroline was absent. Susan had considered Greenwood Hall her home. She had been upset when Caroline took her away after Eleanor's stroke and the closing of the nursery. Caroline hadn't wanted to burden her much younger sister with the whole story of Greenwood's downfall, which had perhaps been a mistake, because Susan had continued to idolize Mabel, who had run off to get married.

"Susan slept in this room with three other girls." Rose Harris stopped at a door on the second floor and opened it.

The room was surprisingly tidy. Caroline assumed that was enforced when the girls' space was so limited. Each girl had a bed, a small table, and the ability to store whatever they wished under their bed. There was one double wardrobe with four drawers beneath it.

"Susan had the bed on the right and the fourth drawer in the cabinet. She hung her clothing on the far right in the closet." Rose opened the cupboard and the drawer so Caroline could look inside. "We have searched all the most obvious places, but so far we haven't found anything untoward."

"She must have found a way to continue to communicate with Mabel," Caroline said as she looked through Susan's meager possessions.

"I doubt she was able to write to her today," Rose said. "Mrs. Forester told Susan you would be visiting her only yesterday afternoon at tea. If she left last night, she might have done it without any help."

"Are there ways to leave the grounds without passing through the main gate?" Caroline asked as she sat on Susan's bed.

"Several gates lead out into the fields and the hamlet down the road. Most of them are locked, but the wall isn't very high in some places. Even I could climb over parts of it."

"Would it be possible to speak to the girls who share this room with Susan?" Caroline asked. "With you in attendance, of course."

"I can't see why not." Rose considered her. "Perhaps I should ask Mrs. Forester."

"Or simply bring them in here?" Caroline suggested. "They might be more willing to be honest if their headmistress isn't present."

"That is certainly true." Rose hesitated. "But I can't afford to lose this job, Lady Caroline. It is all I have."

"Why don't you send in the first girl and then go down and ask Mrs. Forester if she has any objections to me speaking to the girls. If she wishes to be present, we can start again."

While Rose was gone, Caroline took the opportunity to have a thorough search of Susan's bed. Knowing her sister's favorite hiding places, she soon found a letter between the mattress and the bed frame written in Mabel's distinctive hand. She heard Rose returning and quickly tucked the letter in her pocket.

"This is Emma Delaney, Lady Caroline." Rose ushered a girl into the room. "She and Susan were best friends."

"Good afternoon, Emma," Caroline said.

"You're Susan's sister," Emma said. She had fair hair and frosty blue eyes that were currently glaring at Caroline. "You're the one who forced her to come here."

"Emma!" Rose said. "That was extremely rude. Apologize to Lady Caroline this instant!"

A faint flush gathered on Emma's cheeks. "I don't have to do what you tell me, Miss Harris. I only answer to Mrs. Forester."

"Then I'll go and fetch her, shall I?" Rose asked. "I'm sure she'll be delighted to hear how you've just spoken to one of her staff *and* a guest at our school."

Rose left the room. Emma bit her lip before tossing her hair and returning her attention to Caroline.

"Susan didn't want to see you."

"So I understand. Did you know she planned to run away last night?"

"I might have done." Emma shrugged. "What else was she supposed to do?"

"I hoped she would be brave enough to face me," Caroline said. "Running away always seems . . . childish to me."

"She's hardly a child," Emma retorted. "If you hadn't incarcerated her here, she would be having her London Season."

For a moment Caroline didn't know what to say. Susan's dream was so detached from their current reality she couldn't possibly believe it was true.

"There's plenty of time for that after she's finished her education," Caroline said.

"You had a Season."

"Yes, but I'm ten years older than my sister. My situation was quite different from hers."

"You were considered a diamond of the first water." Emma frowned. "If you'd hurried up and married someone, Susan wouldn't be in these straits."

Caroline was surprised how much Emma had learned about her from Susan. She reminded herself to stay on task, but it appeared that Emma wasn't willing to give up her defense of her friend.

"You were engaged to a titled gentleman and you let him go. Susan was very upset about that."

"I'm sure she was," Caroline said. "Now, do you know where Susan was heading when she left last night?"

Emma raised her chin. "Why would I tell you that?"

"Because it is extremely unwise for a young lady to be out by herself in the dead of night near a port," Caroline said briskly. "For all we know, Susan could be lying dead in a ditch after being set upon and robbed."

There was a flicker of uncertainty in Emma's eyes as she stared at Caroline. "That isn't true."

"You don't know that. If you have any idea where Susan was heading and who she was attempting to meet, I think you should tell me."

"You'll force her back here."

Caroline looked around the sheltered room. "There are far worse places Susan could be than here, Miss Delaney. Or do you not wish her to be found?"

"I . . ."

Mrs. Forester came in with Rose behind her. "Emma, enough of this. If you know where Susan has gone, please tell me immediately."

"I promised her I wouldn't say."

"She's been missing for hours. She could be injured or dead on the roadside. If she truly is your friend, how can you want that for her?"

Caroline wasn't impressed by Mrs. Forester's forthright way of dealing with the girl. Emma's expression became almost regal, and she pressed her hand to her heart.

"I made a promise not to betray Susan You can do anything you like to me, and I will *never* tell!"

"Don't be ridiculous, child," Mrs. Forester snapped. "We aren't in one of your ridiculous novels. This is real life, and Susan might be in real danger."

Emma raised her eyes to heaven in a manner very reminiscent of Joan of Arc. "Do what you wish to me! Cast me into your darkest dungeon! I will never tell!"

"Susan's probably gone to the Mermaid's Kiss. In Folkestone," a voice said from the doorway.

Mrs. Forester spun around. "Harriet! I didn't know you were there."

Harriet, who was a tall, dark-haired girl with spectacles, sighed. "No one ever does, which is why I know everything that goes on in this school, and no one thinks to ask me about it."

"Harriet is another of Susan's roommates," Rose explained to Caroline as the girl came into the room.

Caroline smiled at Harriet. "It is a pleasure to meet you, Harriet."

"You're Susan's sister, aren't you?" Harriet stared critically at Caroline. "She said you were quite beautiful, and she was right. I never believed all her stories about your wickedness, because if you really were evil, you wouldn't have placed her in the best boarding school in Kent. You would've left her to rot in a deserted Scottish castle."

"That is remarkably observant of you." Caroline nodded. "I have always tried to do my best for my sister."

"I told her she was a fool for running away, but she didn't listen to me."

"When did you speak to her?" Mrs. Forester asked.

"Last night," Harriet said. "She woke me up when she was leaving. I asked her where she was going, and she blurted it out before looking absolutely mortified."

"Did it not occur to you to mention it to one of the teachers this morning?"

Harriet frowned. "No, why would it? I've only come forward now because Susan appears to be in some peril, and I wouldn't wish harm on her."

"You hated her!" Emma spun around to confront Harriet. "You've never forgiven her for becoming my best friend."

Harriet raised her eyebrows. "That's silly."

"It is not!" Emma gestured wildly. "That is why you're betraying her to her sister she loathes!"

Caroline winced.

"I'm worried about Susan, not you, Emma," Harriet said. "It is all very well to playact and imagine that running away will lead to a glorious future. The reality is that Susan has very little money, no idea of the geography of the area, and no transport to take her somewhere better."

Emma burst into tears. Rose handed over her handkerchief and sat down beside the sobbing girl.

"Well, it's true, isn't it?" Harriet looked at Caroline and Mrs. Forester. "That's why I'm speaking up."

"I, for one, am very glad you did," Caroline said. "Susan told you directly that she was going to the Mermaid's Kiss?"

"Yes, she instantly tried to take it back, but I heard her quite clearly." Harriet nodded.

Caroline rose to her feet. "Thank you. At least it gives me a place to start."

Mrs. Forester turned to the door. "I will speak to you both later, girls. Please go and rejoin your classes."

Harriet sighed, and Emma sobbed even harder.

Caroline followed Mrs. Forester down the stairs to the morning room, where Dr. Harris was happily drinking tea. Mrs. Forester excused herself to go and speak to her secretary, leaving Caroline and Dr. Harris alone.

"Any luck?" he asked, setting down his cup and standing.

"I believe she's in Folkestone."

"Then we'll go back there."

"Dr. Harris, if you wish to remain here and continue your visit with your sister, I will quite understand—"

He gave her a long-suffering look. "It's bad enough that there's one Morton running around Folkestone unsupervised without adding another. I will be accompanying you. Mrs. Frogerton would murder me if I left you to your own devices. Rose will understand."

He handed her a cup of tea. "Drink this before we go. It's not very warm, but it will give you some energy."

Caroline obediently drank the warm, milky tea. "It's very sweet."

"It's a shame we weren't offered any cake." Dr. Harris sighed. "We could've taken it with us. Where's Rose, by the way?"

"Consoling one of the pupils." Caroline finished the tea and set the cup down on the tray. "I must speak to Mrs. Forester before we leave and give her the name of the inn where we are staying."

"Are you hoping Susan will come back of her own accord?" Dr. Harris asked as he followed her into the hall. "If Mabel has her, I doubt that will happen."

Caroline grimaced. "I'd rather Susan was with Mabel than alone, but I am concerned about Mabel's intentions."

"Justifiably," Dr. Harris said. "The only good thing is that we can assume Mabel will be kind to Susan until she gets what she wants, which gives us some time."

Unfortunately, Dr. Harris's reasoning was sound but hardly reassuring.

Mrs. Forester approached them, her expression worried. "I trust you will keep me informed as to your search. I cannot apologize enough for what has occurred. You left your sister in my care, and I have failed you."

Caroline shook Mrs. Forester's hand. "I will write to you the moment I locate her. If she returns here, I would like to know as soon as possible."

"Of course," Mrs. Forester said. "Let us hope we can resolve this matter quickly with no harm done."

Dr. Harris bowed to the headmistress. "Don't worry, ma'am. We'll find her." He looked around the hall as if expecting his sister to magically appear. "Tell Rose I'll be back to see her when this matter has been resolved."

"I'll do that." Mrs. Forester nodded. "And thank you for your assistance in this matter."

Chapter 12

"Let's go back to the Rose & Crown and decide how we wish to proceed," Dr. Harris said the moment the carriage left the school.

"Surely we should go straight to the Mermaid's Kiss?" Caroline asked. "The driver knows where it is located."

"He told me it's not in a part of town that a lady like yourself should be frequenting."

"I don't particularly care—"

"Well, I care, and Mrs. Frogerton would have my head if I let you enter an establishment where you'd be either robbed or seen as a woman of ill repute."

Caroline glared at him. "One might think that a man such as yourself would be protection enough!"

"I can't be worrying about what you're getting up to while I'm trying to find out what Mabel has done with Susan."

"And what if Susan is there? Don't you think she should be taken out of such a dangerous place with all speed?"

"I suspect Mabel knows how to protect her," Dr. Harris said.

"How about we compromise?" Caroline asked.

Dr. Harris looked skeptical. "What are you proposing?"

"What if we drive to the Mermaid's Kiss and I stay in the carriage while you go in and ask if Susan is there?"

"That seems reasonable." Dr. Harris considered her. "Although I doubt it will be that easy."

"If Susan is there, and Mabel is not, then you can persuade her to leave."

"I doubt she'll want to do anything I say."

"Then you'll have to . . . make her."

Dr. Harris's brows drew together. "You're not suggesting I knock her out, are you?"

"You're a physician."

"Who swears an oath to first do no harm."

"I'm sure you can think of something," Caroline said. "Or perhaps I should accompany you after all."

"I'll get her out if she's there, Miss Morton." Dr. Harris opened the window, letting in a gust of sea air. "We're approaching the town. I need to speak to our driver."

Despite her brave words to Dr. Harris, Caroline was quietly appalled by the state of the waterfront near the docks and could only hope that Susan had arrived at her destination unscathed. Several large ships were anchored in the harbor docks, involved in the laborious task of loading or unloading their cargo. Cranes swung overhead, and a multitude of men toiled up and down the gangplanks, carrying goods on their backs.

The Mermaid's Kiss was a low-set, thatched-roof timbered building that leaned drunkenly to one side and was held up only by its obliging neighbor. An archway over filthy cobbles indicated that stabling was behind, but Caroline doubted it operated as a coaching inn.

Their hired carriage stopped farther down the street beside a ship that lay in its berth with no signs of life onboard, the only sound the slap of the wash against the hull as the boat bobbed in the current. This ship was considerably smaller than the tall-masted ones down the line.

"Stay here," Dr. Harris said as he got out. "Do not attempt to follow me." He stared at Caroline. "I'll have your word on that."

"What if you don't come back?" Caroline asked.

"I will." He took out his pocket watch. "If I don't return in half an hour, go back to the Rose & Crown and alert the authorities."

"What authorities?"

"How in God's name would I know how they manage such things in this part of the world? Ask at the inn. I'm sure they'll help you."

"By which time it will be far too late to stop you having had your throat cut or being press-ganged," Caroline retorted.

"Your faith in my abilities is somewhat lacking, Miss Morton, but I'm fairly certain I'll survive." He bowed. "Now, for once, do as I ask. I beg you."

Caroline moved across the carriage so that she could watch Dr. Harris's progress. He disappeared into the inn, and she realized she was holding her breath. He emerged five minutes later, and after speaking to the driver, he got back in with Caroline. The carriage moved off before he spoke.

"The innkeeper denied seeing Susan, or Mabel for that matter."

"Well, he would, wouldn't he?"

"On further questioning and with a substantial bribe, he indicated that a young lad *did* arrive at the inn very late at night and that the lad was taken away by a lady he seemed to know." Dr. Harris paused. "It sounds like Susan had the sense to disguise herself as a boy."

"I wonder if Mabel made an arrangement with Susan to be at a certain place every night in case Susan was able to get away," Caroline mused. "Wait . . ."

She found the note she'd taken from Susan's bedchamber and opened it. "Yes, that's exactly what they agreed." She raised her head. "If only I'd read this before we left the school."

"It would certainly have saved you a lot of worrying and doubting me, Miss Morton," Dr. Harris agreed. "I don't suppose the letter gives Mabel's real address in Folkestone?"

"Unfortunately, not."

"But at least we can assume your sister is safely with her cousin and not lost in the countryside."

"That's something of a mixed blessing," Caroline said. "But at least it gives us time to come up with a plan to separate them again."

The carriage arrived at their temporary place of residence. After viewing the dilapidated Mermaid's Kiss, the Rose & Crown looked positively magnificent. The moment the carriage stopped in the stable yard, an ostler opened Caroline's door and helped her descend.

"Good afternoon, my lady. Will you require the carriage again today?"

Caroline looked at Dr. Harris, who had joined her.

"No, I think we're done for the day, thank you." Dr. Harris offered Caroline his arm. "Shall we go inside? I'm famished."

"Trust you to think of food at a moment such as this," Caroline murmured.

"It's not my sister who is missing, Miss Morton," Dr. Harris pointed out.

"I'm well aware of that." Caroline stripped off her gloves as the landlord approached them.

"Lady Caroline, you have received some mail. I took the liberty of placing it in your bedchamber. Would you like me to send a maid up to assist you before dinner? It will be served in your own private parlor at six." He turned at Dr. Harris. "We have some excellent lamb tonight."

"I don't think I can last until six." Dr. Harris sighed. "We haven't eaten since breakfast."

"Then I'll get my wife to lay out a small repast in your parlor, shall I? We can't have you starving. We pride ourselves on feeding our guests well here."

Dr. Harris looked pleadingly at Caroline.

She nodded and said, "I'll meet you in the parlor in a quarter of an hour, Dr. Harris." Caroline turned to the landlord. "Thank you, Mr. Landon."

He bowed. "Anything for a friend of Mrs. Frogerton's, my lady."

Caroline went up the stairs and into her bedchamber, which was as large as the one she currently occupied in Half Moon Street. It was at the back of the inn overlooking the relative quiet of the stables. After taking off her bonnet and tidying her hair, she spied two letters on the desk. One was from Mrs. Frogerton and the other from Inspector Ross.

After penning a quick note to be delivered to Mrs. Forester, Caroline took the letters down with her to read. Their private parlor was currently unoccupied, but a fire burned in the hearth. The enticing scent of beef and spices emanated from the kitchen, which was at the end of the corridor.

She opened Mrs. Frogerton's letter and was relieved that her employer had spared no expense in sending her a missive of several pages and hadn't crossed her pages. An alarming number of blots and exclamation marks were within the widely spaced lines, which reminded Caroline that Mrs. Frogerton wrote in a similar manner to how she talked.

Dr. Harris came in and held the door open for the landlady, who carried a tray full of food.

"I was just helping Mrs. Landon in the kitchen, Miss Morton."

"So, I see." Caroline smiled at the innkeeper's wife. "Thank you, Mrs. Landon. This is very kind of you when I'm sure you're busy cooking dinner."

"It's no trouble, my lady. Mrs. Frogerton told us to treat you right, and we will." She winked at Dr. Harris as she set down the tray. "I like a man who appreciates good cooking, sir." She went to the door. "I'll bring you a pot of tea, my lady."

Dr. Harris rubbed his hands together. "There's beef, pork pie, even some bread and cheese I'm sure you'll like, Miss Morton."

He offered her a plate. "Please go ahead."

"Why don't you start, Doctor? I'm still reading Mrs. Frogerton's letter."

"Anything interesting?" he asked as he piled his plate high.

"Oh, dear," Caroline said. "Mrs. Frogerton has arranged to meet Mrs. DeBloom at her offices."

"For what reason?"

"I suspect she wants to take a look at all the DeBloom employees and work out which one threatened me."

"I can't argue with her reasoning, but I'm not sure she should be poking her nose in there."

"She says she intends to invite Mrs. DeBloom to join her on a charitable committee dedicated to educating factory children." Caroline reread the paragraphs and tried to paraphrase. "It is a real committee, and it's headed by one of the queen's cousins. Mrs. Frogerton believes Mrs. DeBloom is enough of a snob to want that royal connection."

Dr. Harris nodded as he chewed.

"Mrs. Frogerton has made an appointment to visit the DeBloom offices to discuss the matter, although why she couldn't have asked Mrs. DeBloom to visit her at home, I'm not sure."

"Perhaps she didn't want Mrs. DeBloom to know you'd

gone away," Dr. Harris said. "And if you were there when a DeBloom visited, that might inflame the man who threatened you."

"I do hope Mrs. Frogerton will be careful." Caroline set the letter aside. "I'll write and remind her of her promise."

Dr. Harris snorted as he slathered horseradish sauce on a piece of beef. "The woman has no sense. She's bound to make everyone suspicious."

"Please don't say that." Caroline helped herself to a plate of food. "I would never forgive myself if she was hurt because of her association with me."

"Bit late for that, isn't it?" Dr. Harris said far too cheerfully. "And I don't think she'd thank you for suggesting you dragged her into anything. From what I've observed, the shoe is very much on the other foot." He gestured with his bread. "Is that from Mr. DeBloom?"

"No, it's from Inspector Ross."

"Oh, him." Dr. Harris busied himself cutting more cheese. "How does he know where we are?"

"Because he is dealing with the murder investigation into Mr. Smith and the assault on me." Caroline paused. "It seemed . . . prudent to let him know I was leaving London for a few days."

"Prudent." Dr. Harris looked at her. "Interesting choice of word. What does he have to say for himself?"

For some reason, Caroline was remarkably reluctant to open the letter in Dr. Harris's presence, but if she demurred, he might draw all the wrong conclusions.

"I haven't read it yet."

"Then go ahead. We have plans to make regarding Susan. The sooner we know how things are in London, the sooner we can get on."

Caroline broke the seal imprinted with Inspector Ross's family coat of arms and opened the single written sheet. To her relief, the letter was strictly impersonal. She read it through and looked up at Dr. Harris.

"Mr. Thettle has been found dead at home."

"From your expression, I doubt he died unexpectedly in his sleep." Dr. Harris set down his knife. "Do they know how he died?"

"He was strangled." Caroline swallowed hard. "His lodgings were ransacked and the furniture overturned. His landlady came up the stairs to complain about the noise and was practically thrown down the stairs by a masked man as he left Mr. Thettle's room."

"Good lord."

"Inspector Ross said that in Mr. Thettle's desk they found Mr. Smith's appointment diaries and various pieces of correspondence that should not have been in Mr. Thettle's possession."

"I don't suppose one of those was your father's will?"

"Apparently not. Even the copied notes he was supposed to have were not there. Inspector Ross checked very carefully."

"Then, that's it, isn't it?" Dr. Harris grimaced. "With no will and no living witness to the will even existing, the De-Blooms—if it is the DeBlooms—have won."

Caroline finished her tea and ate some of the pie Dr. Harris had put on her plate, but her appetite had gone. Her relief at not being in London had intensified. She wished Mrs. Frogerton had come with her.

"Now, as to Susan's whereabouts," Dr. Harris said briskly. "I've had some thoughts on this matter."

"So have I." Caroline set down her cup. "If you are certain Susan isn't at the Mermaid's Kiss, we need to see if Mabel's husband, Harry, has his ship in dock."

"That would be helpful," Dr. Harris agreed. "Except we don't know the name of it."

"Yes, we do." Caroline took out Mabel's last letter. "This doesn't have an address, but it does have the name of Harry's ship, *The Good Fortune*. We can take a stroll together after dinner and see if we can find it."

Dr. Harris glowered at her. "Unless you want the sailors

thinking you're displaying your wares, we are *not* strolling on the dock in the dark."

"But I'll be with you," Caroline pointed out.

"Have you looked at yourself, woman? Any sailor fresh off a six-month voyage will take one look at your face and kill me to get his hands on you."

"That is quite ridiculous, Dr. Harris."

"It's the truth. Here's what we'll do. You'll stay safely in the parlor, and I will ask Mr. Landon if *The Good Fortune* has docked here. If he doesn't know, I'm fairly certain he'll be able to direct me to someone who will. I'll confirm the ship is in port, and then I'll find out as much as possible about its future plans."

"Do you really think people will just tell you these things?" Caroline asked.

"Yes, if they think I'm a surgeon willing to go to sea. We are in much demand, you know."

For once, Caroline couldn't see a single fault in Dr. Harris's plan, apart from the fact that she wasn't involved in it.

"Fine," she said with something of a snap. "I will stay here and write to Mrs. Frogerton and Inspector Ross. I will expect a full report before you go to bed."

"Fair enough." He grinned at her. "And thank you."

"For what?"

"Admitting that I was right for once."

After an excellent dinner, Dr. Harris spoke to the innkeeper and set off for the docks and taverns that lined the seafront, leaving Caroline ensconced in the parlor. After writing a lengthy letter to Mrs. Frogerton and a shorter one to Inspector Ross, she resumed her seat by the fire and picked up her embroidery. She was concentrating on fixing a mistake when the door opened.

"You're back earlier than I expected." Caroline looked up after she'd finished speaking and went still. "Mabel."

Her cousin smiled. She wore a simple faded-blue gown

with a woolen shawl wrapped around her shoulders and head. Her skin was brown from the sun, and she appeared much older.

"Surprise! How *are* you, Caroline?"

Caroline stabbed her needle randomly through her embroidery and set it aside. "Where is Susan?"

"Why would you think I know that?" Mabel raised her eyebrows. "Harry and I have just arrived in England on his ship. Imagine my surprise when I heard that a lady was looking for me."

"I'm looking for Susan. I have no interest in what you do or where you go, Mabel." Caroline stood and faced her cousin. "Susan is not old enough to make decisions for herself, and nothing you can say will change that."

"She's old enough to know whom she wishes to be with, and it certainly isn't you," Mabel said. "In truth, she hates you."

"Her feelings are irrelevant. She is legally under my control."

"I wonder what the courts would say about that?" Mabel smiled. "It almost sounds as if you are forcing her to stay where it suits you."

"At a very expensive boarding school in Kent," Caroline said. "The poor, poor girl." She took a steadying breath. "I want you to return Susan to me. If you do that, I promise I will never speak your name again."

"Why would you be speaking my name in the first place?" Mabel asked.

"Because the authorities in Norfolk would very much like to talk to you and Harry." Caroline held her cousin's gaze. "There are questions to be asked about what happened at Greenwood Hall. I'm sure they would be delighted to know you are both in England again."

"Are you threatening me?" Mabel's smile disappeared. "That's . . . silly, seeing as I *might* know where your sister is."

"If you know where Susan is, Mabel, please stop playing games and take me to her."

Mabel smiled. "But I don't think I want to do that, Caroline. We're having far too much fun without you."

"You cannot keep her."

"Oh, I think I can." Mabel almost seemed like her old self now. "She is very excited about the possibility of leaving these shores for good and setting up home with me and Harry."

"I will not allow you to take her anywhere."

"I'm not sure how you intend to stop me." Mabel laughed. "You've lost her trust, Caroline. You forced her out of the only home she'd ever known and took her away from the cousin she adored."

"You were the one who ran away, Mabel. I stayed behind to pick up the pieces."

"Please don't expect me to feel sorry for you, cousin, when I have been denied my birthright." Mabel raised her chin. "Nick won't release a *penny* of my inheritance to me!"

"I can't say I blame him."

"It's not fair!"

"He's hardly going to come around if you kidnap Susan."

"Oh, I don't know. He might be willing to pay to get her back." Mabel looked speculatively at Caroline.

"I don't have any money, and as your brother is still embroiled with his bank sorting out your father's affairs, I doubt he has any, either."

"That's not quite true, is it, Caroline?" Mabel said. "Susan told me she received an inheritance from my mother."

"She might be the beneficiary, but the money has not been released from your mother's estate yet. You must know it can take months or years, and even when the money does arrive, I will be the recipient on Susan's behalf."

"Only if she's in your care," Mabel said.

"She *is* in my care. No court in this land would dispute that." Caroline held her cousin's gaze. "We both care deeply for Susan, Mabel. Will you at least allow me to see her so we can sit down and sort this out?"

Mabel smiled. "I'm glad you're finally acknowledging that *I* am the one who will allow you to see Susan. That's progress, at least."

"Then tell me where you're staying and arrange a time for us to meet," Caroline suggested. "I can't make any decisions until I hear Susan's own thoughts on this matter."

"I'll have to speak to Harry," Mabel said. "I'm not sure he'll agree."

"Surely this is between us?" Caroline suggested.

"Don't be naïve, Cousin. Harry and I intend to live in America. If Susan wishes to accompany us, we're happy to take her."

"As long as she brings the money to furnish your ambitions," Caroline said.

"It would certainly help, and Susan is very enthusiastic about the notion." Mabel smiled. "Come now, Caroline, it's not such a bad idea, is it? Susan would be in a safe place, she'd be happy, and you'd be able to live your life without having to worry about your little sister."

"I have already explained this," Caroline said steadily. "Susan has no money to bring with her."

"But you could borrow some." Mabel paused. "I'm sure Mrs. Frogerton would lend you money against Susan's expectations?"

"I wouldn't ask that of her."

Mabel sighed. "Then you won't be seeing Susan, and if we can't finance her voyage with us, I'm not sure what Harry will do with her."

Caroline took two hasty steps forward, and Mabel

started in surprise. "Is that a threat?" Caroline asked. "Pay up, or you won't see your sister again? Is that what you've become, Mabel?"

There wasn't a flicker of remorse on Mabel's face when she spoke. "We need at least a thousand pounds."

"That's *twice* what Susan was left in your mother's will."

"I assumed you would be willing to give us your half of the money to safeguard Susan's future."

Caroline stared at her cousin.

Mabel shrugged. "Let me know when you have the funds, and I will be delighted to let you say your goodbyes to your sister in person."

A door banged in the inn, followed by the sound of male voices.

"I'd better go," Mabel said, glancing at the door. "Don't follow me, or Harry might get upset."

"If he touches Susan, I will—"

"You'll do what, Cousin? It's very simple. Talk to the Frogertons, bring the money, and nothing bad will happen to Susan. You can leave me a message at the Mermaid's Kiss, or if it's too rough for you, send Frogerton again."

She left the room, leaving Caroline shaking with a com- bination of rage and fear. By the time she recovered enough to run after her cousin, it was far too late to see where she'd gone. Caroline returned to the parlor, her thoughts in disarray, even as she wondered why on earth Mabel had mentioned the Frogertons.

The owner of the Mermaid's Kiss must have told Mabel about Dr. Harris's visit. Had the doctor mentioned where they were staying in an attempt to contact Mabel? It seemed possible, but she couldn't blame him for that. Nei- ther of them could have expected Mabel to be so brazen that she'd turn up to hurry things along.

But why had Mabel been in such a hurry? Caroline pon- dered that as she sat down. Was Harry contracted to go back to sea on his current ship, or had the couple already booked passage to America? Caroline glanced at the clock on the mantelpiece. Where was Dr. Harris? She needed to speak to him immediately.

The clock was striking midnight by the time Dr. Harris came into the parlor. He was whistling and smelled of wood fires, cigars, and beer.

"Where on earth have you been?" Caroline snapped as she shot to her feet.

He raised his eyebrows. "Good evening to you, too, Miss Morton."

"While you've been sampling ale at every hostelry in Folkestone, I had a visit from Mabel."

"I know." Dr. Harris grinned as he sat down beside the fire and warmed his hands. "I was coming in earlier when I saw her, bold as brass, in the stable yard. That's where I've been."

"You followed her?"

"Yes."

"Thank God." Caroline sank back down into her seat. "Did you see Susan?"

"I didn't dare go inside, but I waited around long enough to see Harry turn up. They aren't staying at an inn. It appears to be some kind of boarding house."

He stretched his booted feet out toward the fire. "I wonder if there is anyone in the kitchen who might make me some coffee. I'm quite parched."

"I'll go and inquire." Caroline headed for the door. "Do not leave this room until I return."

He sighed and waved her off.

She returned with a tray of coffee she had made with the help of one of the chambermaids. Dr. Harris started as if he'd been asleep.

"Thank you, Miss Morton. This is very welcome." He helped himself to the coffee. "What did Mabel want?"

"Money," Caroline said succinctly. "She and Harry have decided to go to America. According to Mabel, Susan wishes to accompany them."

Dr. Harris made a face. "She probably wasn't lying about that. From what I understand, Susan blames you for all the upheaval in her life."

"That isn't exactly helpful, Dr. Harris."

"I didn't mean it to be. In truth, it makes our task much harder because Susan won't want to be rescued."

He had a point, but Caroline refused to dwell on it.

"Mabel wants me to give her a thousand pounds."

Dr. Harris whistled. "That's a lot of money. Where on earth does she think you'll get that from? You work as a companion, and your father left you with nothing. Surely, she knows that?"

"Susan told her about the bequest from our aunt Eleanor, which—between me and Susan—would come to one thousand pounds."

"How convenient." Dr. Harris frowned. "Mabel can't possibly think you carry the money around with you. How does she expect you to access the funds?"

"She suggested I ask Mrs. Frogerton for a loan."

"Of course." Dr. Harris nodded. "Mabel's always been the cleverest of the Greenwood children. I should imagine that if you did ask Mrs. Frogerton, she'd be more than willing to accommodate you."

"Mabel intimated that if I did not come up with the money, they would abandon Susan to fend for herself." Caroline struggled for a moment to regulate her voice. "She tried to suggest it would be Harry's doing, but I know her rather too well to believe that."

"She certainly lacks a conscience," Dr. Harris agreed. "Where did you leave things with her?"

"She told me to contact her via the Mermaid's Kiss when I had the money and that she would then 'allow' me to speak to Susan."

Dr. Harris frowned. "You can hardly force your sister to leave with you in the middle of afternoon tea."

"I am well aware of that."

"We'll have to try to take her when Mabel and Harry aren't there."

"I suspect that might be difficult," Caroline acknowledged. "Mabel knows both of us rather too well to be fooled."

"She doesn't know me very well. I didn't live at Greenwood Hall for long, and she was a child at that point. And I gave a false name when I asked for her at the Mermaid's Kiss and at the other pubs."

"What name did you use?"

"I said I was Mr. Frogerton." Dr. Harris shrugged. "It seemed appropriate somehow."

"*That's* what Mabel meant when she mentioned a Mr. Frogerton at the Mermaid's Kiss. I thought it was a slip of the tongue." Caroline smiled approvingly at Dr. Harris. "You have been wonderfully clever."

He nodded. "I do my best, Miss Morton."

"I wonder if that is why Mabel thinks I can access money so quickly?" Caroline asked. "If she thinks I came with Mr. Frogerton, she might assume it would be easy for him to access any sum of money he requires in an instant."

"If she thinks that, she doesn't know Mrs. Frogerton very well at all," Dr. Harris commented. "Not that it matters. If Mabel believes the money can be made available to her at speed, then that's all that counts."

"As to that—did you find out how long Harry's current ship will be in port?"

"It's due to leave in less than a week, I believe."

"Which might explain their haste," Caroline said. "Harry will either have to leave Mabel and Susan in Folkestone or take them with him."

"It's not a ship built to take passengers," Dr. Harris said. "It currently carries grain between here and the

French coast. If they're planning to leave for America, they'll have to book passage from Liverpool or Bristol."

"Would they need to pay for their tickets in advance?" Caroline asked.

"I don't think so." Dr. Harris considered her. "If you're going steerage, I think you can just turn up, find a ship that is leaving, and pay to get on the passenger list. There might even be options for credit, and don't forget Harry is an accomplished sailor who could get taken on as ship's crew."

Caroline stared down at her coffee cup. "I must confess that I am at a loss as to what to do."

"That's most unlike you, Miss Morton."

"If Susan truly doesn't wish to live with me, should I stop her going with her cousin whom she loves?"

Dr. Harris's brows drew together. "You're giving up?"

"Perhaps if I offer Mabel Susan's bequest, that will satisfy her."

"Wait a moment—are you mad? None of that money would be used for Susan's benefit. As far as we know, they could get into the middle of the Atlantic Ocean, toss Susan over the side, and proceed merrily without her."

Caroline looked up. "Mabel is very fond of Susan."

"Mabel is fond of Mabel, and we already know she is willing to do whatever it takes to get what she thinks she deserves." Dr. Harris was scowling now. "This is *not* the time to give up and hand your sister over to a woman like that."

"Then how do you think we proceed?"

"You agree to give Mabel some of the money and spin a tale about how complicated it is to get the rest of it sent down from London. You push for a meeting with Susan where you will do your best to make her see sense. If you slow things down sufficiently, Harry will have to go on his next voyage without Mabel or Susan."

"And what will you be doing?"

"I'll be watching their lodgings, and when you entice Mabel here with the promise of more money, I'll nip in and get Susan."

"Who won't want to come with you."

Dr. Harris shrugged. "She might be having second thoughts by then, if you've played your part well."

"And if she isn't?"

He raised an eyebrow. "Do you *want* your sister back or not, Miss Morton?"

"Of course I do."

"Then you will have to allow me to . . . improvise if necessary."

Chapter 13

Caroline spent a restless night trying to think of any other way to get Susan back and eventually concluded that Dr. Harris's plan was the only viable one. She'd written a long letter to Mrs. Frogerton before she went to bed. She knew it had gone off to London at dawn, which might mean she'd hear from her employer the very same day.

Mrs. Frogerton had generously given Caroline a large sum of coin to pay for special messengers and other expenses she might incur on her journey to Kent. There was not enough to tempt Mabel to release Susan, and Caroline was averse to wasting it in case they were forced to leave Folkestone in a hurry and had to hire a chaise and four fast horses.

When she went down to breakfast, there was no sign of Dr. Harris. Mrs. Landon handed her a note that informed her he'd gone off to visit his sister at the school and would update Mrs. Forester on the search for Susan.

"There's a letter for you, too, Mrs. Morton," the landlady said. "Came with the first London coach." She delved into the pocket of her apron and found it. "Now will you be wanting eggs and porridge for breakfast like yesterday? Or do you fancy some ham?"

"I'll happily eat anything you put in front of me, Mrs.

Landon." Caroline smiled. "The sea air is giving me an appetite."

"You should take a walk along the battlements, ma'am. You'll get a fine view of the coast and the town," Mrs. Landon suggested. "I can pack you some victuals in a basket for your lunch if you like."

"That would be very kind of you," Caroline said.

She took the letter into the parlor and opened it while she waited for her breakfast. The handwriting was unfamiliar, which gave her pause until she glanced down at the signature.

> *My dearest Miss Morton,*
> *Thank you for your letter. I am shocked to my soul to find out that someone chose to abuse your person in <u>my family's name</u>. I shall endeavor to find the culprit and discover what is going on with <u>all haste.</u> I <u>pray</u> you have recovered from your injuries and that the assault has not blackened my reputation beyond all redemption. The fact that you chose to write to me gives me hope that is not the case and that you still trust me, for which I am profoundly grateful.*
> *Rest easy, Miss Morton. I shall ensure that you are never troubled in this manner again.*
> *Yours,*
> *Philip DeBloom*

Caroline acknowledged it was a well-written letter that expressed all the right sentiments, but could she trust him? For all she knew, he was the one paying the man to frighten her. Did he think it might drive her into his arms to seek his protection? Despite his professions of shock and sympathy, he had not offered any evidence that he knew who it was, and in a small company like the DeBlooms, that seemed unlikely. Either his mother had sanctioned the violence or he had. It was impossible to believe that out of the entire population of London, a rogue South

African had chosen to threaten her and that he somehow knew the DeBlooms.

Caroline read the letter again and found it even more unsatisfactory. She folded it up and was just about to put it in her pocket when she stopped to read the direction on the front. She'd written to Mr. DeBloom from Maidstone and not included a forwarding address or expected a reply. How had he known how to find her in Folkestone?

After eating her breakfast, she took her landlady's advice and went for a walk away from the harbor and the bobbing ships and out along the northeast pier. The wind buffeted her and tugged at her bonnet strings, but she enjoyed the activity and certainly appreciated the view of the sea. There was something about the enormity of a stretch of water that reminded her that her problems were very small indeed.

She found a more secluded spot to eat her luncheon and then walked back to the Rose & Crown. A church bell sounded twelve times as she passed beneath it, making the seagulls squawk as they dipped and dived between the buildings and riggings of the tall ships.

Dr. Harris was just coming down the stairs when she arrived back.

"Miss Morton. I see you've been out."

"Yes, I walked along the new defenses. Mrs. Landon suggested it."

"You look . . . very well."

"I'm glad to hear it." Caroline paused. "Is there something the matter? I can assure you I made no attempt to find Susan or Mabel."

He gave himself a little shake. "That's not it. Sometimes I just forget how pretty you are."

Caroline took longer than necessary untying her tangled bonnet strings to avoid having to answer Dr. Harris or look at him.

"While I was with Rose, I had a thought about Susan's possessions." Dr. Harris walked along the corridor and opened the door into their private parlor for her. "I asked Mrs. Forester to pack them up so I could bring them here." He paused. "It occurred to me that you might take Susan to London rather than return her to the school, where she might run away again."

"That was an excellent idea."

"I had the maid put them in your room. I thought you might want to go through them—make sure everything is there." He handed her the key.

"I'll do that." Caroline sat down. "I had a letter this morning."

"From Mrs. Frogerton? That was quick. Or did your letters cross in the post?"

"It was from Mr. DeBloom."

"Ah." Dr. Harris came to sit opposite her, his gaze alert. "What did he have to say for himself?"

Caroline handed him the letter. He read it quickly and gave it back to her. "The fellow uses too many long words to say absolutely nothing of substance."

"He certainly doesn't name any names, which would have been helpful."

"I'm sure that was deliberate," Dr. Harris said. "I mean, if he doesn't want you threatened, he must know there's only one person who could have given that order."

"Perhaps he is loath to believe his mother has gone this far."

"Or that someone he employs has exposed their company to the scrutiny of the Metropolitan Police." Dr. Harris shoved a hand through his hair. "I hope he does *something,* but I'm not convinced he has the nerve to stand up to his mother."

"I suspect we'll find out whether our suspicions are correct when we return to London," Caroline said. "There is nothing we can do about him now, and we do have more important things to worry about."

"Have you decided how you wish to proceed with Mabel?" Dr. Harris asked.

"I'm going to write to her, enclose five pounds as a token of good faith, and ask to see Susan."

"She probably won't fall for that."

"I know, but it will establish that Mabel is picking up her messages from the Mermaid's Kiss and win us some time." Caroline paused. "I wonder if she is working there. Is it far from the lodging house?"

"It's quite close." Dr. Harris nodded. "Yes, the more we delay handing over any money, the sooner Harry gets back on that ship without them." He held out his hand. "Do you want me to deliver the letter for you?"

"I think it might be better to send someone else," Caroline said. "Mabel knows I'm staying at the Rose & Crown and won't be surprised if a messenger comes from here. I don't want to risk her seeing you in case she remembers you from Greenwood Hall and realizes you aren't Mr. Frogerton."

"I suppose I am quite distinctive," Dr. Harris said. "I'll ask Mr. Landon to send one of his boys."

Caroline gave him the letter she'd written to Mabel and a coin for the delivery boy, and he went to find the innkeeper. He was gone for so long that Caroline finished her tea. She was just about to go upstairs and sort through Susan's belongings when the door opened, and he stuck his head inside.

"Guess who just turned up in the mail coach?"

"Mrs. Frogerton?" Caroline asked. "It would be just like her."

Dr. Harris looked back over his shoulder. "I had the same thought, but it appears she's sent her deputy." He stepped to one side. "Good afternoon, Mr. Frogerton. What brings you to Kent?"

Mr. Frogerton came into the room and bowed to Caroline. He still wore his outdoor garb and looked tired and extremely cross. "Miss Morton. My mother has informed me that you need my help."

"That is very kind of her, sir, but—"

He held up his hand. "I know you didn't specifically ask for me to descend on you, but considering the situation with your sister, my mother decided it would be better if one of us was here to provide any necessary funds to secure her release."

Dr. Harris grinned at Caroline. "Basically, Mr. Frogerton is here to act as your own personal bank."

Caroline's first thought was to send Mr. Frogerton right back to London, but could she afford to do so?

"I didn't intend to involve your family in this matter, sir. If you are needed elsewhere, please don't feel obliged to stay," Caroline said carefully.

Mr. Frogerton sighed. "I'm here because my mother insisted, and to be frank, Miss Morton, if my sister was missing, I'd take all the assistance I could get."

She met his resolute gaze. "I appreciate that, Mr. Frogerton. I would be delighted if you were prepared to stay and help."

"Good lass." He bowed. "As Dr. Harris mentioned, I've brought funding."

"I would be happy to accept any money from you as a loan—with the properly drawn-up paperwork in place, of course," Caroline said.

Mr. Frogerton looked grimly amused. "I wouldn't lend it to you otherwise. My mother says you can pay her back when your inheritance comes in."

"Susan's inheritance," Dr. Harris said. "Don't use your own, Miss Morton."

"For once we agree about something." Mr. Frogerton turned to Dr. Harris. "Now, will you escort me to my room and tell me exactly what's going on? I'm sure you'll make much shorter work of it than Miss Morton." He nodded to Caroline. "I'll see you at dinner, Miss Morton. Six o'clock would suit me."

He headed for the door, and Dr. Harris followed him.

Caroline waited until their voices faded before she left the parlor and went up to her own bedchamber. It appeared Mr. Frogerton had been given the second-best room, which was next door to hers. She could hear him talking to Dr. Harris as she passed by on the landing.

She wasn't quite sure how she felt about his arrival. It was typical of Mrs. Frogerton to want to be helpful even while she had to remain in London to deal with Dorothy. But Mr. Frogerton was a man who knew his own mind, and Caroline suspected he might be difficult to deal with. She couldn't deny that having immediate funds to tempt Mabel into giving Susan up made her chances of succeeding immeasurably better. Mabel was very fond of Susan, but given the choice between gold coin and her cousin, Caroline was fairly certain which Mabel would choose.

Of course, Mabel planned to have everything. Caroline sighed as she sank down onto the floor beside Susan's trunk. Negotiating any deal when her sister wanted to leave with her cousin wouldn't be easy. How could she show Mabel in an unflattering light and make Susan change her mind without alienating her completely? Perhaps a few days hiding in a cheap lodging house near the docks might make Susan think differently, but Caroline couldn't assume anything.

She opened the trunk with the key Dr. Harris had given her, and the scent of lavender washed over her. She'd spent hours sewing pouches to fill with Susan's favorite scent before sending her off to school. Not that Susan had appreciated it; she'd still been furious about being uprooted from Greenwood Hall. Tears crowded Caroline's throat at the thought she might never see her sister again.

If Mabel allowed Caroline to speak to Susan alone, Caroline had already decided to tell her sister everything that had happened to the Greenwoods and her cousin's part in it. She doubted she would be offered such an opportunity. It was in Mabel's best interests to keep Susan believing that Susan and Mabel had been terribly wronged by the rest of the family—including Caroline.

From what she could see, someone had packed Susan's

trunk with great care and nothing appeared to be missing. There were two dresses unaccounted for, which meant her sister had at least remembered to take a change of clothing. Susan had escaped dressed as a boy. It would've been easy to drop a parcel containing boys' attire over the school walls that could be picked up and concealed beneath a cloak.

After checking the time, Caroline glanced over at her bed. A restorative nap was in order if she was going to have to deal with Dr. Harris *and* Mr. Frogerton at dinner.

"I forgot to give you this." Mr. Frogerton took a letter out of his coat pocket. "It's from my mother."

"Thank you." Caroline set the letter on the table beside her.

She was currently enjoying the roast beef Mrs. Landon had produced from the kitchen along with a variety of side dishes. So far, the conversation had centered mainly on the weather and the dubious delights of Folkestone, which had allowed her plenty of time to eat.

"She visited the DeBlooms, you know," Mr. Frogerton said. "I accompanied her."

Caroline set down her wineglass. "Did anything untoward happen?"

"She didn't find the scoundrel who attacked you, Miss Morton. She was very disappointed about that, but I think she convinced Mrs. DeBloom to join her on the charity committee. For a business owner, Mrs. DeBloom seemed remarkably uninformed about her own company. She said she left most of the day-to-day running to her business manager, Mr. Kruger. I think my mother was horrified at the very idea." He finished his tankard of ale. "I can't say that Mrs. DeBloom looked thrilled to see us, but she was very polite, and she didn't set the dogs on us."

"There were dogs?" Dr. Harris asked.

Mr. Frogerton gave him a look. "Not real ones, Doctor."

"Did Mrs. Frogerton hear anything more about Mr. Thettle?"

"Inspector Ross came round to speak to her." Mr. Frogerton pointed at the letter. "I'm sure she's told you all about it in there. In truth, she wrote so much that it was probably cheaper to send me with the letter than mail it." He laughed heartily at his own joke.

The letter did look rather bulky. Caroline was looking forward to reading it. Mrs. Frogerton was usually far more enthusiastic about Caroline's suggestions than her son and far more informative as well.

There was a knock on the door. Mr. Landon came in to clear away some of the plates and offer rhubarb pie, thick cream, and some excellent cheese and port.

He took a letter out of his pocket. "This came for you, Miss Morton. The boy didn't wait for an answer."

"Thank you."

Dr. Harris barely waited until the door closed before speaking. "Is it from Mabel?"

"Yes." Caroline opened the folded note. A five-pound note fluttered out. The letter was short and to the point. Caroline read it out loud to her companions. " 'I am insulted that you think I can be bought for five pounds, Cousin. If you truly wish to see your sister, I suggest you take this matter seriously.' "

"You sent her five pounds when she's asking for a thousand?" Mr. Frogerton whistled. "I'm all for starting with a low bid, Miss Morton, but that *is* insulting."

"We were merely attempting to gauge how quickly Mabel responded to a message left for her at the Mermaid's Kiss," Dr. Harris spoke up before Caroline could reply. "By the way, Mabel thinks I'm you."

Mr. Frogerton's brow creased. "We look nothing alike and she already knows who you are."

"We barely saw each other at Greenwood Hall. I wasn't considered a guest."

"That still doesn't explain how you came to present yourself as me." Mr. Frogerton looked affronted.

"I used your name when I first went into the Mermaid's Kiss in an attempt to be anonymous," Dr. Harris said. "I wasn't expecting you to turn up in Folkestone and complicate matters. I left Mabel a message and only spoke to the landlord."

"You're suggesting your cousin thinks I'm here with you?" Mr. Frogerton addressed Caroline. "And believes I have been from the start?"

"She certainly believes there is a Frogerton in the vicinity," Caroline said. "I did not attempt to disabuse her of the idea."

"Next thing you know, she'll be trying to kidnap me." Mr. Frogerton refilled his ale.

"It's not a bad idea—you in exchange for Susan," Dr. Harris said. "Good of you to suggest it."

"I have no intention of offering myself up like a sacrificial lamb to a pair of blackmailers," Mr. Frogerton said. "From what you told me, they have no moral conscience."

"Could we perhaps get back to the matter in hand?" Caroline suggested. "How much should I offer Mabel to get her to allow me to see Susan?"

Mr. Frogerton considered her, his fingers drumming on the tabletop. "A hundred pounds? You can tell her that's all you have until you speak to your banker in London, and that it will take at least three days to release any more capital to you." He glanced at Dr. Harris. "You did say we're trying to stall them until Harry gets back on his ship?"

Dr. Harris nodded. "That is correct."

"Then that's what I'd do," Mr. Frogerton said. "And I'd make your letter more conciliatory."

"Maybe even try to sound a little flustered or desperate," Dr. Harris added.

Caroline looked at them both. "You wish me to appease her."

"Exactly," Mr. Frogerton said. "When is her husband's ship due to leave on its next voyage?"

"In three days."

"Then that excuse should serve you well. A hundred pounds is nothing to be sniffed at. I can't imagine they have much if they live on a seaman's wages."

"I think Mabel must have taken her jewelry and other valuables when she left Greenwood Hall," Caroline said. "I had a letter from her older sister at one point accusing me of stealing them when I left."

"That doesn't surprise me at all," Dr. Harris murmured. "I've never encountered a more unpleasant bunch of people in my life." His gaze fell on Caroline. "Present company excepted, of course."

Mr. Landon returned with the promised pie, cheeses, and port. For a while, Caroline was able to forget about the terrible tangle she found herself in and just enjoy the novel sensation of dining with two men who made no attempt to curate their conversation simply because a lady was present. It was quite refreshing; although, if she'd still been a member of society, her reputation would've been completely ruined.

When they moved on to discussing politics, Caroline left the table to sit down at the writing desk near the window. She spent some time attempting to write a suitably fawning letter to Mabel. Mr. Frogerton came and looked over her shoulder and told her to grovel more, whereas Dr. Harris, who joined them, said she was being too obsequious.

Eventually, a letter was produced that satisfied them all. Mr. Frogerton went upstairs to retrieve the necessary sum of money from his strongbox. He returned with a leather pouch full of clinking coins that he informed them were sovereigns.

"I will take the money to the Mermaid's Kiss myself, Miss Morton," Mr. Frogerton announced as he sat down.

"Not at this hour, you won't," Dr. Harris said. "You're

in a port teeming with sailors. You'd be knifed and robbed within five feet of this inn."

"I can defend myself." Mr. Frogerton sat up straighter.

Caroline decided it was time to intervene. "We don't want to capitulate too quickly, Mr. Frogerton. Harry's ship is still in port, and we want him to be on it when it leaves."

"Then I'll walk around to the Mermaid's Kiss in the morning." For all his bluster, Mr. Frogerton wasn't stupid.

"That sounds most satisfactory, sir."

He took the letter and put it in his pocket along with the coins. "I'll bid you both good night. I have to write a note to my mother to let her know I arrived safely and give her an update on our plans."

Caroline remembered she hadn't yet read her own letter from Mrs. Frogerton.

"May I put my letter to your mother in with yours, Mr. Frogerton? I'll have it ready by the morning."

"Aye, of course." He smothered a yawn with his hand. "But don't wake me up to do it. Slide the note under the door."

"Miss Morton is hardly likely to creep into your bed-chamber while you're sleeping, Frogerton. She's a lady, not a chambermaid," Dr. Harris said.

"I'm fully aware of that." Mr. Frogerton headed for the door. "My mother blathers on about it every day. Good night, Miss Morton. Dr. Harris."

Caroline inclined her head. "Good night, sir, and thank you again for your assistance in this matter."

She took out Mrs. Frogerton's letter and unfolded it. There were at least ten sheets of paper.

"Don't take any notice of Frogerton, Miss Morton," Dr. Harris said after a while. "He doesn't mean anything by it. He's from the north."

Caroline looked over at him.

He shrugged. "He can be quite rude."

"He's willing to help me save my sister from Mabel. I

am prepared to forgive him the occasional harsh word."
Caroline returned her attention to the letter. "I am quite
used to dealing with gentlemen who make unfortunate remarks."

There was silence as she read the next page.

"I suppose you're referring to me, Miss Morton."

"Now why would you think that?" She didn't look up.
"Mrs. Frogerton says the weather in London has been dread-
ful and that she hopes you remembered to bring your umbrella."

"I don't own one anymore. I kept forgetting where I put
it, and one day it simply disappeared."

Caroline read on as Dr. Harris took a turn around the
room. "She says that the coroner has confirmed Mr. Thettle was strangled. They think someone came up behind
him when he was sitting at his desk and took him by surprise. There are no other injuries or signs of a struggle."

"It makes you wonder whether it was someone he knew
that he'd allowed into his lodgings." Dr. Harris frowned.
"Someone he didn't think would attack him if he turned
his back on them."

"Or he was genuinely unaware that someone had
come in."

"Unlikely, Miss Morton. When you live in lodgings, you
are acutely aware of what goes on around you in case
there is trouble."

"Mrs. Frogerton says that none of his valuables, such as
they were, are missing."

"Which unfortunately indicates he was killed for what
he knows rather than what he had."

"Yes." Caroline paused her reading. "I almost wish
you'll be right and this will mean the end of it."

"That hardly seems fair on you, Miss Morton."

"How so?"

"The will could've given you financial independence
again."

"I sincerely doubt that. My father's bank was very insistent that there was no money in the accounts for me or Susan."

"There must have been something to draw all this attention to the damned thing," Dr. Harris said.

"I suspect it's about the fake shares my father bought in the DeBloom mines," Caroline said. "The DeBloom family do not want them to come to light and are willing to do what is necessary to preserve their reputation."

"Murder people? That's no laughing matter, Miss Morton. I'm surprised you're being so sanguine."

"I'm hardly that. I don't understand it either, Doctor. But I can't think of any other reason why the DeBlooms are so interested in my father's will, can you?" She met his gaze.

"Not yet, but surely there should be a better reason to murder innocent men than hurt pride over a bad decision made years ago." He turned to the door. "I think I'll go to bed. Good night, Miss Morton."

"Good night, Dr. Harris."

Caroline finished reading her letter and wrote a reply. She thanked Mrs. Frogerton for sending her son to Folkestone and promised to repay any bills incurred on Susan's behalf. She updated her employer on everything that had happened with Mabel and asked for advice about her negotiating strategy when the hostage was unwilling to be saved.

By the time she'd finished writing, Mr. Landon had been in to clear the table and lay the fire for the morning. She took the candle he offered her and went up the creaking stairs to bed. The scent of burned ash from the fire and the smell of ale followed her up. She paused to slip the note under Mr. Frogerton's door, which was gently vibrating from the loudness of his snoring, and continued on her way.

The clock downstairs struck twelve as she unlocked her door. In two days, Harry's ship would depart, and if they were lucky, neither Mabel nor Susan would be on board. With Harry out of the way, their chances of reclaiming Susan increased substantially. Caroline could only pray that Mabel's greed would overcome her desire to keep hold of Susan. She hoped her cousin's true nature would be revealed and that Susan would realize she was being used. But how to achieve that still eluded her.

She prayed the solution would appear to her after a good night's sleep. She cast an eye toward the wall she shared with Mr. Frogerton. If she was able to sleep at all . . .

Chapter 14

"What on earth did you do to yourself?" Caroline hadn't meant to blurt out her question, but the sight of Dr. Harris minus his beard was slightly shocking.

"I thought it might help my disguise." Dr. Harris smoothed a hand over his chin. "I can't say I like the sensation of bare skin, and my face feels cold."

It was early afternoon. The tide was out, and the weak sun was lighting the seascape in interesting ways that made Caroline yearn for the ability to paint. Mr. Frogerton had gone out to take a stroll along the seafront after delivering Caroline's note to Mabel earlier that morning. He'd asked Caroline if she'd like to accompany him, but she'd declined. She was rather too anxious to make good company and preferred to wait at the inn for Mabel's reply to her more generous offer.

"I need to visit some of the taverns on the docks again to make sure Harry's boat is expected to leave on time," Dr. Harris said. "I don't want to bump into Harry and have him recognize me."

"It's probably too late for that," Caroline said. "We've been here for days."

"And we'll stay here until we have Susan safely back with us."

Caroline looked up at Dr. Harris. "If you need to return to London—"

"I'm not going anywhere. You forget I have a very good reason for wanting to see your cousin thwarted for once."

Remembering Dr. Harris's difficult relationship with the Greenwood family, Caroline couldn't disagree with him.

"And I wouldn't leave you alone with Frogerton," Dr. Harris continued. "He's far too impressed with the sound of his own voice, and he doesn't listen."

"If Mabel allows me to see Susan, we'll be able to return to London very shortly," Caroline stated.

"She won't let Susan leave with you. I can promise you that."

"I tend to agree." Caroline sighed. "At this point I'd be happy just to see she is alive."

"Mabel's hardly going to mistreat her when she needs her money," Dr. Harris pointed out. "I'll go and visit the docks after dinner."

"I thought you said it wasn't safe."

Dr. Harris went toward the door. "For Frogerton, not me. If I carry my doctor's bag the sailors tend to leave me alone."

"You mean they give you a wide berth."

He shot her a look. "Very funny, Miss Morton. I'll see you at dinner."

Just after they sat down for dinner, a message was delivered for Caroline. Mabel's note was typically short, but not as damning as the first one. Caroline read it out to her companions.

"She writes, 'You may come to the Mermaid's Kiss at three o'clock tomorrow afternoon where you will have the opportunity to say your farewells to your sister. Do not bring anyone with you, or you will suffer the consequences.'"

"I wonder what she means by that," Mr. Frogerton said.

"I don't intend to find out." Caroline folded the note up and put it in her pocket. "I will go alone."

"I'd be happy to accompany you," Mr. Frogerton offered. "To underline the seriousness of the matter to your cousin and to confirm the availability of funds."

"That's very good of you, but I can relay all that information to her myself," Caroline said.

"Miss Morton is perfectly capable," Dr. Harris interjected.

"I know that," Mr. Frogerton said.

"Then try not to treat her like she's a fool."

"I'm not."

Before Dr. Harris could reply, Caroline hurriedly spoke up. "Could you pour me a glass of wine, Doctor? I'm looking forward to trying this fish pie."

"Remember—tell Mabel you can't get all the funds until the bank agrees to release your capital," Mr. Frogerton said as he served the pie. "That should buy us a few days."

"Unless Mabel thinks you can hurry things along, Frogerton," Dr. Harris said. "She might suspect you already have the funds available, and she might demand payment in full." He paused. "Perhaps *you* should be the one going back to London."

"I'll have to if Miss Morton wants me to release the whole amount," Mr. Frogerton said. "My money works for me in the business. It doesn't lie around in a bank. I'll have to get my mother's signature on any documents to release capital."

"I . . . didn't realize it would be so difficult, Mr. Frogerton," Caroline said.

"It's not." He set down his knife. "It's just a process that needs to be followed. There's no need to fret, lass." He reached across the table and patted her hand. "You never know, you might persuade Mabel to give Susan up with far less than a thousand pounds."

* * *

Caroline approached the Mermaid's Kiss with some trepidation. In the daylight, the place looked even more run-down—the roof needed rethatching, the front door had a crazy lean to it where it had been kicked in, and all the upstairs curtains were drawn. Caroline had left Mr. Frogerton at the corner of the street after trying to persuade him to go back to the Rose & Crown. He'd refused and said that if she needed help, she was to run outside and scream at the top of her lungs, and he'd be there.

Despite his stubborn refusal to be dismissed, she was secretly grateful he'd decided to remain close by. Dr. Harris had gone to wait outside Mabel's lodgings in case Harry appeared or something untoward happened.

Caroline gripped her reticule hard and approached the front door. There wasn't a lick of paint left on the door, and the brass knocker sounded loud when she used it. Despite the sunniness of the day, the sharp breeze blowing off the sea made Caroline shiver and wish she'd worn her cloak as well as her coat.

Eventually the door opened a crack and, with much cursing and kicking, was forced open until there was room for her to step inside.

The landlord, who was younger than Caroline had anticipated, looked her up and down. "I suppose you're the lady Miss Mabel's waiting for, are you?"

"Yes."

"She's in the best parlor." He pointed to a dark corridor beyond the public bar. "You can't miss it."

"Thank you."

The ceiling beams were so low over the doorways that Caroline had to bend her head to get through. She considered knocking on the parlor door but decided not to and lifted the latch. Mabel sat in front of a table with a teapot, three mismatched china cups, and a bowl of sugar. The fire hadn't been lit, and the room smelled of damp and bad drains.

"Where is Susan?" Caroline didn't bother with the pleasantries.

"She'll be here in a minute." Mabel smiled. "I thought you'd prefer it if we concluded our financial business in private."

"Why would you think that?" Caroline asked. "Surely Susan should be involved in any decision as to her inheritance."

"As you keep reminding me, she's still a child. We can settle this matter between us." Mabel gestured at one of the chairs. "Would you care for some tea?"

"I would not." Caroline turned to the door. "I came to see Susan. If she's not here, I'll leave."

"Oh, sit down, Cousin. I'll call her. You've become quite a different person since you've taken up with Mrs. Frogerton." Mabel went to the corner of the room where a small door concealed a narrow spiral staircase. "Susan! Your sister's here."

Caroline remained by the door until Susan came down the stairs and then rushed over to her. "Oh, my goodness, it is so good to see you unharmed! We have all been so worried!"

Susan didn't return Caroline's embrace and remained stiff, her arms by her side, until Caroline reluctantly released her.

"Please sit down," Mabel said. "Susan, would you like some tea?"

"Yes, please."

She sat beside Mabel and Caroline reluctantly joined them. Susan looked remarkably well—her gown was clean, her fair hair was styled, and she looked rested. Her hopes that Susan would have been treated badly enough to want to leave faded rapidly.

"How have you been, Susan?"

"Very well." Susan didn't look directly at Caroline. "Better, since I escaped that horrible school you forced me to attend."

"I sent you there to complete your education when the nursery at Greenwood Hall was shut down." Caroline wanted to make sure her sister had all the facts before she made a decision Caroline was certain she'd come to regret. "You only have a few months left and you will be free of it."

"To do what, exactly? Live with you?"

"I had hoped you would wish to do that." Caroline paused. "We are sisters."

Susan raised her chin. "You're going to give me my Season in London, then?"

"There is no money," Caroline said gently. "Father left us with nothing." She turned to Mabel. "Surely you haven't been telling her otherwise?"

"I haven't been telling her anything." Mabel smiled. "She is old enough to understand that an injustice has been perpetuated against her."

"Not by me."

Susan glanced quickly at her sister and then away as Caroline continued speaking. "I'm hardly living in luxury. I have to work for my living to survive."

"Which is entirely your own fault," Mabel said. "If you'd just kept quiet and stayed at Greenwood Hall as my mother wanted, none of this would have happened."

"I beg your pardon." Caroline met her cousin's wide gaze full-on. "You're blaming *me* for everything that has gone wrong in your life?"

Susan and Mabel both nodded, leaving Caroline with a terrible sense of helplessness. How could she prevail when her sister and her cousin insisted on holding her responsible for all the ills in their own lives?

"Aunt Eleanor would've given me a Season," Susan said. "Mabel said so."

"On my last visit to Greenwood Hall, Aunt Eleanor told me she wanted you to become a governess in the nursery," Caroline said. "She believed you had a natural ability to keep the younger children in order and thought she could save money by using you in the role. She had no intention of finding you a husband or launching you into society."

Mabel sighed. "Well, you would say that, wouldn't you, Caroline? In truth, you probably begged my mother to employ Susan in some way so that you wouldn't have to bother about her any longer."

"That's not true." Caroline directed her attention to her sister. "You are my only sister. All I want is your happiness."

"Then why are you here?" Mabel asked sweetly. "Susan has made it very clear who she believes her real family are."

Caroline focused on Susan, who was biting her lip. "Is that true, Susan? Do you wish to leave England with Mabel and Harry forever?"

"You've never wanted me," Susan said. "You left me at Greenwood Hall and didn't come back for months!"

"I had to arrange our father's funeral and speak to his solicitors and his bankers," Caroline said. "I discovered he had used our dowry money and sold our family jewelry to finance his last years, leaving us with *nothing*. At that point I could have resigned myself to living on my aunt's charity for the rest of my life—my future and yours hers to dictate—or I could learn to take care of myself."

"This is all very edifying, but hardly relevant," Mabel interjected.

"It explains why I couldn't come back," Caroline said. "My entire goal has been to make enough money so that Susan and I aren't dependent on anyone."

"Which my mother has just made possible by giving you a bequest," Mabel said. "Not that I've been allowed to take my own share of the family pot. Oh no. Nick won't even speak to me."

"You ran away and left him in a very difficult position," Caroline reminded her. "He's struggling to hold the estate together."

"I have no sympathy for him," Mabel snapped. "I am owed that inheritance."

"So you thought you'd take mine and Susan's instead?" Caroline met her cousin's furious gaze. "Does Susan know that if I hand over her inheritance she won't see a penny of that money—that it will all be used by you?"

"It will be used for all of us!" Mabel raised her chin. "Susan will want for nothing!"

"But what about me?" Caroline asked. "You intend to take my money, leaving me with nothing."

Susan shifted in her seat. "I don't want Caroline's money, Mabel. My five hundred pounds will be enough."

"Don't be silly, darling." Mabel laughed. "Caroline owes you that money for deserting you. Surely she deserves to stay in Mrs. Frogerton's employ until she's old enough to be pensioned off or left to die at the poorhouse?"

Caroline finally caught Susan's eye. "Is that truly what you wish, sister? What you think I deserve?"

Susan's lip trembled, and she looked away.

Sensing an advantage, Caroline leaned forward. "Perhaps you need more time to decide how you wish your life to proceed. You could go back to school, keep corresponding with Mabel, and make a decision once she is established in America as to whether you want to join her."

"Don't try to confuse her with your false sympathy. You know we can't leave if we don't have the money." Mabel's complacent smile had finally disappeared.

Caroline drew an unsteady breath. "Then take my inheritance and let Susan return to school."

Mabel stared at her. "Do you think I am a fool? Once you have Susan back in your clutches, you'll never let her go."

"I can have the money here in three days," Caroline said.

"Why will it take so long?" Mabel asked. "Surely, Mr. Frogerton can find such a sum in his coat pocket."

"As it is my entire capital, I will have to sign papers to acknowledge that I am taking it all from the bank and give them notice to provide the correct amount of coin."

Mabel looked skeptical. "I thought you said the money wasn't available yet?"

"If it isn't, Mrs. Frogerton has agreed to loan it to me."

"How nice for you to have such rich acquaintances, Caroline. You should set your cap at her son. Then that five hundred pounds you begrudge giving me would mean nothing to you."

"Do we have an agreement, then?" Caroline resolutely refused to be baited. "I will give you my entire inheritance if you allow Susan to return to school, where she can await your instructions about joining you when you are settled."

Mabel glanced at Susan. "What do you think?"

"This isn't what I want. It should be *my* money that was given to *me*," Susan said. "If Caroline has control of that, she should hand it over."

"Then that's how it will be," Mabel said. "Now, why don't you give your sister a kiss goodbye and go upstairs to fetch your cloak. I'll join you in a moment."

Susan stood up and so did Caroline.

"I . . ." Susan's voice stumbled into silence.

Caroline cupped Susan's cheek so that she had to look at her. "I know we have had our differences, Susan, but I swear on our mother's grave that I only want the best for you."

Her sister's eyes filled with tears and she stepped away. "Don't."

"I love you very much." Now Caroline's voice was wobbling. "I want you to take your time to decide what's right for you. If you still wish to leave after you finish school, I won't stop you."

Susan turned and ran for the stairs, her sobs echoing as she ascended.

"Now look what you've done." Mabel pouted. "It's

taken me days to make her stop sniffling, and now you've started her off again. I don't know how I'm going to put up with her on such a long sea voyage."

"If you accept my terms, you won't have to," Caroline said. "As we just agreed, you get five hundred pounds, and Susan stays here."

Mabel looked thoughtful. "I'll have to talk to Harry. He has the final say about such matters." She rose to her feet. "Goodbye, Caroline. I'll inform you of our decision when I've discussed it with my husband."

"The longer you delay, the longer it will take me to go to London and start the process of obtaining the money."

Mabel set the cups back on the tray. "As I said, I'll speak to Harry. Now excuse me. I need to take this back to the kitchen."

Caroline opened the door and let Mabel go past her into the corridor. She waited a second until her cousin turned the corner and then hurried back into the parlor and up the stairs. She found Susan standing at the window with her bonnet and cloak on ready to leave.

"What on earth are you doing here, Caroline?" Susan asked. "Mabel will be cross."

"Please listen. What Mabel doesn't want you to know is that if I don't produce the money, she and Harry plan to abandon you to your fate. She believes the threat will make me do as she wants."

Susan recoiled as if Caroline had attacked her. "She would never do that! She loves me."

"I'm staying at the Rose & Crown. If you need me or change your mind, just come. I promise I'll keep you safe." Caroline spoke rapidly as she heard Mabel calling from below.

"Susan? Bring my cloak and come down so I don't have to climb those stairs again." Mabel laughed. "I think that went remarkably well, don't you? I almost wish I could see her face when we wave goodbye and leave her in floods of tears."

Susan's gaze returned to Caroline and then she picked up Mabel's cloak.

"I'm coming," she called down the stairs.

Caroline held her breath as Susan left, but her sister didn't betray her presence, and she heard the two cousins leave, chatting amiably.

She waited a few minutes to make sure they were gone and then left the inn herself. There was no sign of the land-lord or any of his staff, which was fortuitous. As she turned the corner, Mr. Frogerton appeared and took hold of her elbow.

"From your expression, I gather it didn't go well."

Caroline sighed. "I tried my best to negotiate a compro-mise, but I am fairly certain Mabel was enjoying giving me hope just so she could dash it to pieces. She says she needs to speak to Harry to consider my proposal and will give me her answer tomorrow."

"After his ship has sailed," Mr. Frogerton said. "I as-sume that means she's the one who will be making the de-cision?"

"She's a very clever woman."

"So it seems. Did your sister seem set on leaving?"

"Unfortunately, yes."

They walked in silence until they reached the front door of the Rose & Crown.

"Have you considered just letting her go?" Mr. Froger-ton asked.

"With *them*? I'm not sure she'd survive the voyage, if it didn't suit Mabel's plans."

"Are you sure about that?" Mr. Frogerton persisted. "Perhaps Mabel genuinely cares for your sister."

"She does care for her. One assumes she cared for other members of her family until she decided they were no longer of use to her." Caroline looked up at Mr. Froger-ton. "I *can't* let Susan leave with her."

He held her gaze. "I admire your devotion to your sister, Miss Morton."

"I'm certain you'd feel the same if it was Miss Frogerton, sir."

He smiled, a rare thing that transformed his hard face.
"I'm not so sure about that, lass. It might be a blessing in
disguise."

Behind them, someone cleared their throat. "Are you
two going in, or do you intend to stand on the step chatting forever?"

Caroline turned to find Dr. Harris wearing a frown.

"We're going in, Doctor. I will tell you what happened
with Mabel after I've taken off my bonnet."

She arrived at the private parlor to find Dr. Harris had
ordered her tea and was already sharing a pot of coffee
with Mr. Frogerton.

"I assume Mabel wasn't willing to let go of either Susan
or the money?" Dr. Harris said as he poured her tea and
offered her a fresh scone with jam.

"She pretended to consider my proposal, and said she
would consult with Harry, but I fear you are right."

"What did you propose?"

"I offered her my entire inheritance if she'd let Susan
stay here and finish school while they established themselves in America."

Dr. Harris and Mr. Frogerton shared a glance.

"That was very . . . good of you," Dr. Harris said.

"Foolish more like." Mr. Frogerton snorted. "You
should have let me come with you to negotiate, lass."

Dr. Harris intervened. "How was Susan?"

"Resentful and reluctant to believe I spoke a word of
truth." Caroline tried to keep her tone light, but her sense
of betrayal made it difficult. "I managed to speak to her
privately for a second. I told her where I was situated and
that Mabel didn't have her best interests at heart. I don't
think it did any good."

Dr. Harris grimaced. "Then it looks as if we're going to
have to kidnap her after all."

"Is that allowed?" Mr. Frogerton asked.

"I am Susan's legal guardian until she is eighteen," Caroline pointed out. "It is Mabel who is doing the kidnapping."

"Can't the authorities do anything to aid you?" Mr. Frogerton frowned. "There must be some other way to get your sister back rather than taking the law into our own hands."

"I am perfectly within my rights to bring her home," Caroline assured him. "And there is no need for you to be involved. Dr. Harris and I will deal with the matter."

Mr. Frogerton didn't look convinced. "It doesn't sit right with me."

"If we assume Mabel will decline your proposal, Miss Morton, we'll need to move swiftly to take Susan while Harry is away," Dr. Harris said. "I had a stroke of luck today. I was loitering around the boarding house where Mabel is living when the landlady came out and asked me if I was wanting a room."

"That doesn't speak well to your ability to loiter unseen, Dr. Harris, but please continue."

"The room she offered me is directly below the one occupied by Harry and Mabel," Dr. Harris said. "I saw them come in after you'd met them. Neither of them recognized me."

"I assume my mother is already paying for your lodging here, Dr. Harris. Why should she pay for another?" Mr. Frogerton asked.

"Because it makes it far easier for me to get hold of Susan." Dr. Harris was looking very pleased with himself. "The landlady told me Mabel goes out most days and leaves her cousin in the rooms alone."

"You intend to knock on Susan's door and just persuade her to leave with you?" The skepticism in Mr. Frogerton's voice was hard to miss.

"I can pretend I have a message from Miss Morton."

"I do have her trunk," Caroline said slowly. "You could ask her whether she wishes me to have it sent round to her."

"It certainly might help facilitate the conversation," Dr. Harris agreed. "But I can ensure she'll come with me without a fuss."

"How? With a gun?"

"No, something far more effective." Dr. Harris paused impressively. "Chloroform."

"What the devil does that mean?" Mr. Frogerton asked.

"It's a form of anesthesia developed by a Frenchman," Dr. Harris continued. "I've seen how it works in laboratory testing. I simply place a few drops of the liquid on my handkerchief, press it to Susan's face, and she'll be out like a light."

Both Caroline and Mr. Frogerton stared at Dr. Harris.

"I can assure you it's quite safe." He paused. "At least we think it is."

"I'm not sure you should be trying out an experimental drug on Miss Morton's sister," Mr. Frogerton said. "There must be another way."

"Fine. I'll use it as a last resort." Dr. Harris looked disappointed. "I intend to occupy the room immediately. I'll let you know when Harry departs for his ship and Mabel goes out. That would be a perfect time to steal Susan away."

"And if Mabel doesn't leave her?" Caroline asked. "One might think that this close to getting what she wants, she would prefer to keep an eye on her prize. She might even be expecting us to attempt to rescue Susan."

"I agree with Miss Morton," Mr. Frogerton said. "But I think I know how we might manage this without resorting to experimental substances or blind luck."

Chapter 15

Two days later Harry's ship sailed with him on it. Mabel had politely declined Caroline's offer on Susan's behalf and insisted on the full amount being delivered to her without delay. Caroline had countered with the need to go to London and had left it at that. In truth, Mrs. Frogerton had made certain that neither Caroline nor Mr. Frogerton needed to make that trip by sending by armed messenger enough money to pay the amount in full.

Mabel hadn't left the lodgings since Harry's departure, meaning Susan was with her at all times. It also meant Mr. Frogerton's plan was now their most likely option.

Mr. Frogerton came into the parlor where Caroline waited, ready to leave in her bonnet and cloak. All her possessions were packed and stowed in the carriage he had hired.

"Good morning, Miss Morton. As agreed, I left an urgent message for Mabel at the Mermaid's Kiss that you would meet her there with the money at eleven o'clock."

Caroline rose to her feet. With the stakes so high, the thought of encountering her cousin made her feel physically sick. Mr. Frogerton looked at her closely before clasping her shoulder.

"You'll do fine, lass. Just keep her talking for a quarter

of an hour and we'll do the rest." He paused. "If she insists on checking every coin, then you might have to take off, but I doubt she'll waste the time when she'll want to get back to Susan."

"I hope you're right," Caroline said. "Shall we go?"

Mr. Frogerton told the driver to take them to the Mermaid's Kiss. He remained inside the carriage while the coachman helped Caroline bring the strongbox into the parlor. The carriage drove off, and Caroline sat down to await her cousin, who arrived shortly afterward.

"You came in a carriage," Mabel said. "Very fine."

"I've been to London. Mrs. Frogerton insisted on hiring it to bring me back, which shortened my journey considerably," Caroline said. "Is Susan upstairs? May I see her?"

"You paid your hundred pounds to say goodbye to her. That's good enough," Mabel said. To Caroline's relief, her cousin seemed calm and indifferent to the thought that she might not succeed in all her aims.

"That's cruel and unfair," Caroline said.

Mabel shrugged. "You agreed to those terms, not me."

"I thought—" Caroline paused. "I thought you'd be kinder than that. I might never see her again."

"You want to make one last desperate attempt to make her stay, and although that might be amusing to watch, I couldn't guarantee you wouldn't try something stupid like knocking me out and forcing Susan to leave with you."

Caroline moved her hand toward her pocket, and Mabel tensed.

"*Is* Susan here?" Caroline asked.

"No, and if you actually have a pistol and are foolish enough to shoot me, you'll never find her."

"I could just wound you." Caroline studied her cousin. "I'm sure you'd rather tell me where she is than bleed to death."

"If you dared to shoot me, the landlord would be in here in a trice to subdue you. I told him you were unstable, and that if you did anything to harm me or Susan, he had my permission to deal with you as he thought fit." Mabel smiled. "He used to be a professional boxer, did Rob." Her gaze turned to the small strongbox. "Give me the key."

Caroline took as long as she dared finding the key in her reticule. There was no clock in the disused parlor. But she was painfully aware of time moving onward and that every second was valuable.

"Mrs. Frogerton thought you would prefer gold coin to notes," Caroline said. "I had to borrow from her, as the solicitor still hasn't released the monies to me."

"How lucky you were to find Mrs. Frogerton, Caroline." Mabel took a deep breath, picked up a handful of coins, and let them fall through her fingers. "She will take care of you even though you have nothing to your name."

"Mabel."

"Yes, Cousin?" Mabel closed the lid of the box and locked it.

"Now that you have my money, and I have nothing, will you at least leave me Susan?" Caroline held her cousin's gaze. "She is worth all the coin in the realm to me."

"And that's why she's coming with me," Mabel said. "Because I can't allow you any happiness when you have caused so much damage in all our lives."

"You decided your fate, Mabel, when you chose revenge," Caroline said. "I had nothing to do with your plans to right your perceived wrongs."

"I don't regret anything." Mabel considered her. "Except my share of the family inheritance. I fully intend to take my brother to court until he releases my funds. Hopefully I'll be as successful with him as I've been with you."

"You've only succeeded in denying me a life with my sister," Caroline said. "I'm not sure I'll ever forgive you for that."

Mabel's indifferent glance shifted to the door. "Enough of this. I need you to leave."

Caroline reached into her pocket, and Mabel held up her hand.

"You cannot intend to shoot me now."

"I have a letter for Susan. If you give it to her before you . . . leave, will you allow her to come back to me if she changes her mind?" Caroline hoped she sounded desperate enough. "And if you do take her, will you promise me you'll keep her safe and allow her to write to me?"

Mabel angled her head. "You're upset."

"Of course I am! You're taking away the one person in the world I truly love."

"Good. I can't think of anything you deserve more. Go away, Caroline. We are done."

Caroline threw the letter on the table, stifled a sob, and ran from the room. Her tears weren't feigned. Her cousin's callousness was truly terrifying. She had barely rounded the corner before a piercing whistle split the air.

"Miss Morton!" Dr. Harris was gesticulating at her from the carriage. "Come on, we have to leave!"

She'd barely been hauled inside before the carriage moved off and turned toward the main London Road at a smart pace. Dr. Harris and Mr. Frogerton stared at her, but her attention was on Susan, who appeared to be sleeping peacefully between them.

"What did you do to her?" Caroline scrambled to sit beside her sister.

"Not what you think," Dr. Harris said as both gentlemen hurriedly moved across to the opposite seat. "She opened the door and had such a shock seeing me that she slipped on the rug, went down, and hit her head on the table."

"I don't believe you." Caroline drew Susan's limp form onto her lap and smoothed her hair. "You gave her that medicine."

"Look at her forehead! There's a bump the size of an egg." Dr. Harris pointed at Susan. "She recovered consciousness very quickly but was dazed enough that I could pick her up, shut the door behind us, and get her into the carriage without drawing attention to myself."

"I doubt that," murmured Mr. Frogerton. "Not that it matters at this point. I don't think Mabel has the means to outrun a coach and four."

"She has the means," Dr. Harris said. "Didn't you leave her with a thousand pounds?"

"Not quite." Mr. Frogerton looked quite pleased with himself. "The top layer might be real gold, but the rest are forgeries."

"Of course," Dr. Harris said. "Mrs. Frogerton thinks of everything."

There was a groan from Susan, and Caroline returned her attention to her sister. "Susan?"

Her eyes opened and eventually fastened on Caroline. "Help!" she screamed. "I'm being kidnapped."

As Caroline attempted to remonstrate with her, Mr. Frogerton looked over at Dr. Harris. "Do you have anything in that bag of yours that might keep her quiet other than chloroform? Because if not, it's going to be a very unpleasant journey."

Even though Mr. Frogerton paid the coachman extra to procure the fastest horses and passage to London, all the occupants of the carriage were exhausted by the time they arrived at Half Moon Street late that night.

Dr. Harris jumped out the moment the carriage came to a stop. "Right," he said, his hand on the carriage's door. "I'll leave you here, Miss Morton. I have to get back to the hospital."

Caroline, who was still dealing with an inconsolable Susan, looked out at him. "Thank you, Dr. Harris."

"You're welcome, Miss Morton." He nodded to Mr. Frogerton. "Sir."

Mr. Frogerton nodded in return and knocked on the front door. He also looked like a man who wanted to escape. The butler opened the door, and Caroline persuaded Susan to get out of the carriage and go inside. Mrs. Frogerton appeared at the top of the stairs surrounded by her dogs and came down with some haste.

"Well done, Samuel!" She kissed her son's cheek.

"Mother." Samuel returned the kiss and stomped up the stairs. "I'll speak to you in the morning."

Susan pushed herself away from Caroline and faced Mrs. Frogerton. "You have to help me. I've been kidnapped." Susan shot a hostile glance at Caroline. "She's a terrible, awful person!"

Mrs. Frogerton's face softened. "She is not, lass. She loves you dearly."

"She *stole* me!"

"From someone who wished you harm," Mrs. Frogerton said. "And once you calm down, you'll realize just how lucky an escape you've had."

Susan drew herself up. "If you don't send me straight back, I'll . . . call the police."

"And say what, lass? That your sister saved you from being taken away to a foreign land without her permission?"

"You're as bad as she is," Susan retorted. "You believe all her vile lies about Mabel."

Caroline reached for her sister's arm. "Susan . . ."

"Don't touch me!" Susan screeched. "I hate you!"

Mrs. Frogerton stepped between them. "That's enough. I'll take you up to your room. Maybe a night of quiet reflection will ensure you'll be more willing to listen to reason tomorrow."

"You can't keep me locked up for the rest of my life, Caroline." Susan turned toward the stairs, Mrs. Frogerton beside her. "The moment you become distracted, I'll go straight back to Mabel, who loves me."

"Get on with you." Mrs. Frogerton chivvied her up the stairs. "Will you order some tea, Caroline? I'll meet you in the drawing room."

Half an hour later, Mrs. Frogerton came into the room and sat opposite Caroline.

"She's quite safe, lass. I've a maid stationed outside her room. Every door is locked, and the keys are safe with the butler. She looked too exhausted to try to escape, especially after I gave her a piece of my mind." She took the tea Caroline poured for her. "One has to wonder why you didn't tell Susan what Mabel was up to at Greenwood Hall. She had no idea. I think she was quite shocked when she realized her cousin wasn't the shining example of goodness she thought she was."

"I suppose I didn't want her to know," Caroline confessed. She was surprisingly close to tears. "Susan always adored Mabel."

"People like that love their acolytes." Mrs. Frogerton sniffed. "A child, whose whole world was torn apart because of her father's reckless spending, would be easy to beguile into worshipping someone."

"When Susan turns eighteen, I might not be able to stop her leaving," Caroline confessed.

"Then let's do our best to keep her here until she can make that decision with all the facts in front of her," Mrs. Frogerton said.

"That's the compromise I offered Mabel." Caroline swallowed hard. "But she wanted everything. She . . . said I deserved to lose everything I loved."

"I hope you didn't believe that for one second," Mrs. Frogerton said briskly. "I've met people like your cousin before. Nothing is ever their fault and they are always the ones who are being persecuted."

"But I *did* leave Susan at Greenwood Hall." Caroline stared into her tea as a wave of tiredness engulfed her.

"Did you have a choice?"

Caroline looked up. "No."

"Then you did the best you could in the circumstances, and you can't do better than that," Mrs. Frogerton said. "You made sure your sister had a roof over her head and you took on the responsibility of making a living. That is admirable. I told Susan so myself."

"I do hope she wasn't too rude to you, ma'am," Caroline said. "After all you've done for us."

"No ruder than Dotty. It doesn't bother me. I'd rather a girl show a bit of spirit than be mild as milk." Mrs. Frogerton set her cup back down. "I think you'll sleep well tonight. You look worn out."

"It was somewhat . . . trying in the carriage," Caroline admitted.

"I can imagine, especially with Samuel and Dr. Harris trapped in there with you." Mrs. Frogerton shuddered.

Caroline rose and set her cup back on the tray. "I'll take this down to the kitchen."

"No need. Ring the bell, and the butler can manage." Mrs. Frogerton looked up at her. "You did well, lass. Don't let anyone tell you any different."

"Thank you for everything, ma'am." Caroline was too tired to do much else than sleep. She could only hope Mrs. Frogerton was right and that things would make more sense in the morning.

Caroline woke up in something of a fright. It took her a confused moment to remember where she was, and that her cousin Mabel, who'd been pursuing her through her dreams, was nowhere in sight. The sun was streaming through the gaps in the curtains, and she had a sense that it was late. Without bothering to ring for Letty, she washed, got dressed, and went down the stairs. She found Mrs. Frogerton in the dining room eating her breakfast.

"Good morning, my dear. You look much refreshed." She waved a hand toward the sideboard. "I told the butler to leave everything out until you and Samuel came down, so help yourself. You must be famished."

"Thank you, ma'am."

Caroline was surprisingly hungry. Although they'd stopped regularly on their journey up from Kent to change the horses, her attention had been on Susan rather than her own needs.

"You'll be pleased to hear that neither Mabel nor Harry have been banging on our front door demanding we return Susan to them." Mrs. Frogerton sipped her tea. "I'm fairly certain they are too busy booking themselves passage to America to worry about her."

"Have you seen Susan this morning?" Caroline asked.

"Yes, Letty is keeping her company. She was far more subdued today," Mrs. Frogerton said. "She asked whether Mabel had come to get her. I told her no, and that I wasn't expecting her to. Susan said she'd stay in her room until Mabel arrived. I left it at that."

"I fear Susan will have a long wait." Caroline sighed. "It's infuriating because this is exactly what happened when Mabel first ran away. Mabel made promises to return for Susan that she didn't keep."

"I suppose she kept them eventually, but only when she thought she'd get some benefit for herself," Mrs. Frogerton remarked. "One might have hoped Susan would've been less trusting than she was."

Caroline ate her food while Mrs. Frogerton read the newspaper and had several more cups of tea. She regaled Caroline with tales of Dotty's social activities, her disagreements with her future mother-in-law, and the sumptuous wedding Dotty wanted that would probably offend half the *ton*.

"I assume Samuel told you about my visit to the De-Blooms' place of business?"

"He did mention it, ma'am."

"Mrs. DeBloom is a strange woman. It's almost as if she hates running that company. Makes me wonder why she doesn't simply hand it over to her son and her business manager to run it for her."

"Mayhap she doesn't trust them?"

"It's possible, I suppose. She mentioned Mr. Kruger's name

several times during our visit, and her son's only once." Mrs. Frogerton paused. "Perhaps that's the problem."

"How so, ma'am?"

"Maybe Mr. DeBloom and Mr. Kruger don't get along, and Mrs. DeBloom feels she has to be there to stop them fighting. I've seen it before." Mrs. Frogerton nodded. "She might be afraid Mr. Kruger will take over the business entirely, or that her son will fire the manager, and the business will fail."

"I don't believe Mr. DeBloom is stupid," Caroline said. "If he could only apply himself to his work, I'm sure he'd succeed."

"The person he needs to convince of that is his mother," Mrs. Frogerton said. "As Samuel had to do for me."

"What did I do?" Mr. Frogerton came in. He bent to kiss his mother's cheek and nodded to Caroline. "Good morning, all."

"You showed me you were worthy of running the family business." Mrs. Frogerton smiled fondly at him.

"I assume you're comparing me to Mr. DeBloom, who seems singularly inept," Mr. Frogerton said as he went to get his food. "If I had the chance to run a company such as that, I'd be busy proving my worth all over the place. I hear rumors that there are exciting new finds in the mines in South Africa. I wouldn't mind some of that wealth."

"Perhaps you should speak to Mrs. DeBloom. I'm sure she could help you," Mrs. Frogerton said.

Her son snorted as he sat down next to her at the table. "How is your sister, Miss Morton? Has she calmed down at all?"

"I believe so." Caroline smiled at Mr. Frogerton. "Thank you for your help in this matter, sir. I doubt we could have succeeded without you."

He waved off her thanks with his usual brusqueness. "I'd do the same for anyone, Miss Morton. Do you mean to find her another school in London?"

"I'm not sure yet," Caroline said.

"Fair enough." Mr. Frogerton nodded. "You probably can't trust her not to run off. Did Miss Morton tell you about Dr. Harris wanting to try a new kind of sedation on her sister?"

"No!" Mrs. Frogerton looked intrigued. "How very like him."

The butler came in with Mr. Frogerton's coffee. "There is a young lady asking for admittance in the hall, ma'am. Do you wish to speak to her, or shall I turn her away?"

Mrs. Frogerton pressed her hand to her bosom. "Dear Lord! Is it Mabel?"

"No, ma'am. I believe it's Miss DeBloom." The butler paused. "Shall I ask her to come back at a more convenient time? She was quite insistent about seeing you."

"Send her in," Mrs. Frogerton said.

Mr. Frogerton poured himself some coffee as they waited for the butler to reappear with Miss DeBloom, who arrived behind him in something of a rush.

"Mrs. Frogerton, have you seen my brother?"

"Not today, Miss DeBloom." Mrs. Frogerton exchanged a startled glance with Caroline. "In truth I haven't seen him in days."

"He hasn't been home." Miss DeBloom wrung her gloved hands together. "I'm very worried about him."

"Young gentlemen do have a tendency to, er . . . disappear occasionally, Miss DeBloom," Mr. Frogerton said. "I wouldn't worry too much about it."

"He would have told me where he was going." Miss DeBloom's lips trembled. "He always tells me so I won't worry."

"Has he perhaps gone away on business for your mother?" Mrs. Frogerton suggested.

"I doubt Kruger would trust him to do that." Miss De-Bloom turned to Caroline. "Do you know anything, Miss Morton? Philip often confided in you."

"I've been away in Kent visiting my sister at school," Caroline said. "I only returned last night." She hesitated. "The last I heard from him was by letter, and that was several days ago."

"If I might be so bold, what did he write to you about?"

Caroline pressed her lips together.

Miss DeBloom took a step toward her, her hand outstretched. "*Please* tell me. It might have some bearing on what has happened to him."

As Caroline hadn't told anyone except Dr. Harris about her recent correspondence with Mr. DeBloom, she considered how best to frame her reply.

"We were discussing the business relationship between my father and your mother."

"Oh dear," murmured Mrs. Frogerton.

"Your brother indicated he intended to speak to your mother about the matter. He was quite upset."

"The last time I saw him, he was very angry about something," Miss DeBloom said. "He actually swore in my presence."

"What did he say?" Mrs. Frogerton asked with great interest.

"Something about 'those damn shares,' I believe." Miss DeBloom sighed. "I'll have to speak to my mother again. Thank you for your help."

She exited, leaving the room silent.

Mr. Frogerton stirred. "I wonder what's happened to the man."

"It sounds like he's incurred his mother's wrath." Mrs. Frogerton made a face. "Did you also mention your assault when you corresponded with him, Caroline?"

"That's primarily why I wrote to him, ma'am. It seemed an obvious way to invite him to clear himself of blame for the murders."

"How so?"

"If he did nothing and my assailant turned up again, I

would assume he was the guilty party. If he didn't know what was going on and was rightfully angry, he'd try to find out the truth from his mother."

"And now, after asking his mother, Mr. DeBloom has apparently disappeared. Who's hare-brained idea was that?" Mr. Frogerton demanded.

"Dr. Harris and I—"

Mr. Frogerton spoke over Caroline. "Harris, of course. The man is a fool."

"I disagree. How else are we supposed to get to the truth if everyone is lying to us?" Caroline asked.

"How about leaving it to the authorities?" Mr. Frogerton asked. "Although you and Dr. Harris have a tendency to do things just as you please."

"There is no point in arguing about what has brought us to this point," Mrs. Frogerton said before they could continue the conversation. "We need to act. Let's get our bonnets on and pay a visit on Mrs. DeBloom."

"Are you quite sure—" Caroline's question was ignored as both the Frogertons nodded.

"Weren't you just saying that we needed answers, lass? Well, here's an opportunity to find some." Mrs. Frogerton finished her tea. "Samuel will ensure Susan doesn't leave the house while we are out."

Mr. Frogerton nodded. "I can do that. What a shame I don't have Dr. Harris's fancy chloroform handy."

His mother shot him a look as she rose from her chair. "You're a clever lad. I'm sure you can think of something. Now, come along, Caroline."

Their first stop at the DeBloom town house wasn't successful. None of the DeBloom family were at home to visitors. After the bestowal of a liberal bribe, the butler admitted that Mrs. DeBloom was at her offices.

When the carriage moved off, Caroline asked her employer a question. "What are we going to say to Mrs. DeBloom when we see her?"

There was a glint in Mrs. Frogerton's eye that didn't bode well for the DeBlooms.

"I think it's time to hear the truth, don't you, lass? About your father's will and particularly those shares."

"And what if Mrs. DeBloom refuses to answer and calls on my assailant to teach us a lesson?"

"We'll take George in with us."

"George?"

"The coachman. He has a thick cudgel to deal with thieves and a blunderbuss full of birdshot under his seat. If either of us utters a squeak of discomfort, he'll know what to do."

Chapter 16

Mrs. Frogerton ignored all calls to stop and barged into Mrs. DeBloom's office, startling the lady as she sat behind her desk.

"What on earth?" Mrs. DeBloom shot to her feet. "Get out! Kruger!" She looked around as if her manager would magically appear from under the desk. "Where is the man?"

"Good morning, Mrs. DeBloom." Mrs. Frogerton advanced toward her. "I understand your son is missing. Would that have anything to do with you?"

"How dare you barge in here!"

"I've tried being polite," Mrs. Frogerton said. "I've even invited you onto a committee where I'm sure you won't be much help, but it appears I need to be more direct. What is your involvement in the matter of the late Earl of Morton's will?"

Mrs. DeBloom's wary glance flicked to Caroline. "I don't know what you're talking about."

"Are you denying you had a relationship with my father?" Caroline asked.

"A business relationship, possibly, but it was fleeting."

"That's not what my father said."

"As if he'd confide in you," Mrs. DeBloom scoffed. "You were a child at the time."

"Perhaps you didn't realize that I have his personal papers, ma'am." Caroline held the other woman's gaze. "He was quite eloquent about your . . . relationship."

Mrs. DeBloom looked toward the door. "Kruger!" she shouted as loudly as she could.

"He doesn't appear to be here, Mrs. DeBloom," Mrs. Frogerton said. "Now, what have you done with your son?"

"I have done *nothing* with him. How dare you." Mrs. DeBloom's color rose alarmingly.

"Did he not come and speak to you about what happened to Caroline?" Mrs. Frogerton asked. "He intended to."

"I don't know what you're talking about. If you refuse to leave my office, I will leave instead, and if you try to stop me, I'll call the police." Mrs. DeBloom took a step toward the door.

"Someone in your employ assaulted her," Mrs. Frogerton said.

"That's . . . ridiculous!" Mrs. DeBloom said.

"She was warned to keep away from your family, or she would be killed. If I was being generous, I might assume you simply didn't like your son's interest in Caroline, but I suspect it was more than that." Mrs. Frogerton paused. "You didn't want the contents of the earl's will coming out and were determined to stop it."

Mrs. DeBloom paused at the door, her face curiously blank. "You are completely wrong about everything, ma'am. Please excuse me."

"Then explain it to me," Mrs. Frogerton said. "Or promise me nothing else will happen. I will not allow Caroline to be threatened again."

"I will give your unwanted advice the attention it deserves." Mrs. DeBloom wrenched the door open and discovered George standing in front of it, his cudgel in his hands. "Get out of my way."

George looked at Mrs. Frogerton. She nodded, and he stepped aside.

"Mrs. DeBloom. I will have your promise." Mrs. Frogerton followed her through the door. "Or I will lay a formal complaint against you with the Metropolitan Police."

"You can have my promise." Mrs. DeBloom looked back over her shoulder. "Not that you need it. I would never lay a hand on another."

"Thank you for that, at least. Perhaps you might also tell us what has become of your son? I understand he's been missing for days."

"That is a lie. He's been working with Mr. Kruger all week."

"Your son told you that?"

Mrs. DeBloom stiffened. "Of course he did. Now leave this office. I've had quite enough from you for one day. I've made countless allowances for your lack of gentility, but your conduct is unforgiveable."

"You made allowances when you wanted my money for your son, Mrs. DeBloom," Mrs. Frogerton said. "Funny how that's changed now that you've lost hope of Dotty's fortune and your son is interested in the daughter of your former lover."

"Get out." Mrs. DeBloom pointed at the front door.

Mrs. Frogerton smiled. "We shall leave, but we would appreciate hearing from Mr. DeBloom when he has a moment."

Mrs. DeBloom didn't reply. Caroline and Mrs. Frogerton left the building accompanied by George.

"That was most unsatisfactory," Mrs. Frogerton said as they drove away. "I probably shouldn't have gone in without a proper plan, and I did slightly lose my temper with her."

"You were justified in doing so, ma'am," Caroline said. "She was quite rude. We did learn something, though. Mrs. DeBloom isn't a very good liar."

"She did look quite shocked, didn't she?" Mrs. Frogerton mused. "I wonder how little she knows about what goes on in her company."

"Did Mr. DeBloom confront her about what happened

to me, and she immediately sent him off with Mr. Kruger to keep him occupied and out of her way?"

"That sounds likely." Mrs. Frogerton nodded. "It would also explain why Miss DeBloom doesn't know where her brother is."

"Then perhaps we have done all we can," Caroline suggested. "We could involve the police, but I fear we don't have any new evidence to convince Inspector Ross that the DeBlooms are responsible for the deaths associated with my father's will."

Mrs. Frogerton sighed and folded her hands in her lap. "I suspect you are right, lass. But at least we have Mrs. DeBloom's word that you won't be attacked again."

After a fairly subdued luncheon—for which Susan refused to join them—Dorothy turned to her mother. "I need you to come with me and visit the dowager Vicountess Lingard this afternoon. Apparently, there is a family tiara and a wedding veil I am supposed to wear. I am not sure I want to do that."

Mrs. Frogerton looked at Caroline. "Is that usual?"

"It is fairly common in titled families," Caroline said. "It's considered a seal of approval if the bride is offered the family jewels to wear on her wedding day. If I were you, Dorothy, I would accept them."

"But what if they are hideous?" Dorothy asked. "What if they don't go with my wedding gown?"

"A lot of brides design their dress around the family jewels and veil," Caroline said. "Perhaps when you see them, you can consider them as inspiration for your gown?"

Dorothy didn't look convinced.

"I'm sure it would mean a lot to Augustus if you accepted his mother's offer," Caroline added.

"I suppose I should go and look at them." Dorothy pouted. "But I won't wear them if they make me look like a hag."

226   *Catherine Lloyd*

"And you'll thank the dowager countess nicely for the offer regardless," Mrs. Frogerton said. "If I were you, Dotty, I'd take the jewels. I'll come with you and we can take a look at them together."

"Thank you," Dorothy said. "I'll send her a note to let her know we're coming."

Mrs. Frogerton turned to Caroline. "Perhaps you'd like to stay home and spend some time with your sister? You must have a lot to say to each other."

"If you are certain you don't need me, ma'am?" Caroline's dubious gaze rested briefly on Dorothy.

"I'll make sure she does the right thing," Mrs. Frogerton said. "Don't you fret."

An hour later, after a fruitless attempt to talk to Susan, Caroline went to the drawing room, where Mrs. Frogerton's dogs were curled up in a disconsolate pile on the hearthrug waiting for their owner's return. They looked up when Caroline entered and wagged their tails but didn't get up. Without Mrs. Frogerton's exuberant personality filling the space, the house felt far too quiet. Caroline assumed Mr. Frogerton had gone out as well.

She had barely settled into a chair and picked up one of Mrs. Frogerton's gothic novels to read when the butler entered.

"A note was delivered for you, Miss Morton."

"Thank you."

She opened the single sheet, which wasn't sealed, and read the contents.

I need to speak to you immediately. Come to my mother's business address.

The note wasn't signed, but Caroline recognized Mr. DeBloom's handwriting from his previous correspondence. Mindful of her promise to keep Mrs. Frogerton informed of her doings, Caroline scribbled a note and left it beside her employer's chair. She ran upstairs to put on her bonnet while the butler found her a hackney cab.

When she reached the DeBloom offices, she discovered the exterior door was unlocked. She entered to find one elderly clerk manning the desk.

He looked up as she came in. "May I help you?"

Caroline smiled. "I'm Miss Morton. I've come to see Mr. DeBloom."

"I'm not sure if he's available, miss. I shall inquire."

He disappeared into the back offices, and she heard the murmur of voices before he returned.

"Come this way, miss."

She followed him to a different office than Mrs. DeBloom's. He knocked on the door and stood back.

"Thank you."

She was already inside before she realized the man behind the desk wasn't Mr. DeBloom.

"Excuse me, sir. I think I am in the wrong place."

"No, you're exactly where I wanted you." The man sitting behind the desk rose.

Caroline took an involuntary step back as he smiled. He was tall and extremely wide, with the coldest gray eyes she'd ever seen.

"I'm sure you remember me, Miss Morton."

The hairs on the back of her neck rose as he gestured to the chair in front of his desk. "Please sit down."

"I prefer to stand, Mr. Kruger."

He raised an eyebrow. "If I want to hurt you, Miss Morton, I'll do so whether you're standing or sitting. You already know my strength far outweighs yours."

"Perhaps I prefer to give myself a chance to avoid that fate now that I know who you are, and what you are capable of," Caroline said.

"You're intent on running away before you ask me about Mr. DeBloom?" Mr. Kruger looked pained. "And I thought you liked him."

"I am always concerned about the safety of my acquaintances, sir." She looked back at the door. "Is Mr. DeBloom here?"

"You'll not be seeing him until you've dealt with me. Sit down like the well-brought-up young lady you are, and listen."

A hint of violence hung in the air as Caroline considered her options. If she tried to run, she was fairly certain Mr. Kruger would catch her, and she already knew that wouldn't be pleasant. If she complied with his request, she might find out where Mr. DeBloom was, and exactly what part Mr. Kruger had played in Mrs. DeBloom's schemes. Also, the longer she was absent, the sooner Mrs. Frogerton would become concerned and send reinforcements.

Caroline sat down.

Mr. Kruger smiled and resumed his seat behind his desk, his work-roughened hands folded in front of him. "You have upset my employer."

Caroline pressed her lips together.

"You and that woman who employs you came here and made accusations. I won't stand for it."

"Mrs. DeBloom seemed unaware that you had attacked and threatened me, Mr. Kruger. Was she angry with you?" Caroline asked. "Is that why you made Mr. DeBloom summon me here today?"

"Who said she was angry?"

"She was certainly shocked."

He shrugged. "She doesn't always appreciate my methods, but she likes the results. That's why we make an excellent team. Your father tried to come between us. I'll not stand for his daughter interfering as well."

Caroline took a moment to digest that before she ventured a reply. "Was she angry with Mr. DeBloom for expressing his distaste for my treatment at your hands?"

"Mr. DeBloom does what he's told, Miss Morton. I don't recall him coming to your defense at all."

"Then perhaps you don't know as much as you think you do," Caroline said. "He assured me—"

He spoke over her. "Trust me. Philip's a weak man who is too cowardly to stand up to his own mother."

"Then let me speak to him, and we can set matters straight."

"Not until we've concluded our business, Miss Morton." He looked down at his hands. "You must stop all investigations into your father's will."

"How on earth do you expect me to do that?" Caroline asked. "I can hardly tell Inspector Ross and my solicitors what to do."

"I beg to differ." Mr. Kruger looked at her. "Inspector Ross will do anything for you. And your solicitors? They simply wish to avoid any more damage to their professional reputation and will be more than willing to drop the matter if you ask them to."

"But what about my financial status? If the new will—"

He cut her off again. "It provides you with *nothing*, Miss Morton."

"How would you know?"

He held her gaze. "Perhaps you might reconsider that question? I'm unwilling to reveal my methods, but rest assured, I have read the will, and you have nothing to gain from it."

"Perhaps I would prefer to read it for myself."

His sigh was patently false. "From all accounts, the will was lost when your solicitor was robbed in Shoreditch."

Silence fell as they considered each other.

"What exactly are you offering me in return for my compliance?" Caroline asked.

"Your continued existence?"

"I doubt you'd murder me, Mr. Kruger. I'm not some obscure clerk or solicitor. I'm the daughter of a peer."

"I'm fairly certain I could still dispose of you."

Despite the chill that shot through her, Caroline raised her chin. "If the whole point of this exercise is to stop people talking about the will, surely killing me would be counterproductive?"

His smile this time was approving. "You're not stupid, I'll give you that, Miss Morton." He glanced down at the papers on his desk. "There might be some financial return for your continued silence."

"That would be most welcome," Caroline said. "Perhaps you might draw up an agreement between us to that effect and send it to my address?" She rose from her seat, her knees shaking. "Now, if you can guarantee Mr. De-Bloom is still living, I would be most happy to take my leave. Mrs. Frogerton will be worried."

Mr. Kruger stood, too, and she tensed, but he simply nodded.

"I can confirm that Mr. DeBloom is alive. He's been on a business trip with me." He paused. "And if you think to persuade him to marry you *and* take my financial offer, I'd advise you to think again."

"I have no marital designs on Mr. DeBloom, sir." Caroline held his gaze. "I do not appreciate weakness. Good afternoon."

She turned and walked toward the door, aware he might change his mind and prevent her from leaving but determined not to display any fear, because she knew he would enjoy that. She nodded graciously to the clerk who escorted her out of the building, and she faltered only when she was on the street and her knees threatened to give way.

She somehow managed to hail a hackney cab and was soon back in Half Moon Street. She didn't remember much about the journey, because she still felt hunted, her senses too sharp, the taste of fear in her mouth.

There was some confusion when she went to knock on the door, as the butler was in the process of opening it to allow Mrs. Frogerton out.

"Caroline!" She rushed forward and caught hold of Caroline's arm. "I was so worried!"

"I'm quite well, ma'am," Caroline said. "Might we go inside?"

"Of course! I had just ordered my carriage to take me to

the DeBlooms' offices." Mrs. Frogerton turned to the butler. "You may tell the coachman to take the carriage around
to the mews. I won't be needing it again, after all."

She followed Caroline up the stairs, clucking like an
anxious hen, and then watched her take off her bonnet.

"You look like you are about to swoon, lass. Do you
want my smelling salts?"

"No, I'll be fine in a moment," Caroline said. "I just
need to . . . collect my thoughts."

"What happened? Dorothy and I returned about ten
minutes ago. As soon as I saw your note, I decided to go
out again and find you."

"I finally met Mr. Kruger." Caroline briefly touched her
throat. "He's . . . the man who threatened me."

Mrs. Frogerton uttered a shriek and abruptly sat down.
"Goodness gracious me! Did he threaten you again?"

"He offered me a bargain." Caroline swallowed hard.
"My silence over my father's will in exchange for money."
She paused, surprised at the calmness of her voice. "He
did suggest that killing me was still an option, but I think I
talked him out of that."

Mrs. Frogerton's mouth formed a perfect "O." "Did he
admit to murdering anyone?"

"Not in so many words, but he implied that he had read
the whole will. He assured me I had nothing to gain from
it. Which I assume means the opposite."

Mrs. Frogerton flapped her hand in front of her face.
"I'm surprised you're still alive, lass. Were you terrified?"

"I was, but I tried not to show it," Caroline said. "He
struck me as a man who disdained weakness and admired
strength."

"How did you escape?"

"I simply told him to send me any financial arrangement he proposed, and I left." She paused. "I did ask after
Mr. DeBloom. Mr. Kruger assured me he was quite well
and that they had been on a business trip together."

"Which is what Mrs. DeBloom said." Mrs. Frogerton

nodded. She rose to her feet and went to pull the bell. "I don't know about you, lass, but I think I need something stronger than tea. I'll get the butler to bring up the best brandy."

"Mrs. Frogerton?" Caroline looked over at her employer as she resumed her seat. "May I ask you to keep this between ourselves? I don't wish to upset Mr. Kruger."

"I can see why. The man's probably a murderer!" Mrs. Frogerton frowned. "But what shall we do about Inspector Ross? Surely we should inform him of these threats?"

"That's exactly what we shouldn't do," Caroline said. "If we truly want this matter to die, then we cannot tell anyone anything."

Mrs. Frogerton looked at her. "I must say I am somewhat surprised at you, Caroline."

"About what, ma'am?"

"You seem to be suggesting you're willing to take a murderer's money rather than bring him to justice."

"I haven't agreed to anything yet."

"Are you quite sure about that, lass?"

"I asked Mr. Kruger to draw up an agreement between us. I didn't say I would sign it," Caroline countered. "We still don't know how deeply Mrs. DeBloom and her son are involved in this matter. Mr. Kruger seemed to suggest that Mr. DeBloom knew very little. All I have done is buy us more time to find out."

"If you say so." Mrs. Frogerton still looked slightly dubious.

The butler delivered the brandy, and they both had a small measure.

"To be honest, ma'am, I would almost have agreed to anything to get out of that office with my life intact." Caroline shivered. "Mr. Kruger is quite intimidating." She stood up. "Will you excuse me? I need to go upstairs to take off my outdoor things and change my boots."

"Yes, of course." Mrs. Frogerton looked up at her. "Are you truly all right?"

"I think so," Caroline replied. "Although it might take a while for my limbs to stop shaking."

"You were very brave," Mrs. Frogerton said. "I would've gone to pieces!"

"No, you wouldn't, ma'am. You would've made the same bargain and walked out of the door with your head held high."

Caroline left her employer—who was looking pensive—and went up the stairs. On impulse, she passed her room and went down the corridor to Susan's. She knocked on the door and went in to find her sister sitting by the window staring out at the street.

"Good afternoon, sister."

Susan scowled. "I don't want to talk to you."

"That's quite all right, because all you have to do is listen." Caroline sat on the end of the bed. "It occurred to me earlier that if Mr. Kruger had intended to kill me, then his next victim would be you."

"What on earth are you talking about?"

"I realized I should stop treating you as a child and tell you exactly what has been going on with our late father's will. If I am no longer here, you need to be prepared for the worst." Caroline took a deep breath. "It all began when I had a letter from our family solicitor . . ."

Caroline felt well enough to attend dinner that evening. Although Susan had decided not to join them, Caroline felt she'd made some progress by sharing the news about their late father's new will. All the Frogertons were present, as Mr. Frogerton was leaving the next day to attend to his businesses up north. Dorothy was intent on dominating the conversation as she discussed her visit to the dowager viscountess Lingard to view the family jewels.

"They were huge!" Dorothy said. "Diamond and rubies as big as boiled peas! The viscountess said I had the stature to carry them off as well."

"She's right about that," Mr. Frogerton said. "You've always had a big head, Dotty."

"She did look rather splendid in the tiara," Mrs. Frogerton said. "I almost shed a tear, and the *veil* . . . handmade lace and over ten yards of it, I reckon."

"Much cheaper to make on the machines in our mills," Mr. Frogerton commented.

"But not as nice," Dorothy countered. "I really did feel like a queen when I tried it on." She turned to Caroline. "You were right to tell me to consider it. I can't imagine not wearing the tiara now."

"Dotty's got a taste for diamonds," Mr. Frogerton said. "Augustus had better watch out."

They were just finishing their dessert when the butler came in. "I have a message from Miss DeBloom, ma'am. She asks if you and Miss Morton could come to her house immediately. Her mother is unwell."

Mrs. Frogerton set down her napkin. "If you will excuse us, Samuel? Poor Miss DeBloom has very few friends in London, and I think we should go to her. I know it is your last night, but I promise we'll be back before you leave."

"I've seen quite enough of you recently, Mother." Mr. Frogerton winked. "And I'll see more of you when you come back home and start criticizing everything I've done at the factories."

He turned to Caroline and surprised her by planting a kiss on her cheek. "Miss Morton. A pleasure, and I never thought I'd be saying that when I arrived."

Dorothy smiled at her brother. "I'll keep you company, Samuel. Shall we retire to the drawing room and have our coffee there?"

Mrs. Frogerton didn't waste time calling for her carriage but got the butler to find them a hackney cab. The journey to the DeBloom residence only took ten minutes in the late evening traffic, and they arrived before the light went completely.

Miss DeBloom opened the door herself. It was obvious she'd been crying, but she greeted them calmly. "Please come in. It's the staffs' half day, so I'm the only person here."

She started up the stairs, bypassing the drawing room on the first floor, and continued on up. "Mother's in her bedroom. I didn't know what to do."

Caroline and Mrs. Frogerton exchanged an uneasy glance as they followed Miss DeBloom up the stairs. There was a light on in Mrs. DeBloom's bedroom, and she appeared to be sleeping. Caroline set her hand on Mrs. Frogerton's arm, holding her back as Miss DeBloom lit another lamp closer to the bed.

"I can't wake her up."

There was a note propped up against Mrs. DeBloom's empty glass. Miss DeBloom appeared not to have noticed it.

Mrs. Frogerton moved forward. "Clarissa, dear, why don't you sit with Caroline while I take a look at your mother?" She passed the note to Caroline, who went to sit with Miss DeBloom in the chairs by the window.

It didn't take more than a moment for Mrs. Frogerton to straighten and turn to Clarissa. "Will you send for your physician? I believe Mrs. DeBloom is dead."

Chapter 17

Two hours later, Caroline and Mrs. Frogerton arrived back at Half Moon Street with Miss DeBloom, who still appeared to be in shock. Despite several attempts to contact Mr. DeBloom and Mr. Kruger, they had not yet been located. Mrs. Frogerton hadn't wanted to leave Clarissa alone with the servants and her mother's body, so she had insisted Clarissa come home with them.

Miss DeBloom hadn't argued. She allowed Caroline to take her up to the best guest bedchamber and provide for her needs. She sat listlessly on the bed watching as Caroline laid out the contents of her hastily packed bag.

"Was your mother unwell this evening?" Caroline asked.

"She said she had a headache. That's why she went to bed so early."

"Did she have any guests at dinner?"

"We didn't have dinner together. She was speaking to Mr. Kruger and Philip in her study while I ate alone. When they left, she came into the dining room and told me she was going straight to bed." Clarissa shook her head. "I wish I'd gone and checked on her earlier. She might have told me something was wrong."

"It is easy to have regrets when such tragedies occur, Miss DeBloom, but you should not blame yourself." Caroline placed a hairbrush and comb on the dressing table.

"We were planning our voyage home just yesterday. She said she had decided to leave Philip here to run the London business. I was so pleased for him." Clarissa sighed. "What will I do now?"

"I'm sure Mr. DeBloom will look after you," Caroline said. "He is very fond of you indeed."

"That's true. I don't think he'll desert me." She paused. "But I am beginning to wonder where he is right now. Mother didn't mention that he was leaving town again."

"As soon as he hears the news, I'm certain he'll be knocking on our door, eager to see you." Caroline finished her preparations and turned to Clarissa. "Do you wish to come down to the drawing room, or would you prefer to remain here?"

"I'll stay here." Miss DeBloom shivered. "I think I might go to bed."

"I'll send a maid up to assist you," Caroline said. "And if you have any concerns during the night, please do not hesitate to wake me."

"You are very kind."

"I know how it feels to lose one's mother, Miss De-Bloom. You have all my sympathy."

Caroline went down to the drawing room, where Mrs. Frogerton awaited her. She had her favorite pug, Max, on her knee and was stroking his fur, a thoughtful expression on her face.

"How is she?"

"Still subdued." Caroline sighed. "I cannot blame her for that."

"And I cannot help but be suspicious of the timing of Mrs. DeBloom's death," Mrs. Frogerton said. "Do you still have the letter?"

Caroline produced it from her pocket. "Don't you think we should give it to Miss DeBloom or the authorities?"

"We shall do both those things in good time." Mrs. Frogerton held out her hand. "If you are having an attack of conscience, give it to me. I'll read it."

Caroline gave her the note and sat down.

"Well." Mrs. Frogerton looked up after reading it.

"What does she say, ma'am?"

"That she's the one who orchestrated the whole scheme to get hold of your father's will and that she takes responsibility for the deaths of Mr. Smith and Mr. Thettle." Mrs. Frogerton shook her head. "That's absolute nonsense."

Caroline agreed. "I can't imagine her stalking Mr. Smith through London and robbing him. Or having the strength to strangle Mr. Thettle."

Mrs. Frogerton consulted the letter again. "She *does* say she takes responsibility for the deaths, not that she actually carried them out. It still doesn't ring true to me, lass."

"Miss DeBloom said the last people her mother spoke to before she went upstairs to bed with a headache were Mr. Kruger and her son."

"Kruger again." Mrs. Frogerton shook her head. "That man is a menace."

Caroline heard voices in the hall and turned to see the butler ushering Inspector Ross into the room. Mrs. Frogerton quickly refolded the letter.

"Good evening." He bowed. "I apologize for the lateness of the hour. I was informed Mrs. DeBloom had died and that her daughter is currently residing with you."

"We're always pleased to see you, Inspector," Mrs. Frogerton said. "Would you like some refreshments?"

"Not while I'm on duty, ma'am."

Mrs. Frogerton offered him a seat.

"This is a sorry business," he said as he sat down.

"Indeed." Mrs. Frogerton shot Caroline an apologetic glance. "I was just about to write you a note, Inspector, so I am glad you are here."

"Miss DeBloom asked us to come to her house because she feared her mother was ill," Caroline spoke up. "We realized almost immediately that Mrs. DeBloom was dead."

"I hate to ask, but were there any signs of violence? Did she have any marks on her body that would be indicative of a struggle?"

"None at all," Mrs. Frogerton said. "I helped the doctor lay her out, and there wasn't a mark on her. Her cheeks were a very hectic red, but other than that she looked her normal self." She paused. "There was one anomaly, Inspector."

"What was that?"

Mrs. Frogerton held up the letter. "This. It was propped up against her water glass beside the bed."

Inspector Ross took the note. "I assume you've read it?"

"Yes, I didn't want Clarissa to have to do it." Mrs. Frogerton held his gaze. "It is not easy reading."

Inspector Ross unfolded the note and read it. "It seems to be a confession."

"That was also my conclusion, Inspector."

"And perhaps an admission that she chose to end her own life." Inspector Ross grimaced. "I wish she'd come to me and told me the truth rather than this."

Caroline felt so sorry for him that she almost blurted out that she didn't believe any of it was the truth.

"I'm not sure I believe Mrs. DeBloom carried out those murders herself," Inspector Ross said, justifying Caroline's faith in him. "But in this city, it's easy to find someone willing to do your dirty work for you."

"I quite agree, Inspector." Mrs. Frogerton nodded. "It was probably the same man who attacked Caroline."

Inspector Ross looked at Caroline. "If that is true, then she really did have a lucky escape."

"I am well aware of that, Inspector," Caroline said. "Does this mean you will close the investigation into the deaths of Mr. Smith and Mr. Thettle?"

"I expect it will." He looked down at the letter in his hand. "It's hard to ignore a confession, even when everything inside me is saying I should. Would it be possible to speak to Miss DeBloom and her brother?"

"Miss DeBloom is already in bed, and Mr. DeBloom has not yet been located," Caroline said.

"I'll come back and speak to Miss DeBloom in the morning to get her statement," Inspector Ross said. "If Mr. DeBloom turns up, will you ask him to come and speak to me?"

"Of course," Mrs. Frogerton said. "If Mrs. DeBloom did end her own life, do you think she used poison?"

"It's highly likely." Inspector Ross pressed two fingers to his temple. "You mentioned there was a glass beside her bed?"

"Yes. As soon as I saw the note propped up against it, I wondered what the glass had contained." Mrs. Frogerton put down her dog and rummaged in her large reticule. "I have it here. I was worried that someone in her household would inadvertently take it down to the kitchen and wash it."

Inspector Ross accepted the glass with some reluctance and wrapped it in his handkerchief. "Thank you, but may I remind you that you are not supposed to remove items from another person's house?"

"I was just trying to be helpful, Inspector."

"I'm sure you were." He rose to his feet. "I will take my leave. I need to speak to the coroner and make sure he looks for signs of poisoning in Mrs. DeBloom's body."

Caroline stood as well. "I'll see you out, Inspector."

They walked down the stairs into the deserted entrance hall.

"Did you enjoy your trip to the coast, Lady Caroline?" Inspector Ross asked.

"Not particularly. I had to rescue my sister from a relative who wanted her inheritance and intended to take her to America."

He raised an eyebrow. "I thought you were recuperating after your ordeal."

"I wish that had been the case, sir, but things were far too perilous for resting."

His smile was a delight. "You do live the most exciting life, my lady."

"I wish I did not," Caroline confessed. "And I hope I'll never hear another word about wills, inheritance, shares, or bequests again. Money really does bring out the worst in people."

"I agree with that." He paused. "One day I'd like a nice quiet life in the countryside with my wife and children, in a smallish house with just enough money never to have to worry about it again."

"That sounds lovely," Caroline said.

"Yes." He was looking down at her. "It absolutely does."

For a fleeting moment, she thought he was going to kiss her, and she wondered what she might do if he did.

He was the first to step away. "I'll wish you good night, Lady Caroline."

"Good night, Inspector."

She closed the door behind him and leaned against it, imagining herself in that rose-covered country house while their dark-haired children played around their feet.

"Miss Morton?"

She looked up to see Letty staring at her.

"Are you stopping someone getting in, miss? Because it's much easier to just lock the door."

"I was just about to do that."

Letty helped her lock up. "I was looking for you. Miss DeBloom's gone to sleep, and Lady Susan is tucked up in bed, too."

"Thank you for looking after them so well."

"It's all right, although I'm not looking out for you much, am I? I've hardly seen you for days, and you're not doing your hair right. "

"I'm managing fine," Caroline reassured her maid. "As you know, my needs are quite simple."

"That's cos you've got a beautiful face. It makes up for everything," Letty said as they went up the stairs together. "By the way, a parcel came for you when you were away. The butler had to pay extra for it, and he was quite cross. I left it in the butler's pantry and forgot all about it. I'll bring it up to you tomorrow when I have a moment."

"I can collect it from the butler myself."

"Don't do that, or he'll tell me off for not doing my job properly." Letty paused in front of the drawing room door. "I'll bring it up. I promise."

Caroline went into the room. "I sent Inspector Ross on his way."

Mrs. Frogerton looked up at her. "I hope you didn't mind me giving him that letter."

"Why would I mind, ma'am?"

"Because you said you wanted to keep matters between ourselves."

"Mrs. DeBloom's murder is slightly more important than that." Caroline sat down. "And, in truth, if Inspector Ross closes the case, it means he will no longer be involved."

"You don't want him coming round, lass?"

"I'd prefer it if he wasn't coming round to deal with police matters concerning me."

"I see. I suppose it is hard for him to come courting when he might literally have to call on you to testify in court." Mrs. Frogerton chuckled at her own joke. "He is a fine gentleman, Caroline, I'll give you that."

"I thought you approved of him, ma'am."

"Oh, I do." Mrs. Frogerton paused. "I just wonder what Dr. Harris would think of that."

Caroline chose to change the subject. "I am not at peace with Mr. Kruger getting away with murder, ma'am."

"Neither am I, but what can we do? As Inspector Ross said, with Mrs. DeBloom confessing all, there is little need to look for other suspects."

"Mr. Kruger practically confessed to me that he was responsible for those deaths, and I can do nothing about it."

"And if you did attempt to accuse him, Mr. Kruger might say that you were in cahoots with him because you accepted a bribe."

"Hardly, ma'am. It just seems far too convenient that Mrs. DeBloom suddenly decided to take all the blame and kill herself." Caroline sighed. "And with Mrs. DeBloom out of the way, Mr. Kruger has complete control of the company."

"You forget Mr. DeBloom. Surely he is his mother's heir?"

"Mr. Kruger believes Mr. DeBloom is weak. I wouldn't be surprised if he eventually contrives to do away with him, too."

Mrs. Frogerton gasped. "Perhaps he already has. No one has seen Mr. DeBloom since last night, and he left his mother's house in Mr. Kruger's company."

"None of this makes sense," Caroline said. "I keep thinking I am missing something obvious." She pressed two fingers to her temples. "I'm also rather tired."

"I think we should both go to bed and pray for some clarity in the morning." Mrs. Frogerton stood up. "Samuel is leaving at eight. I intend to be up to say my goodbyes."

"I will join you, ma'am," Caroline said. "In both endeavors."

After waving Mr. Frogerton off, Caroline, Mrs. Frogerton, and Dorothy returned to the house to have breakfast. Dorothy was full of plans for her wedding gown and chattered away, while her unusually subdued mother bemoaned the loss of her son. Both Susan and Miss DeBloom had opted to have their breakfast in their rooms.

Caroline remained quiet, her mind still full of her dreams, which had consisted of endless documents falling on her until she was buried up to her neck.

She felt a sense of restlessness that had her rising to her feet. "If you will excuse me, ma'am. I'll go and ask the butler to bring you some more toast."

"Thank you, Caroline." Mrs. Frogerton smiled wanly as she dabbed her eyes with her lace handkerchief. "That would be kind of you."

Caroline went into the kitchen where the staff were clearing up after cooking breakfast and sent the butler back to the dining room with the promised toast. While he was occupied, she popped into his pantry and found the parcel Letty had mentioned the previous day and had still forgotten to bring up to Caroline.

It was quite a bulky package, and she decided to take it up to her room to open it. She didn't recognize the handwriting, but it had been posted and stamped within the confines of London. Its slow delivery was probably due to its excess weight. She could see where the extra postage had been calculated before it had been sent out again for delivery.

She went up the back stairs and entered her bedroom. Letty had obviously been in and laid a new fire, made her bed, and opened the window to let in fresh air.

Caroline carefully broke the seal on the back of the letter

and removed the covering. There was a single sheet of paper folded around some parchment.

Dear Lady Caroline, I don't trust the DeBlooms or my employers. I'm sending this to you for safekeeping. J. Thettle Esq.

Hardly daring to breathe, Caroline spread out Mr. Thettle's copies of her father's will on the bed and started to read.

Chapter 18

It was hard for Caroline's patience to wait until Mr. De-Bloom finally came to Half Moon Street to claim his sister. She'd realized that at some point he and Mr. Kruger would have to act, or their lack of interest in Mrs. DeBloom's death would start to look suspicious.

She was surprised that both men presented themselves in Mrs. Frogerton's drawing room dressed in funeral black and wearing somber expressions to match the tragic events.

"Mrs. Frogerton." Mr. DeBloom rushed forward to clasp Mrs. Frogerton's hands. "I can't thank you enough for taking care of my sister!" He gestured at the man standing silently behind him. "Mr. Kruger and I were on a business trip to Scotland. It took days for the news to reach us and for us to arrange our return. I was beside myself with worry, wasn't I, Kruger?"

"Indeed." Mr. Kruger inclined his head. "It is a pleasure to finally meet you, Mrs. Frogerton, despite the tragic circumstances. Mrs. DeBloom thought very highly of you."

Mrs. Frogerton's eyebrows rose, but she simply nodded. "Good morning, sir."

Mr. Kruger's gaze turned to Caroline. "Miss Morton."

"Mr. Kruger." She held his gaze. "If you will both excuse me, I'll go and fetch Miss DeBloom."

Caroline paused on the landing to speak to the butler, and then went up the stairs and knocked on Miss De-Bloom's door. When she received no reply, she went in, her heart almost stopping when she realized no one was there.

"Are you looking for Miss DeBloom?" Letty came in behind Caroline, carrying fresh pillowcases. "She's in with your sister. They're becoming fast friends."

"Thank you." Caroline let out a breath. "Her brother has arrived. You might need to pack up her things to ready for her departure."

Letty heaved a sigh. "I just put them all away."

Caroline went down the corridor. Voices sounded from behind the closed door. She knocked and went in to find Susan and Clarissa sitting together by the window. Clarissa still looked frail, her black clothing only emphasizing the delicacy of her fair hair and pale skin.

"I'm pleased to tell you that your brother has arrived, Miss DeBloom."

"Oh, thank goodness! I was so worried . . ." She shot to her feet. "Is he downstairs now?"

"He's in the drawing room paying his respects to Mrs. Frogerton."

"Then I'll come down." Clarissa turned and embraced Susan. "Thank you for listening to me."

She rushed past Caroline, leaving the sisters staring at each other.

"It was kind of you to comfort Miss DeBloom, Susan."

Her sister shrugged. "She was upset." She turned her back on Caroline and looked outside. "Did you tell Mabel not to come here for me?"

"No," Caroline said simply. "I even left her my address in a letter I wrote to you. If she wishes to find you, there is nothing stopping her."

"You'd stop her from seeing me."

"Actually, I wouldn't." Caroline considered her sister. "You'll soon be an adult and free to make your own decisions. If Mabel wants you, then you'll be free to go."

"So this was always about thwarting Mabel and never really about me."

"On the contrary," Caroline said. "This is understanding that loving you means trusting you to do what is best for *yourself*. If you truly believe you'll be happy with Mabel, despite all you've learned about her, then I have to make my peace with that. I don't want you to leave, and I'll be devastated if you go, but I can't force you to stay, love."

Susan turned away, a glint of tears in her eyes that made Caroline want to hold her.

"I'll wait. I know Mabel will come."

Caroline turned to the door, her heart hurting for her sister. Every instinct she possessed told her Mabel wouldn't come, but Susan would never believe that. Only time would bring such realization, and then it would be up to Susan to make her choice as to what to do next.

Caroline went down to the drawing room. Clarissa was weeping in her brother's arms, and Mr. Kruger stood by the door, his expression unreadable as he studied Miss De-Bloom. For the first time, Caroline wondered if he was married or if he planned one last act to cement himself into the DeBloom family business by taking control of the vulnerable Miss DeBloom.

Mr. DeBloom persuaded his sister to stop crying and sit next to him on the couch. He kept hold of her hand.

"We have a lot to deal with regarding Mother's death, love. But luckily, we have Mr. Kruger and Mrs. Frogerton to aid us." He glanced around the room. "I suspect we will need all the help we can get. I never expected my mother to die in a foreign land."

"We will certainly help you," Mrs. Frogerton said. "Do you intend to hold a service here? I am sure there are many people in society who would appreciate the opportunity to say their last goodbyes to your beloved mother."

In Caroline's opinion, the only things that brought out the crowds to a funeral were excellent catering, the best wine, or a hint of scandal, which meant that a DeBloom memorial might do very well.

"I will gladly be guided by you in this matter, Mrs. Frogerton. I have no real knowledge of English society and its customs," Mr. DeBloom said. "I do intend to take her back to our homeland, where she can be buried in our family plot."

Miss DeBloom sniffed into her handkerchief. "She was planning on going home. She told me so herself."

Caroline didn't miss the swift, apprehensive glance Mr. DeBloom shared with Mr. Kruger.

"She said she thought you more than capable of running the London office," Miss DeBloom continued.

"She did?" Mr. DeBloom failed to conceal his surprise.

"Are you intending on returning to your town house, Mr. DeBloom?" Mrs. Frogerton asked. "If so, we will need to have Miss DeBloom's bags packed."

"I don't want to go back there." Miss DeBloom burst into noisy sobs.

Her brother looked appealingly at Mrs. Frogerton. "Is it possible she could stay here, ma'am, among friends? I know it is a lot to ask, but—"

"Of course, she may stay," Mrs. Frogerton said. "You are most welcome, as well."

Mr. DeBloom looked at Mr. Kruger. "Do you think that is a good idea, or would you prefer me to stay at the town house?"

"It doesn't bother me where you stay, Mr. DeBloom." Mr. Kruger paused. "I'll always find you."

"Yes, of course, then perhaps I'll stay here as well— as long as that won't be inconveniencing you, Mrs. Frogerton?"

"Not at all. My son, Samuel, has just left. It will be nice to have a man around the house again." Mrs. Frogerton turned to Caroline. "Would you speak to the butler, lass? He'll need to get one of the maids to air out a room."

Miss Frogerton went off with Miss DeBloom to fetch more of her belongings from the town house, Mr. Kruger left to inform the company of Mrs. DeBloom's demise, and Mrs. Frogerton went to consult with her housekeeper, leaving Caroline with Mr. DeBloom in the drawing room.

Eventually, he set down his cup and cleared his throat. "Thank you for your care of Clarissa. She always speaks very highly of you." He paused. "Did you have a pleasant trip to the coast?"

"Yes, thank you."

"And . . . you have recovered your health?"

"I am quite well."

He grimaced. "You must think me a fool not to have realized that my mother would turn to Kruger with her grievances against you."

"I hesitate to speak ill of the dead, sir, but one might think Mrs. DeBloom's response somewhat overwrought when there has never been anything between us except friendship."

"I suspect she knew me well enough to realize that my feelings were truly engaged." He paused. "I suspect you know that, too, Miss Morton, despite your denial."

"I have never encouraged your attentions, Mr. DeBloom. A woman in my position is extremely vulnerable to the judgment of others. I cannot afford to lose my reputation or my livelihood."

"That is all very well, Miss Morton, but you don't seem to have the same scruples when it comes to Dr. Harris or Inspector Ross."

"Neither of them has ever expressed any romantic interest in me, sir, or made me feel . . . pursued."

He stared at her. "If I have done that, I apologize, but it

is simply a measure of how deeply I feel about you. With my mother dead, I—"

Caroline interrupted him. "Have you forgotten that my life was threatened because I became involved with your family?"

He set his jaw. "As I have been trying to say, that threat has now gone."

"Perhaps you should speak to Mr. Kruger about that, sir." Caroline held his gaze. "He is still very much alive."

"I . . . am aware of that. I will speak to him. I fear my mother allowed him rather too much leeway."

Caroline raised her eyebrows.

He shrugged. "I can't just dismiss him."

"Why not?" Caroline asked. "If you truly believe you and I are meant to be together, one might think it essential."

"I only wish it were that simple."

Caroline folded her hands on her lap. "With all due respect, sir, this conversation is meaningless without the intention to change."

"Are you saying you would consider my suit if Mr. Kruger was no longer part of the company?"

"I am saying nothing of the sort, sir. We are merely talking in hypotheticals, because you have no intention of doing anything of the kind." Caroline stood up. "Now will you excuse me? I need to make sure that Letty is prepared for Miss DeBloom's return with her luggage." She went to walk past him.

He shot to his feet and grabbed her arm, his fingers biting painfully into her skin. "I never saw you as a tease, Miss Morton. Is this what you do to your other gentlemen? Make them dance to your tune?"

"Let me go, or I will scream the place down."

He released her but didn't step back. "You ask the impossible. I can't get rid of Kruger. He knows too much. I am . . . somewhat afraid of him."

"Aren't we all?" Caroline moved past him.

"If I disappear, Miss Morton, will you tell Inspector Ross to question Kruger very closely? I am in fear of my life, as should you be."

Caroline kept going until she was at the door, and then she turned to look at Mr. DeBloom. "Perhaps I have already made my peace with Mr. Kruger, sir. Did you ever think of that?"

She shut the door firmly behind her but not before she'd seen his appalled expression. Mrs. Frogerton hadn't approved of her plan to put herself firmly between Mr. Kruger and Mr. DeBloom and reveal him as the murderer. But Caroline had insisted the only person in danger would be Mr. DeBloom, and as he was safely ensconced in Half Moon Street, Mr. Kruger's opportunities to kill him were very limited indeed.

Now, if they could just persuade Mr. DeBloom to gather his courage and confront Mr. Kruger, Caroline's plans might come to fruition after all.

The butler stopped her in the hall as she went to ascend the stairs. "Inspector Ross said he will be happy to join Mrs. Frogerton for dinner this evening, Miss Morton."

"Thank you." Caroline smiled at the butler. "Please let me know when Dr. Harris replies as well."

Caroline put on her best evening gown for dinner and wore her mother's pearls for courage. She couldn't deny that she was nervous about how matters would proceed, but even if she and Mrs. Frogerton didn't succeed in revealing Mr. Kruger's crimes, she suspected Mr. DeBloom would never trouble her again.

She went down to the drawing room early and was surprised to see Inspector Ross had already arrived. He'd changed out of his working clothes into something more tailored. He looked impeccable.

He bowed as she came in. "I do apologize for arriving so early, but I wanted you to read this note I had from an acquaintance in the mining industry." He handed her the letter. "I believe it confirms your suspicions rather well."

"Thank you." Caroline sat down to read the letter and looked up again when she'd finished. "Mr. Frogerton said something similar just before he left. It sounds as if the faint rumors are growing louder."

Inspector Ross took the note back. "I am somewhat concerned about your plans for this evening, Lady Caroline. I would never recommend that a member of the public take on a murderer."

"I merely wish to point out a few facts to Mr. Kruger," Caroline said. "How he responds is entirely up to him."

Inspector Ross didn't look convinced. "As I often remind you, my lady, you tend to live dangerously."

"With the might of the Metropolitan Police sitting at the table, I am fairly confident nothing untoward will happen, sir."

"I'm more worried about what happens when I go home," Inspector Ross murmured. "I can't protect you from everything."

"And I don't expect you to do so," Caroline said. She looked up as someone else came into the room. "Good evening, Dr. Harris."

"Why's he here?" Dr. Harris pointed at Inspector Ross. "Are you expecting Mabel?"

"Not to my knowledge," Caroline said.

"Good." Dr. Harris nodded. "Because I forgot to mention that I asked the landlord at the Rose & Crown to keep me informed as to Harry's movements when he returned from his voyage. I had a letter today. Apparently, Harry and Mabel left for Bristol, where rumor has it they've booked passage for Maryland."

Caroline grimaced. "I wonder whether I should tell Susan or wait to see if Mabel writes to her."

"I'd wait," Dr. Harris said. "At least until the ship has sailed and she can't run after them. If Mabel wants to write to her, that's another thing entirely."

"Poor Susan." Caroline sighed.

"I'm sure she'll recover," Dr. Harris said bracingly. "Now, why did you invite me to dinner?"

"Mrs. Frogerton invited you." Caroline stood up as her employer came into the room accompanied by her daughter. "Perhaps you might care to ask her that question yourself."

Mr. DeBloom came down from his room just as the clock struck the hour. He was the last person to join the gathering, his sister and Susan having already eaten in their rooms. Mr. Kruger was talking to Dr. Harris, and Mrs. Frogerton was organizing who should go in to dinner with whom.

"You have bruises on your arm," Dr. Harris said to Caroline as he walked over to escort her to the dining room.

Caroline glanced down at her upper arm and readjusted her shawl to cover the marks.

"How did that happen?" he asked.

"I'm not sure." She smiled at him. "Perhaps I walked into something."

"Or someone grabbed hold of you with some force." He frowned. "I work in a hospital, Miss Morton. I see signs of violence against women every day."

"It is of no importance."

"That's what they all say, until they end up dead in the morgue," Dr. Harris muttered as he pulled out her chair with some force.

"I'll endeavor to be careful." She sat down and placed her napkin on her lap.

If Mrs. Frogerton seated everyone according to their plan, she should have Mr. Kruger directly opposite her. She took a moment to steady her nerves, as her opponent took his place at the table.

"Miss Morton." Mr. Kruger nodded as he sat down. "I hear you've been stirring the pot."

She opened her eyes wide. "Stirring? My employment

contract doesn't stipulate that I have to work in the kitchen. I have no idea what you're referring to, Mr. Kruger."

Mrs. Frogerton took her place at the head of the table, and Inspector Ross took the foot. The butler signaled to the two footmen, and they began to serve the soup and pour the first of the three wines that would accompany the meal. Dorothy chattered away about her wedding without any regard as to whether anyone wished to listen to her. Caroline concentrated on charming Dr. Harris, who was looking remarkably suspicious.

Eventually, when the meal was almost over, Mrs. Frogerton looked at Inspector Ross. "As this is something of an informal gathering, Inspector, are you at liberty to disclose when the DeBlooms might claim their mother's body? I'm sure they have arrangements to make to take her back to her homeland, and I would like to organize a memorial before she goes."

"There have been some delays," Inspector Ross said. "The coroner wasn't satisfied with the cause of death suggested by the doctor."

"Typical," snorted Dr. Harris. "What did he think a trained professional might have missed?"

Inspector Ross looked at Mr. DeBloom. "I'm not sure Mr. DeBloom will want to hear this news in the middle of his dinner. Perhaps—"

"Please go ahead," Mr. DeBloom said. "I am anxious to claim my mother's body, so the sooner we can dispense with any nonsense, the better."

"As you wish." Inspector Ross inclined his head. "The coroner detected signs of arsenic poisoning."

"Good Lord." Dr. Harris set his glass down on the table with a thump. "Are you suggesting she imbibed poison before she died?"

"Yes. Which means the death cannot be put down to natural causes," Inspector Ross explained. "Such evidence indicates that either she willingly took the poison to kill herself or someone put the poison in her glass and murdered her."

"I believe there was a note, Dr. Harris," Mr. DeBloom said. "And a confession of some sort."

"That's correct." Inspector Ross nodded. "Mrs. DeBloom said she was responsible for the deaths of a Mr. Smith and Mr. Thettle, who both worked at Lady Caroline's family solicitors."

"Hold on a moment," Dr. Harris said. "You believe she stalked and murdered those two men? How on earth do you think she did that? I saw the condition Mr. Smith was in when he came to our hospital. I cannot imagine Mrs. DeBloom was capable of inflicting such damage on another human being."

"I must confess to having the same thoughts, Dr. Harris," Mrs. Frogerton said. "I can't believe a lady such as Mrs. DeBloom acted in such a way."

"Her note did say that she was *responsible* for the deaths," Caroline said. "I suppose she might have asked someone else to carry them out for her." She let her gaze rest on Mr. Kruger. "Someone who had the brute strength to do what she ordered and who was in her confidence."

Kruger had the audacity to smile at her.

Mrs. Frogerton said, "It still strikes me as most peculiar that almost everyone involved in the matter of the late Earl of Morton's last will has mysteriously died in suspicious circumstances. And let's not forget Caroline was threatened, too."

Caroline gave an exaggerated shudder. "I cannot forget that. If my assailant finds out I have recently received more information about my late father's will, I dread to think what will happen to me."

Mr. DeBloom glanced nervously at Mr. Kruger and frowned. "Perhaps you should keep such matters to yourself, Miss Morton. One would not wish to see you hurt."

"I am extremely unlikely to share such news with society at large, sir." Caroline glanced around the table. "But I am among friends, and I feel safe in expressing my anxiety over this matter."

Inspector Ross cleared his throat. "I am all for informality, Lady Caroline, but it would've been nice if you'd mentioned this development to me in my formal capacity as an officer in the Metropolitan Police."

"I intend to, Inspector," Caroline said. "I will bring the papers to your office tomorrow morning."

"What papers?" Dr. Harris asked. "Don't tell me you found the will?"

"It is all very strange, but while we were away in Kent, I received a package in the post." Caroline paused to make sure everyone was listening. "I discovered that it contained important information about my late father's will."

"As far as I understood it, Miss Morton," Mr. DeBloom said slowly, "your father's will disappeared on the night Mr. Smith was attacked and robbed."

"It appears someone had the forethought to post it to me," Caroline said. "Which is a great relief, because now I can return it to my new solicitor, Mr. Lewis, and he can make sure I receive everything I'm entitled to."

"Isn't it wonderful?" Mrs. Frogerton said.

"Indeed." Mr. DeBloom kept his gaze on Mr. Kruger, who was frowning.

Dr. Harris sat back. "With all due respect, Miss Morton, are you suggesting that a man who ran from his own office in a complete panic had the forethought to stop at some point and post you a *letter*? It sounds quite unlikely to me."

"I don't know when it was posted, Doctor," Caroline replied. "All I know is that after some delay, it arrived here and that I was very grateful to see it."

Mrs. Frogerton rose to her feet. "Shall we leave the gentlemen to their port, ladies?"

Caroline stood up. "I just had a thought, Inspector. Perhaps I could give you the letter to take away with you tonight? The sooner you see it and release it to my solicitors, the quicker this matter will be resolved and the safer I will feel."

"I'd be happy to take it, my lady," Inspector Ross said.

"I'm very interested to see what Mr. Lewis makes of this matter of the shares," Caroline said loudly to Mrs. Frogerton as they left. "After I've settled Mrs. Frogerton in the drawing room, I'll pop up to my room and get the letter, Inspector."

She waited until she heard the gentlemen coming up the stairs from the dining room before she went to her bedchamber. Despite knowing there was help at hand if she needed it, she found it difficult to take her time unlocking her trunk and retrieving the packet. The soft click of her door opening and shutting behind her made her tense as she slid the trunk back under the bed and looked over her shoulder.

Caroline didn't have to conceal her start of surprise as she clasped the letters to her bosom and quickly recalculated. "You should not be in here, sir."

Mr. DeBloom scowled at her. "All you had to do was allow yourself to fall in love with me and accept a marriage proposal, and none of this would have needed to happen."

"I don't understand."

"Don't pretend to be stupid, Miss Morton. I underestimated you once, and then I found out you'd been making a deal with Kruger behind my back. You made me look stupid, and I can't forgive that."

"You seem to be implying that everything is my fault, sir. How can that be true?"

"Because you refuse to let everything go and accept your lot in life."

Caroline frowned. "I am somewhat at a loss to understand your reasoning. You just suggested I should've accepted your marriage proposal. Surely that isn't accepting my lot, but attempting to improve it, which is exactly what I'm trying to achieve with my bargain with Mr. Kruger."

He thrust his finger in her face. "Don't try to be clever with me. I need that will. Give it to me."

"Why would I do that, Mr. DeBloom?"

"Because it is the worthless ramblings of a man who was both delusional and desperate."

"He believed your mother had deceived him by selling him shares in mines that didn't exist. Is that not true?" Caroline asked.

"My mother did what she was told."

"By you?"

He shrugged. "Me and Kruger."

Caroline eased a step away from him. "If the mines were fake and never existed, why is it so important that the issue of these shares to my father doesn't come to light?"

"Because it makes our business look bad just as we are expanding in England."

"You don't want to be seen as a corrupt company." Caroline nodded. "I can quite understand that."

He held out his hand. "Then give me that will, I'll tear it up, and no one will be the wiser."

Caroline considered him. "Mr. Kruger offered me a financial solution to this matter."

"He had no authority to do so."

"It seems fair to me."

"Why?" Mr. DeBloom tried to smile. "Come on, Miss Morton. You're perfectly well situated here with Mrs. Frogerton. You recently received a nice bequest from your aunt that gives you some financial independence. What more do you need?"

"My fair share for not tarnishing your company's reputation?" Caroline asked. "Because despite my current lowly status, I do still have family connections to call upon. My father's banker at Coutts who knew me when I was a child is most obliging."

Even before she finished speaking, Mr. DeBloom lunged at her, ripped the package from her hands, and pushed her against the wall. He ran for the door and barely got five feet before Inspector Ross and one of his constables had him by the collar.

Inspector Ross looked into the room. "Are you all right, Lady Caroline?"

"Yes, I'm fine." Caroline recovered her breath. "Do you have Mr. Kruger secured as well?"

"We do, and I heard every word Mr. DeBloom said to you."

"Would it be possible to speak to both of them before you take them off?" Caroline asked. "There is one piece of this puzzle that still needs to be set in place."

Inspector Ross and his constable escorted their prisoners to the drawing room, where Mrs. Frogerton, Dr. Harris, and Miss Frogerton had gathered.

Caroline took the package Inspector Ross had retrieved from Mr. DeBloom and opened it. "This isn't exactly my father's will, Mr. DeBloom. These are the extracts Mr. Thettle copied for Mr. Emerson Smith." She looked at Dr. Harris. "You were quite right, Doctor. I doubt Mr. Jeremy Smith had time to post anything when he was running for his life from Mr. Kruger. But Mr. Thettle was more cautious and planned ahead."

Mr. Kruger shrugged. "I deny all knowledge of that event. Mr. DeBloom was the instigator of everything."

"Liar!" Mr. DeBloom turned to his business manager. "You killed them both. I had nothing to do with any of this." He looked pleadingly at Caroline. "I *told* you I was afraid of him. Everything I have done has been under threat of violence both to me and my mother. Look what happened to her when she dared to disagree with him about his treatment of you."

"Balderdash. The only person your mother was scared of was you," Mr. Kruger countered. "She knew I was devoted to her. All of this is your fault."

There was nothing so satisfying as watching co-conspirators turn on each other.

Caroline continued, "What I didn't understand was what was so important in the will that made the De-Blooms so eager to prevent it being acted on? Mr. De-Bloom claimed that being exposed for selling fake shares in the past made them look less than respectable when they were expanding their business in England. But surely that doesn't merit murder?" Caroline looked around at the assembled company. "Which made me believe there was something important about those particular shares."

"For a fake mine." Mr. DeBloom shrugged. "Created by Kruger and my mother to con the gullible, which I'm afraid included your father. The only fool here was him, Miss Morton."

"Except that particular mine isn't fake, is it, Mr. De-Bloom?" Caroline turned to Inspector Ross. "We have it on the best of authority that the *Wonderwerk Myne* has the potential to be very lucrative indeed."

Inspector Ross nodded. "There have been rumors flying around for years about new sources of wealth in South Africa from gold and precious stones. That's probably why you came to England to re-register the mine as a going concern, Mr. DeBloom."

Mr. DeBloom went still. "I don't know what you're talking about. If anyone—"

"Mr. DeBloom, I've checked the records. Your signature is on the paperwork," Inspector Ross said.

Caroline faced Mr. DeBloom. "And, as the late Earl of Morton owned almost half the shares in that particular mine, you needed to make sure his heirs were kept in ignorance of that fact. There is also the matter that the very land the mine is beneath belongs to my father, too. There is proof he bought that property in his bank records. In truth, Mr. DeBloom, you were willing to do anything to prevent those facts being known, including pretending to fall in love with me."

Mr. DeBloom took a hasty step forward and was restrained by the constable. "I offered to *marry* you!"

"Is that supposed to make me feel grateful, sir?" Caroline asked. "A marriage offered in such an underhand spirit is unlikely to prosper."

"It was better than the alternative of Kruger killing you like he did to all the others! You should be bloody grateful I saved your life!"

Mr. Kruger lunged for Mr. DeBloom and was held back by the constable.

Inspector Ross bowed to Caroline. "I think we have sufficient evidence to take both of these gentlemen into custody, my lady."

"Thank you."

Caroline went to stand by Mrs. Frogerton, who reached for her hand and whispered, "Well done, lass."

Dr. Harris waited until Inspector Ross and his constables escorted their charges from the house before turning to his hostess. "Why did you invite me to this particular dinner party, Mrs. Frogerton?"

Mrs. Frogerton smiled at him. "Because I knew you'd ask all the awkward questions everyone else was too polite to mention, Doctor."

"I suppose that makes sense, but I can't say I enjoyed being kept in the dark about your plans to expose two murderers." Dr. Harris looked at Caroline. "Another suitor fails to come up to scratch, Miss Morton."

"I never considered Mr. DeBloom as a potential husband, Dr. Harris."

"You could've fooled me." Dr. Harris studied her for a moment. "Was it DeBloom who bruised your arm?"

"Yes, and Mr. Kruger who threatened my life."

"Then they both deserve what they get." He nodded. "I

have to go back to the hospital. Give your sister my re-gards, won't you?"

"I will, Doctor."

He turned to the door and then looked back. "I suppose if that mine does come to fruition, you'll be rich beyond your wildest dreams, Miss Morton."

"I doubt it will happen. With the DeBloom company in disarray, it will never come to pass and will all be forgotten about."

"If there's the slightest chance that it'll make money, someone will take it over." Dr. Harris winked at her. "And then I'll be back to court you properly."

He left, leaving all the ladies staring after him.

"Well!" Dorothy tutted. "The cheek of him!"

"I agree." Mrs. Frogerton shook her head.

"I think Dr. Harris was joking on all fronts, ma'am," Caroline said. "He knows the mine will never open and that he'll never have to propose."

Both the Frogerton ladies looked at her and sighed.

"What?" Caroline asked.

Mrs. Frogerton patted her hand. "Take good care of those shares, lass. I'll wager you might be glad of them in the future."